HELL
OR
HANGOVER

By

Alex Muka

First edition printed in 2025 by:
OME OMY Publishing L.L.C.
Red Bank, NJ

Cover design, and typesetting by Barış Şehri
please visit sehribookdesign.com

ISBN 979-8-9986906-0-0

www.hellorhangover.com

Praise for *Hell or Hangover*

"The most drunken love story I've ever read: never has a novel of drinking, drugs and debauchery failed the Bechdel test with so much heart and good humor!"
— **Peter Shull, author of the novel** *Why Teach?*

"If Jay McInerney hailed from dirty north Jersey instead of genteel New England, worked within the 2010's digital marketing hellscape instead of old media fact-checking, and wrote with zero whiny ploys for reader sympathy, he might have come up with something akin to *Hell or Hangover*. But he couldn't have matched it since Alex Muka is, at base, a much better scribbler."
— **Daniel Falatko, author of** *The Wayback Machine*

"*Hell or Hangover* reads like coke-snorting early Bret Easton Ellis and Charles Bukowski had a wild night in the city with some crazy Cuban cousins, dabbled in santería, and woke up hungover in suburban New Jersey. Alex Muka has written a voice-driven banger about a young man spiraling through shots of booze, lust, and existential angst in search of something real. It's a romance, a reckoning, and a raucous coming-of-age novel full of guts, grime, and poetry. A bold debut from a writer with serious chops and a worldview all his own." — **Andrew Boryga, author of** *Victim*

In your love,
Tara

Friday

APRIL 17TH, 2015

7:19 PM

Every night starts the same. The pregame. The debauchery before the debauchery. An excuse to get drunk before the actual drinking starts. It makes stepping off the PATH train from Hoboken into New York City more difficult than it should be, but it's hard to blame my current state on booze alone.

It began in the liquor store on Washington Ave. As I procured the refreshments my legs turned to jelly, or maybe it is natural to duck when you see a phantom in the store's window. There were the same eyes from ten years prior, brown and chaotic and shaded by dark bangs, then floor. As I stood back up, Arianna, or her doppelganger, had disappeared. I struggled to grasp if what I saw was real or imagined. It was either a ghost from the past or another hallucination, a side-effect of partying for a decade.

My current predicament, the way my lower half feels part elephant and my vision seems to have been set behind an off-kilter gray sheet, could also be blamed on the difference in height New York City maintains over my beloved Hoboken. A quick look up could leave me as dizzy as a tourist. But I am not looking up. The buildings around me are a peripheral blur; a side note to the phone in my hand. It's become a daily chore trying to translate my rambling thoughts into 140 characters.

What to tweet, what to tweet?

My Twitter profile picture shows a twenty-three-year-old male, white enough to have a couple beers, drive, and not worry about acquiring my first DUI, yet Latino enough to have a curly mess of brown hair and an even tan. You can't tell from the picture that I can dance the bachata or cook rabo de toro or that now, two years after this picture was taken, my curls are beginning to thin. Distinguished would be a nice way of putting it. Fun doesn't come without consequences. At the preposterous age of twenty-five, I'm an old man in this game. But what I lack in youth I make up for in dedication.

What to tweet, what to tweet?

I could go with my thoughts on the Israeli-Palestine conflict. Maybe my take on the gender pay gap. I could even enlighten my audience with a small diatribe on the current state of the flailing American empire. But the people don't want that. My followers don't care and neither do I. Give the three hundred loyalists what they want Lou.

I can't help but laugh. Graduating college was supposed to have magically matured me. I took enough social science classes to have crawled from my cave. If the exhilaration of *SOC 2200 – Working Women* didn't get the engines revving on the quest to grow up then nothing would. This was all supposed to end after shutting that last blue book. Looking back on it, college was the perennial pregame. The debauchery before *the* debauchery. An excuse to get drunk before the *actual* drinking started.

What to tweet, what to tweet?

> I wonder what hates me more after college…
> my liver, my wallet, or my parents.
>
> 7:20 PM – April 17th – 2015

Sent.

"Lou, c'mon!"

I know this voice is Kyle Aisle's. It's got that whiny tinge to it, like a child begging for his mom. He knows as much as I do that being late to my sister's party will end in an earful at best.

I shut my eyes, take a deep breath, and try to orient myself. I've been here before. Hopelessly drunk and in the moment. I wonder, for a second, if this night will be just like every other night. The noise, the talking, the noise, the bathroom, the yip, the shot, another shot, the talking, the noise, the drink, the bathroom, the yip, the shot, the drink, another drink…a desperate march.

There's got to be a reason to stop this charade. I just haven't found her yet.

Shit, Freudian slip.

I just haven't found *it* yet.

7 : 21 PM

My legs begin to remember their purpose walking west down 31st. I'm flanked by my two compatriots, Kyle Aisle and Chris VanNeece, who I've dragged to my sister's going away party under false pretenses. This party will surely suck, there's no doubt, which is why I've decided to withhold such information from their pretty little heads.

"So, like I was saying, we went to the bar for a couple of drinks first and then I took her out to dinner. We were talking all night, no awkward silences or anything, which for me is a rarity. She's the receptionist at the veterinarian I go to for my mom's dog, remember?" Kyle asks.

I have no idea what he's talking about. I still can't get past his outfit. I've told him time and again you have a 60% chance of getting laid if you dress in joggers, a hoodie, and some sneakers, but he insists on going with the 70s album cover look. A pleather jacket, baggy jeans, and boots are a sure-fire way to scare any suitors away.

"Sure Aisle, keep going," I say.

"I asked her if her day was 'ruff'. She loved it," he says.

My legs were heavy but now I'm floating, as if gravity shut off or the world stopped spinning on its axis. Learning Santa isn't real was less disappointing than hearing this garbage fall out of Aisle's mouth. Ruff? Fucking ruff? He seems unfazed.

"Jesus bro," VanNeece says.

VanNeece's caterpillar eyebrows touch at the center in concern. He's got so many facial follicles it's hard to tell if he's made of skin or hair. Forgive his father's half-German ancestry, VanNeece is actually a good Italian boy. Even with the Reich-ish last name, VanNeece has the accent of a gumba. It's as if Tony Soprano has been squeezed into chinos one size too small and is stating my sentiments exactly.

"Never mind," Aisle says.

"C'mon bro, just finish the story," VanNeece says.

"No, never mind."

Kyle's got the pout of a giraffe. He wants us to care. It's hard enough to care about myself and now I'm supposed to care about Kyle too? The same Kyle that doesn't heed my warnings. The same Kyle that doesn't take my advice. Kyle, poor Kyle.

"Just finish the story," I say, glancing at my phone.

An email notification pops up from my boss, something about a new phone app being released on Monday. All employees are to promote said app on every social media platform throughout the weekend. I ignore it. Even if the email was life or death and had been sent on Wednesday at noon it would have been just as easily ignored. At work I skirt by, collect my middling paycheck, and try not to get in anyone's way. The key to my professional success as a phone app marketer is keeping a low profile and being the son of a silent partner. Nepotism sounds like a form of government in a struggling Asian country but it is thriving right here in the Garden State.

"Alright, fine," Aisle continues. "I walked her back to her apartment, which is far. All the way down by the movie theatre on 14th Street. I'm figuring, if she made me walk that far she's obviously going to let me up…"

Aisle pauses for dramatic effect. My phone vibrates again. I look down at a notification.

1 Snapchat from Kristen Birdock.

A recent ex.

Odd.

"And…" I say, barely listening.

"She lets me up! Then we start making out on her bed and I start kissing her ears and she loves it. She's making this little moaning sound like ahhuu, ahuuuhaah."

"That sounds like crying, Aisle," I say.

"So, I unbutton her pants and start playing with her a little and she starts to get really, really wet and then…"

"Aright, we get it. Spare us and get to the point. You're no Anaïs Nin," I say.

"Who's Anaïs Nin?" VanNeece asks.

"Just finish the story," I say.

"So, we're about to have sex and she…she starts to cry…" Aisle says.

"Jesus bro," VanNeece contributes to the conversation again.

"See. I knew it," I say.

"She said she just broke up with her boyfriend. That she missed him. She made a compelling argument. Even I shed a little tear," Aisle says.

"You actually cried with her?" I ask.

Aisle's pause leads me to believe the veracity of his statement.

"Jesus bro," VanNeece repeats.

"Why does this shit always happen to me? I can't catch a break," Aisle whines.

"Aisle, let me see this girl," I ask.

"What do you mean?"

"Pull her up on Instagram," I insist.

"I don't have Instagram. I'll look her up on Facebook."

"And you ask me why this always happens to you? A girl can smell that kind of technological desperation the minute you pick her up," I say.

I've broken this down for Kyle thousands of times. Half the battle with women these days is finding out who they are before you even strike up a conversation and Professor Lou is here to illuminate the way.

First, the obvious: is she hot? If she looks good in her pictures hopefully she'll look good in real life. This isn't always the case. If a picture is worth a thousand words then a photoshopped picture is worth a thousand questions. With filters, fillers, jaw-line makeup, and the surgery now available to women, it is almost impossible to tease out the real from the fake. It's not their fault. It's the nature of the medium.

Second, does she have a boyfriend? Most girls that do have a boyfriend incessantly post pictures with them. It's easy to spot the taken from the single. People think this is a bad thing; they're sick of having relationships shoved in their faces at all times. They're wrong. The girls that you have absolutely no chance with are the girls that hardly post pictures at all. These girls aren't looking for any social reassurance. Their confidence is doing just fine and that does nothing for me. It's the ones that need to prove their relationship online that will crash and burn. The key here is to catch one of these girls between boyfriends. The rebound. The breakup back board. If Aisle had paid attention he would have known that there is a Goldilocks zone. Not too soon and not too late post breakup. It's actually easy to know when to swoop in, bringing me to my third, final, and most important piece of advice…

Has she posted any emotional quotes in the last month? If any girl has posted the, "*If you love someone let them go. If they return they were always yours. If they don't they never were*" quote, or other recycled trash then you know the girl needs a helping hand. There's no reason to confuse morality with results here, just read the signs.

Open your myopic eyes. Women are always begging you to pay attention, this is your chance.

You can call me an animal. A misogynist. A misinformed maniac. Say what you want. But this *is* how it works. You don't go into a test without studying, do you? You don't make a speech without practicing it, right? It's called preparation. Why waste all this valuable information people are so intent on throwing at you? Luck is where hard work meets opportunity.

┌─────────────────────────┐
│   7 : 27 PM   │
└─────────────────────────┘

A cab would have been the preferred option, but we somehow make it through the tourist traps of mid-town into Chelsea on foot. The streets become progressively greener. Vendors vanish. Foot traffic thins. The feint hint of river muck begins to overpower the smell of Sabrett. Though it's tough to know where I'm going while viewing a Snapchat, the disappearing I <3 NY signs in my periphery mean I'm headed in the right direction.

The video starts out facing a bathroom stall. There's a dick etched into the door with the words *suck it* in vulgar black sharpie. Maybe I really did screw her over, I wonder, until the camera flips, showing Kristen Birdock sitting on a toilet with her tits out and a hand over her nether region. She giggles. The words "miss me?" slide across the screen. Subtle.

Though I'm tempted to screenshot the last two seconds, I follow the unwritten Snapchat rules. Unless it's your girlfriend, you cannot screenshot nudes. Chivalry is clearly alive and kicking. Just like that, with my pearls clutched and mouth agape, the video disappears.

"I don't think she has a Facebook," Aisle finally says.

"Huh?" I say, staring at my phone.

"What's so interesting down there?" Aisle asks.

"What? Nothing. What were you saying?" I ask.

"No, what's so important?"

"Uh, Kristen sent me a Snap," I say.

"What?!" Aisle yelps.

"Hea we go again," VanNeece says, rolling his eyes.

"What?" I feign ignorance. "It was very low-key. Nothing to see here."

I shoot off a wink at Aisle that will surely make his head explode.

7:31 PM

A block later Aisle looks constipated. He pushes his hands through his slicked back blonde hair, sucking in a breath. His eyes search the ground as if he's lost an earring. An earring is all he's missing with the outfit he's gone with tonight. But lightning does finally strike that thick skull of his.

"She sent you a nude? A *fucking* nude?" he finally yells.

"I am not at liberty to discuss private Snapchats between one consenting adult and another, Aisle. Now please, continue your story."

"I just don't get it," Aisle can't stop himself. "How the hell do you find these girls? After all the shit you did to her she still wants you?"

"What shit did I do to her?" I ask.

"C'mon! The girl wanted to wife you. That little ball of perfection wanted to be with you. Didn't she make you dinner every night for an entire month?"

"Two times a week…10 weeks. And only one dinner," I correct him.

"What?"

"Forget it," I say.

"If you don't want to wife *her* then I don't know up from down," Aisle says.

"Aisle, let me break this down for you. On the surface Kristen might *seem* perfect. On the outside everything goes according to plan. She's short with a set of legs that look good from skirt to legging, a tight yet protruding ass, and tits that are deceivingly large. She even pulls off a bob. Only true beauties can pull off a bob. So far so good, no?"

Aisle nods. Even VanNeece's eyes widen and his head begins to shake up and down.

"Once you go one layer deep it all falls apart," I say.

"How? She's cool, she goes out to the bar with us, she holds her drinks. Shit she even buys us drinks sometimes," Aisle says.

"Fair. Two layers deep then. You guys don't see everything else. You don't get handed the phone to take a thousand pics for the 'gram. You don't watch her brain melt when it comes to writing a caption. You weren't there for brunch that day. I had to end it. I had no choice."

"Aint that every girl?" VanNeece asks.

"That's right, and another reason why I'm not wifing anyone up."

Aisle's thinking again and it looks like it hurts. "You're twenty-five. Your parents got married when your dad was twenty. They're the happiest couple I've ever seen," he finally says.

"That's called an enigma, Aisle."

My parents *are* an enigma. I am constantly reminded of their seven-day "courting." By the end of one week my dad was on bended knee asking my mother to marry him with a ring-pop. This breaks all of Professor Lou's rules and should be considered a dangerous outlier. Looking at a dataset and making policy from one little dot out in no man's land is something a true Professor would never do.

"And besides," I continue, "my mom's the shit. You think there are any women out there as cool as her? Highly doubtful."

"This is true. But don't sell ya' dad short," VanNeece chirps.

My eyes roll back near my occipitalis. My dad has a soft spot for VanNeece for the simple reason that he gives a fuck about his job. He thinks I can learn a thing or two from a semi-successful investment banker. I could tell my pops how VanNeece has taught me how to properly snort drugs. That's a thing or two, I guess.

"Let's get back to the subject, Lou," Aisle says. "I'm talking about you and Kristen."

"There is no subject, Aisle. I'm not wife-ing anyone until I'm at least thirty," I say.

"Right, when all the good ones are gone. Good plan," he says.

It sounds good to me.

7:42 PM

The entrance to my sister's low-rise building is like a maze designed by Kevin McAllister. Avoid the hand-sculpted planters. Duck under the potted banana tree. Miss the cacti set like mouse traps. Make it through the forest and into the loft.

The pregame is supposed to lead to the game but the jungle that greeted us at the door has now turned desert. Though I didn't expect much, a party shouldn't sound like a movie theatre. Half the attendees are hued in blue light, necks bent, phones in hand, glazed over eyes. Leonard Cohen leaks out of the speakers. VanNeece and Aisle look at me as if I were Judas. I avoid eye contact. This "party" resembles a funeral.

What's scarier than my friends' disappointment is my sister making a beeline for us as soon as we walk in. If it came out one day that she is the product of my mother's affair with a large Viking, it would surprise no one. It would be even less surprising if she were, at the bare minimum, adopted. If my mother indeed had Kimberly, I cringe to imagine the pain her pregnancy caused. Not because of the lack of resemblance, but because it's possible Kimberly was taller than my mother at the time of her birth. Long, blonde, and built like a Norse goddess are probably terms you will never hear associated with the woman who gave Kimberly life. My mother is a short woman with dark features born on the island of Cuba. Alas, baby pictures in our mom's palms have surfaced from a time in which photoshop was not possible.

"Why are you late? You killed the vibes," my sister says.

VanNeece yawns while Aisle stares at her with his mouth open.

"There aren't really any vibes to kill sis," I say.

"That's why I told you to come early. Do what you do already!" she says.

Without hesitation, and the faint but all too real prospect of getting beaten up by my big sister, we each man our stations. VanNeece heads toward the iPhone connected to the speakers, prepping anything other than the nap-inducing playlist they've got on. Aisle ravages the place for shot glasses and plastic cups. My job is to get everyone's attention, which shouldn't be too hard. The problem with this "party" is that all of my sister's friends are actually her co-workers.

Kimberly started her business two years after graduating college; two years into the trap they call the "real world." That high-speed car you can see coming from miles away. The options are pretty simple: you can step out of the way nice and early, you can lunge out of the way just in time, or you can get mushed by it.

I'm currently in the mushed phase.

My sister took option number two. If it wasn't for me she might not be so lucky. Her lunge happened when she decided to visit me at college one weekend, long ago. It was a move of desperation. She was a devout disapprover of my shenanigans, but she was fresh off a nasty breakup. I missed the early Friday morning pick up from the train station due to aforementioned shenanigans and she ended up meeting an old man who taught her how to make a simple chair out of wood. Kimberly is lucky like that. Things don't simply fall in her lap, but leap towards it. I didn't see her all weekend, or the subsequent six months, even though we technically lived in the same town. She left with a skill and an idea for a business. I left with a degree and a drinking habit.

That story becomes an anecdote of grand proportions as I walk around her loft. If ever you must live on an island packed with over 9 million souls mashed together into some post-Darwinian hell hole, this is the way to do it – in a loft decorated by the now semi-Instafamous Kimberly Kennedy.

The ceiling is far, far away, aloof to the action below. Tillandsia, peace lilies, and money plants of all different ethnicities, shapes, and sizes pour oxygen into the already airy room. It is like walking into a casino pumped hourly with fresh air but replacing the smell of stale cigarette with soil.

The décor has a warming effect on the room. There is the red oak coffee table made from a tree that fell in the backyard of our childhood home, made by Kim Kennedy. It is surrounded by a group of hand-knitted cushions and pillows like a Bedouin gold mine, knitted by Kim Kennedy. Wheel-crafted pots with Mexican blue patterns hold succulents and ferns with dead ends, made by Kim Kennedy. Uncomfortable, yet beautiful, one-off chairs are scattered around haphazardly to the naked eye, though knowing Kim I am sure everything down to the leaf has its aesthetic purpose. There is even a house phone…yes, a candlestick house phone lined with smooth balsa wood and a rotary dial. It actually works, too. I tested it out one night making random prank calls into the wire-connected microphone.

The true masterpiece is the bookcase covering the entirety of the wall opposite the open kitchen. A work in progress for years, each section is a slightly different color wood filled with juxtaposing colored book sleeves.

"This isn't a library," she told me once. "I can organize my books any way I feel like it. The colors speak to me more than those dead men anyway."

This is where Kim and I diverge in opinion. I am slightly color-blind and would rather read *The Mambo Kings Play Songs of Love* for the fifth time than blankly stare at a Picasso in an attempt to pull meaning from it. This may make me uncultured. I do not argue this point. But I can still appreciate the beauty of the ivy intertwining between shelves of unread 19th century classics as if the entire case and its contents were breathing.

It isn't until I see the newest addition, a rolling ladder, that my infantile joy takes over. Attempting to resist the urge is futile. The momentum of my run and jump propels me and the ladder to the far edge of the masterpiece. The ladder abruptly runs out of track and plants me face first at the bottom of a set of stairs, just a little more disoriented than I already am.

Hoping no one saw my little tumble, I turn to the kitchen. The few glances my way are more out of fear than judgement.

"Who is that feral boy?" I hear in a hushed tone.

This job is going to be harder than I thought.

My phone vibrates.

Kristen: Hi

7:50 PM

Now this, this is more confusing than the Snapchat. At least I understood that video's message loud and clear. It's not the word that is confusing me, it's the meaning behind it. It doesn't get more open ended than 'hi', especially when we haven't spoken in months. But that still begs the question, how do I respond?

I decide to do some more digging to see if I can get closer to the truth of what this "hi" is all about. Kristen's Instagram is a plethora of feminine propaganda but damn if she doesn't look good. There are pictures of her doing that back leg kick in different low-cut dresses, iced coffee selfies, hoodies by a fire, and two or three with that squat pose where one leg is straight and the other is tucked under her ass. If I didn't know any better I would agree with Aisle's assessment that this girl is wife material. But I do know better.

Knowing does little to quell my curiosity though. Her place is in Murray Hell, I mean Hill. Cab distance from my sister's. A hop, skip, and jump from a Plan C...Plan B, let alone Plan A, has eluded me thus far.

7:51 PM

The new Drake wakes me out of my perusal, blasting at a decibel that has the makings of a good time. Thank God. That's my cue to get the party's attention.

"Everyone..."

My voice is cut short by a whisper in my ear.

"Hey..."

Two mounds of fake flesh pressed into a tank top grab my eyes before they can make out the mystery whisperer. These two melons are easily discernable. A birthmark on top of the left breast might as well be a bullseye.

"Bridget. How are you?" I ask.

When I look up her small black eyes are overshadowed by matted-on mascara. Her eyelashes resemble dreadlocks. I'm sure those are fake too but, to each their own. It's hard to focus on lash when there is so much boob.

"Could be better. This party is boring. Nothing like those college parties your sister let you come to. I can't believe I almost took advantage of such a good young boy. How much do you miss me?" she asks.

A memory flashes before my eyes. Bridget, a couch, those large breasts out in the wild, and then my sister and her ex. Yelling, fighting, a push, a shove, my fist landing on the douchebag's chin, my hard on turning into a piece of cooked spaghetti. Nowhere near al dente.

"I miss college...and you, of course," I say.

"I think I'm going to Finale later if you want to come. I know the promoter there," she says.

"Hmm, when are you going?"

"Well, it doesn't really get good until two, so probably three."

I've taken a peek at Bridget's Instagram before and I am starting to connect the dots. Bridget has turned into a bit of a bottle rat. By a "bit of," I mean she's the Master Splinter of bottle rats. The bottle rat is a new species, one evolved from the powder room ladies of the late 1940s. They see themselves as the new Café Society but without the mystique and elegance. The main habitat of this animal is the club, and the club only. We are very lucky to see one so outside of her element. Usually, bottle rats hunt in packs, swarming to the hottest and loudest club. Words like "DJ" and "Bottle Service" are pheromonal to these creatures, attracting different subspecies from far and wide. These subspecies range from The Un-Fuckables (*sexus habere nihil*) all the way to the Two Steppers (*duo gradus*). My sister hiring Bridget to run her social media was probably her smartest decision to date.

As a professor of debauchery, I do get quite pedantic in my observations. Going to a club with Bridget would mean running into all sorts of creatures. But it is something to do if nothing else presents itself.

"I'm down," I'm shocked to hear myself say. "Later, of course."

Knowing my penis was responsible for that answer, I try and stay focused on Bridget's head. The voodoo trickery of her breasts in my face has made a potential late-night Plan B disaster. Plan A still eludes me.

7:55 PM

"Everyone!" I start over. "Let's take a shot for my sister here and wish her good luck on her trip to London. It's been a long road, as you all know. And, really, you're welcome. None of this would have happened if I had just picked my sister up from the train on time. So, cheers to you, and cheers to me. The best of friends, we'll never be. And if we ever disagree, fuck you, and cheers to me."

The shot glasses are already aligned on the table thanks to my trusty sidekicks. Hesitant hands reach out one by one and take the shots which I regrettably find out contain warm vodka. Even I can't hold in a shudder as I give my sidekicks a look of disgust.

As bad as the vodka is, it seems to be working as the party lubricant and, coupled with VanNeece's playlist of new hip-hop, we seem to have this AARP group ready to shake out the cobwebs.

8:21 PM

I take another shot by myself and receive a skeptical look from a couple in the corner wearing matching sweaters. I pour two extras, which their wine glasses are quickly switched out for. All this entertaining makes me fiendish.

I try and force eye contact with VanNeece, who somehow has gotten himself into a heated debate with one of Kimberly's employees. There is a vein popping out of his neck and his hands are flailing and the poor employee looks like he's about to cry. Somehow I am able to pull a Jedi mind trick, or VanNeece is over the argument, and as he looks at me, I lightly tap my nose like a baseball manager throwing up signs to steal second. He nods. We head to the bathroom.

VanNeece deftly crafts two landing strips of white powder on the bathroom sink. He hands me a rolled-up hundred-dollar bill as we look at each other in the mirror and laugh. His smile is somehow soothing. This? It's just a phase, it says.

The bill is in my left nostril. It smells clean. If I didn't know any better I would assume Wall Street prints the bills right there. It's also possible that VanNeece and his Wall Street friends have an ironing board at the office for cash only.

The white line disappears into my nose as the bill moves across the sink. The yip freezes at first, then burns, like running cold hands under hot water. My brain frosts and thaws out within seconds. Breathing deep, I snort in one more time to clear my nose, nullifying the ten plus drinks I've consumed so far. This is the power of the powder.

"This fuckin' guy out there was lecturin' me about capitalism. Said I was something like Hitler fa' working at an investment bank," VanNeece says. "Maybe this'll calm me down."

He taps out another bump on the webbing of his thumb and the little mound rockets up his nose.

"Doubtful," I say.

I could agree with the employee and call my friend a selfish, money-hungry sycophant, but is a man who shares his prosperity with my party-pipe really a selfish, money-hungry sycophant? How dare I even think such filth about such a generous human. A comrade in this same crusade.

"What are we doing here anyway?" he asks.

"We won't stay all night. I just have to see my sister off. She's going to live with her boyfriend in England for a few months."

"But she'll be back?"

"Yea," I say.

"Then what's the fuckin point of a party?"

I shrug my shoulders.

"Anyway, how about that Bridget chick?" he asks me.

He lays out another two lines. I don't object. My body needs more more more now now now always always always.

"Smokin' right?" I reply.

"Yeah," VanNeece says. "I was talking to her before that freak got in my ear. She wants us to go to Finale later. I know the promoter. He could probably hook us up with a table for only like $250 each. Which isn't too bad considering. We'll leave here at like 12 and get there before it gets too packed. We'll definitely get a table."

"We were somewhere around Barstow, on the edge of the desert, when the drugs began to take hold," I say, looking at myself in the mirror.

"What?" VanNeece asks.

"I said, I'm down."

"We'll definitely get a table," he repeats.

His jaws are clenched, making ripples in the sides of his cheeks. He hands me an extra bag for safekeeping. That wondrous powder has a way of solving all problems. In this particular case it's helped me come up with a diabolical plan. A plan that will go down in the record books. A plan that they will write novels about. I text Kristen back.

Me: Hi

Even I am shocked at the subtle genius of such a text back.

VanNeece and I run a nose check before walking out, tilting our heads back and checking to see if there are any white bats in the cave. Drugs aren't so bad as long as no one knows you're on them.

8:30 PM

Aisle just so happens to be waiting for the bathroom. He stares at me as we walk out. I don't know if he's waiting for an explanation or trying to pretend that his puppylike ears weren't perked or his guilting eyes weren't burning a hole through the door. He disapproves of our filthy habits.

"Having fun Aisle?" I ask.

"No," he says.

He brushes past me into the bathroom. The squeak of his jacket has the opposite of his desired effect. It's almost impossible to hold back laughter.

"Fuck's his problem?" VanNeece asks.

I shrug my shoulders.

We creep our way back to a corner of the loft, minds high and ready and focused on nothing at all. It would be best, at this point, to evade all conversation with people who are not on the same level. I don't foresee us staying much longer and the sooner we leave the sooner the night can actually begin.

As we wait for Aisle, my phone vibrates.

Kristen: You like my snap?

Through all this activity I had almost forgot about the wonders of Kristen's earlier gift. I can feel my hard on press against my thigh as if to remind me who's in control here.

Me: My god woman.

Kristen: You like?

Me: Love.

Kristen: I'm actually in Hoboken and thought of you.

Me: I'm in the City.

Kristen: I'll be back later. Am I going to see you?

Me: The odds have increased tremendously.

Kristen: Lol, that's what I thought.

Me: Let me know when you're back.

Kristen: Yes sir.

Aisle's earlier outburst now seems unwarranted. How bad can I be to deserve such a gift? I let the guilt wash away, knowing in the morning it will return with a vengeance.

8:43 PM

I return to the party from the deep, dark recesses of Kristen World and realize my little unit has made a grave mistake. We are in conversation with none other than Christian Antelunes de Miguel. This is one of my sister's employees who I hate to like. Or is it like to hate? I can't tell the difference anymore.

"Cabo was pretty good pero, Puerto Escondido is the place to be," Christian is in the middle of saying. "If you like surfing that is."

"When did you start surfing?" Aisle asks while VanNeece chews on his own tongue.

"On a piece of wood, in Cuba, when I was seven," Christian says.

"On a piece of wood, huh?" I ask.

"Si. It is actually better for learning pero you hab no…"

I have to stop listening. His accent, the Spanglish, the stories of adventure – I've seen it all and heard it all on his Instagram. He is one of those Insta-egos who take selfie videos that start with 'Hey guys' as if he is talking to a legion of fans just desperately waiting on their phones for another Christian post. He's got about 100,000 followers and I am unfortunately one of them. I've never liked a post out of spite.

What he does for my sister is unknown. Is he an influencer? Does he travel the world purchasing stuff for Kim? I have no idea. In order to get him to stop talking about himself I dial up a few tequila shots from a flask I brought. I pour the piss warm liquid into red cups and pass them out like a doctor doling out medicine.

We take the shots and Christian kisses his teeth long enough to stop talking. Aisle's face looks like it's getting sucked in by his nose. VanNeece and I weather the storm with no hint at how awful the drink actually is. They don't call yip a performance enhancer for nothing.

"Man, that is some sheet tequila," Christian says.

He fakes a loogie on the floor.

"I bet if you pour that sheet on a Cadillac, it'll look like a Honda in twenty-four hours. Man, I bet if you pour that sheet on a-a-a como se dice caniche, aaaa a poodle at dinner it'll look like a sphynx cat by morning," Christian says, laughing.

I laugh too. He's got a point. My stomach is in choppy waters and it's possible that this "sheet tequila" is doing a number on my enamel. I try and focus my attention on Christian himself. He's got long hair that begins to curl at his shoulders. His cheek bones are a direct line from ear to chin, his top three buttons undone revealing hard pecs and perfectly manicured chest hair. He looks like he should be on the front cover of a shitty romance novel. In other words, he's everything a woman wants.

"Jyou got anything better than this, my friend?" he asks.

"I think I can find something," I say.

Though Christian is probably asking for some sniffles, I'll do just about anything in order to avoid another story. It's not that I'm bitter or anything. It's just that every time I see a post of Christian in some far-off land like a Dumas-ian hero I lose a little piece of my soul, of which I don't have much left.

I swear…I'm not bitter.

9:01 PM

My sights are now set on Kimberly's liquor cabinet. It has yet to be ravaged, which is not all that shocking.

If there is any real reason to be rich, then Johnnie Walker Blue is that reason. The bottle is hiding in the back of the cabinet, but my sharp, bloodshot, eyes spot the gold. After pouring myself a hefty glass, I offer it to any takers. There are plenty of employees willing to take the whiskey with a vigor they didn't display for the warm vodka. None of their conversations hold me for longer than a sip except for one lesbian couple.

From what I can tell, these two head up the kiln department. No surprise there. The more petite of the two takes the fine liquid down in one gulp and puts her glass out for seconds.

"Finally, some good shit."

I oblige and offer her counterpart a glass as well.

"No, I'm sorry. I don't drink," she replies.

The small voice that comes out in no way matches the stiffness of her handshake. The sides of her head are shaved, her arms are covered in black ink, and her forearm strength leaves my hand cramped.

"Well, what do you do then?" I ask.

"Depends on what you got," the sweet voice says.

Next thing I know, the lesbians and I are nose deep in dashes of white lines. I make a mental note to give these two high praise if my sister happens to ask but, as we exit the bathroom together, Kimberly's disappointed face tells me that my recommendations won't do them any good.

"What are you three up to?" she asks.

"Oh, nothing sis." I wrap my hand around her shoulder, leading her away from her soon-to-be-ex-employees. "You enjoying the party?"

"I guess. Where'd you get that?" She points to Johnnie. "That's Creag's. You might not want to finish the whole thing. And don't get too drunk, please. You need to make sure my apartment is presentable in the morning. My flight's at 6 AM. You promised."

The bottle is halfway empty. Enough for me to put it away and avoid Creag McCullough's wrath. Creag makes my sister look small, which is no easy feat. If I remember correctly, on a drunken night in this very loft, his beard was measured to be bigger than my head.

"Yea, sure. Not too drunk. Clean the apartment. Right. How is Creag anyway? I haven't seen him in months."

"In the beginning it was easy. Almost refreshing. I had all this time for me, for my business. But the apartment doesn't even smell like him anymore..."

Kimberly's eyes begin to deceive her normally stoic nature. I can tell she's been hitting the sauce tonight and I'm devilishly proud. A heart to heart is impending and inevitable. To her point, the apartment currently smells like alcohol and sweat.

"Well, that's why you're going out there, right? You guys can finally have some one-on-one time. How much longer is this job he's working on anyway? I thought he would be back by summer."

"That's the problem. The job is being extended."

"Extended as in…"

"It's going to take another six months to a year," she says.

"Ah."

The things we do for love. Well, not we. But others.

She is holding it together, but a ball of emotion is unraveling behind her placid blue eyes. In my comatose state, a spasm of feeling even slaps at my tear ducts. An architect and a furniture designer. A match made in design heaven. Unfortunately, there are a couple hitches in this perfect gait. This job Creag has been on is in London, his ancestral home. Kimberly's company is here, her newfound home. She's taking a three-month long visit to keep the hope alive.

"Of course, I'm excited to see him. I just hope this isn't his way of trying to convince me to move there. I don't want to give him any false hope. I'm a city girl. A New York City girl," Kimberly says.

"We were raised in the suburbs," I reply.

"Fuck off."

She laughs and punches me in the shoulder. I am sure it will leave a bruise.

"I'm a city girl now," she continues. "You know I've lived in this place almost half as long as I lived at Mom and Dad's?"

"Which makes you only a quarter full of shit," I say.

She doesn't laugh.

"I just don't want to give him any false hope," she says.

Her eyes start to water. She wipes away a stray tear and her finger gets caught pushing back a sweaty bang. I grab her head, pull it down on my shoulder, and squeeze, attempting to cut off any leftover circulation of tears I can't handle.

"Don't worry about all of that Kim. Just go and enjoy your time with the man you love. Who knows, maybe you'll like London. Maybe you'll hate it. But remember, it could always be worse. You could be stuck in an office for 40 hours a week like me."

Usually, comparing my miserable existence to Kim's brings a smile to her face. Knowing she's the successful sibling stacks the chips neatly on her shoulder. But this time her eyes don't light up in vain delight; they stay swollen with held back tears and follow me as I walk outside for a smoke.

9:16 PM

A film has built at the back of my tongue. This is due to the irresistible urge of puffing down back-to-back cigarettes. The wooden planks underfoot along with an Adirondack chair and a lantern hanging from the wall almost lull me into kicking my shoes off, but the sounds don't match. Crashing waves are replaced by the weak and incessant beeps of horns. Wind rattles the high locked fence at the bottom of the set of stairs.

"Who has a deck in Manhattan?" I ask the cosmos.

"That's exactly what I was thinking."

For a second, I wonder if the sky has heard me; that God, in her Spanish accent, has answered my deep and philosophical question of deck necessity in Manhattan. In wonderment, I gaze up at the smog that has answered my prayers.

"What's the purpose?" I ask. "Kim has beach chairs for Christ's...I mean...for damn sakes. Who needs to lay out in Chelsea?"

"Definitely not Jesus," the cosmos says.

Tracking the voice of the universe to ground level, I discover there is another smog admirer in my midst. Her back is toward me, head tilted toward the heavens, and I watch her dark brown hair move back and forth, skimming the straps of her sundress. Back and forth, forth and back; the wind is more confounded than me, having trouble choosing which way is more beautiful. My eyes follow the dress straps down, like two yellow brick roads leading me to the promised land. But her dress is waving too. There's no *body* in sight, no ass to gawk at, no legs to mention. She's enmeshed in a flowing yellow. Her dress and her hair are a moving synchronization, a flow state with the breeze, the shots, the yip.

"Hello?" she asks, still looking up.

After what must be minutes of spectating and simultaneously slobbering over the brown filter of cigarette number three, I remember to speak.

"What are you doing out here all alone?" I ask, popping in a piece of gum.

"'Hello, Clarice' would have made a better first impression," she says. "Are you going to ask me if I want some candy next?"

She's still gazing at the sky. Sounding like a speculative serial killer hasn't scared her off.

"Sky," she continues. "Why are you so creepy?"

"I'm not *always* this creepy," I say.

She turns towards me. The confusion on her face makes it obvious that she was expecting a man in a strait jacket and a hockey mask.

"Just sometimes?" she asks.

Her lightly tanned skin lies under smattered freckles. They run from cheek to nose to cheek like a Jackson Pollock. Her eyes are the piercing green of an apple. She seems foreign, not in country but in time. Mary Magdalene and La Madonna in one. She does know of Jesus' whereabouts after all.

I send up a silent prayer that the curtains match the drapes, which sounds odd in this asexual tone. I pray that the outside matches the inside. I've been tricked there before.

"It's weather dependent," I finally say.

"It depends on the weather?"

"Well…yeah. It happens every winter. My social skills get frozen up. It takes a while for them to thaw out. I'd say I'm melted down to here."

I place my hand at my neck.

"What did it?"

"The alcohol," I say.

Her laugh bursts from her as if even she hadn't expected it. Her teeth shine between dark lips.

"I needed to get some air after whatever it was you poured in there," she says.

"Ah! Warm vodka. My specialty. I can make you another if you want?"

"I'd rather jump into the river."

"You think that was bad? You haven't tried anything yet. Red Bull Vodka, Jägerbombs, Long Island Iced Tea, pick your poison," I say.

She puts her finger in her mouth and pretends to gag, inducing a smorgasbord of disgusting thoughts. One in particular involves tossing her on top of the garbage cans at the bottom of the steps, bringing an entirely new and disastrous meaning to the term dirty thoughts. As my mind races away into its deviant abyss, she smiles, and all the pornographic images fade in comparison to reality.

"You would like what we drink where I am from," she says.

"Where's that?"

"I was born in New York but raised in Barcelona. So that makes me a triple citizen."

"I only counted two there."

"American. Spanish. Catalan."

"Forgive me but, I don't get it," I admit.

"Barcelona is technically Spain but also part of Catalonia," she says.

"I may have just gone cross eyed."

"Poor American," she laughs. "Catalonia is its own nationality."

"Like Texas?" I ask.

"Like Texas," she confirms.

I guide her back to the topic of drinks. Something relatable.

"Gin and tonics. Everyone drinks big gin and tonics," she says.

"And wine. We have some of the best wine that no one talks about but trust me, it is good. Rioja, Tempranillos, Garnacha…"

As she talks, her eyes come alive from their deep sockets. Her arms flail and her lips move with no effort. Her freckles dance.

"What's Barcelona like?" I ask. "I've never been but my mother talks about it like it's heaven on earth."

"She's been there?"

"Lived there for a little while. She was on the Exile Express. Havana to Spain, Spain to Union City," I say.

"So jyou are Cuban?" she asks, loosening her accent.

"Half," I say.

"And half gringo?" she laughs.

"Si…is it that noticeable?"

"¿Por qué no has estado en España?" she asks.

"Huh?"

"Oh no," she says. "Don't tell me you can't speak Spanish…"

I shake my head. My face feels like it's been slathered with hot sauce. The embarrassment of never taking my mother's maiden tongue seriously has finally caught up with me. Hours, weeks, months, even years of learning would have been worth it to speak to this woman.

"Aye, no problema. I don't mind English. It's better for writing than speaking though."

"You write?" I ask.

"Poquito," she says, pinching her pointer and thumb.

"A little bit?"

"See! You're getting it already."

We laugh. Then pause.

"Want to get out of here?" I blurt.

"With you?"

I look around like John Travolta in *Pulp Fiction*.

"And go where?" she asks.

"Anywhere they serve gin."

She smiles and glances inside.

I've secretly been waiting for the other shoe to drop since being hypnotized by the cobra-like movements of her hair and dress. Assuming she is single is nothing short of blasphemy. God forgive us sinners, now and at the hour of our death – which could come at any moment to my poor, pounding, heart.

> ### Beautiful women are not the same species as me.
> 9:20 PM – April 17th – 2015

Sent.

"Huh, did you say something?" I ask.

"Beautiful women are the same species as you," she says.

"Wait, what?"

"I said, phones and cigarettes are bad for you."

Who knew a side effect of cocaine was faulty eardrums.

9 : 48 PM

Half an hour later our conversation is still stuck on the ill effects of cell phones, not cigarettes.

"Cigarettes aren't *that* bad for you," she says.

I find these words as encouraging as her speech on the wonders of Spain's alcohol selection.

"The surgeon general says otherwise, but please enlighten me," I say.

"Well, compared to your phone, the cigarette is almost nothing. That ball of energy in your pocket shooting whatever it shoots right into the place you don't want anything shot and can't be stubbed out," she says.

She looks down at my junk as if she has x-ray vision. A terrifying thought even if I'm semi-erect already. Regardless of how committed

I am to her cause, I take my phone from my side pocket and place it in the back.

"And those thumbs," she continues. "Those poor thumbs. If there was any way to invest in orthopedics on the stock market I would do it."

I note the possible investment while rubbing the base of my thumb.

"But the neck. The neck is the worst. Imagine your head is a bowling ball in the palm of your hand, slowly moving forward. That is what your poor little neck is trying to hold up every time you look down. Now imagine this with two bowling balls."

She points to my head and the curled mess of hair on top of it.

This woman is cutting me to the core. I'm a creepy, two-headed freak who can't speak Spanish. There is little reason for me to be alive and she definitely doesn't want to leave here with the likes of me. But for some reason I can't wipe the dumb smile off my face every time she speaks.

"And don't get me started with how those things screw with our heads."

"You mean from the radiation?" I ask.

"No, our minds. We sit and scroll for hours pretending we are doing something. We get lost in video after video of nothing and the worst part is that it tricks us into thinking we are actually being productive. Think about Twitter for instance. You take fifteen minutes writing a thought that goes into nowhere and just disappears. No one cares."

"No one cares until you become famous and they want to use it against you," I say.

"Exactly!" she laughs. "And then there's Instagram. I actually feel bad for men who have Instagram."

"Please, give me your sympathies. It is a rough life I'm living."

"I'm serious," she continues. "You have pictures of millions of hot women on your phone. Back in the day you'd have to buy a magazine or watch a movie to get a glimpse of such hotness. Or, you'd have to do something even crazier...talk to a real living girl that you find attractive. The horror!"

"Preach," I say. I almost get on my knees and bow.

"It makes every man turn into a little fanboy," she says.

I'm glad I didn't bow.

"Liking pictures of girls you've never met," she continues. "Gawking at women who are photoshopped, thinking that you have a chance with not one but all of them. And meanwhile there are girls out there, real girls, who a real man would kill for and her knight in shining armor has his eyes glazed over looking at the Kardashians."

"I'd rather look at you then anyone on this thing," I say. I chuck my phone over the banister into the pile of garbage bags.

"That's how a woman wants to be talked to."

I smile, lighting a cigarette. "Want one?" I ask.

"No, those are bad for you."

We laugh again.

"But I do like the smell," she says.

A lass after me own heart. I start down the stairs to retrieve my device.

"Don't," she says.

"What?"

"If you leave it there, I'll leave with you," she says.

"If I leave my phone in that pile of trash you'll leave with me?"

"Was I not clear?" she asks.

"Done and done," I say, laughing.

"I'm not joking. Leave it right there in the garbage. All night."

I don't know if I'm fascinated or terrified.

"I'm Lou by the way."

"Marissa."

Her hand is light and warm. Skin soft as a double L. That much Spanish I do know. Bella.

9:55 PM

"Marissa! There you are."

A woman's voice surprises us from the bottom of the stairs.

"I can't bring you anywhere. You're always disappearing. It's my job to keep you safe in such a big bad city. You did it for me in Spain, now I'm returning the favor. Where have you been?"

The voice comes from a girl I can barely register as a human being. In Marissa's light, everything else fails recognition.

"I've been out here. How is the party?" Marissa asks.

"Dead. I think Kim is asleep, and half her staff are arguing about the mayor. This guy Christian and I have been talking. We're going out, do you want to come with us?"

Marissa turns to me: an odd mix of air and earth-like mist. A yellow, freckled mirage. She mouths to me the words *leave it* and smirks.

Plan A.

10:02 PM

I hold the door open for Marissa as we enter our first bar on Professor Lou's New York City bar tour. Shame on me, I know.

"Why thank yjou," she says, an errant j slipping into her y.

As the four of us take seats at an Irish Pub I order four Irish Car Bombs. Marissa looks at me like I have twelve heads, which would mean I now have ten more than she already thinks I have.

"What the hell is this?" she asks.

She's looking at the shot of Jameson and Baileys the color of old milk and a half-filled pint glass of Guinness.

"You drop the shot in and then chug the whole thing. You have to do it fast or the Baileys will curdle," I say.

"Curdle? What do you mean curdle?"

"Just chug it."

She takes the entire concoction down in two seconds. As I'm still chugging, she's wiping her upper lip with a napkin.

"I'm impressed and emasculated all at once," I admit.

"That's not so bad actually. Definitely better than your warm vodka at the party. My choice next."

She orders four gin and tonics and I am thankful.

"They are like a mint for the stomach," she says.

Her taste is impeccable. The drink feels like it's cooling my insides. I lean over to check on Christian and the friend. I haven't had a chance to ask her name and don't foresee any effort being made on that front. Christian is telling a story, his accent and pecs out in full force. If I had my druthers, I would have chosen any other person on planet earth to accompany me on this double date. I run the very real risk of becoming the boring guy next to a person with two last names. Aisle or VanNeece would have been nice, but I have no idea where they are. I don't care either. I try and think of something to say, anything to make me seem interesting, and come up empty.

"What do you want from life?" Marissa asks me.

An abrupt question. One I hadn't really pondered in my twenty-five years on this planet. What do I want from life?

"Another gin," I say. "You?"

She laughs. It's an honest laugh though I can't tell if it is at me or with me.

"When you were on the deck talking to God I noticed that you meant it. Pero, you don't act like you mean anything that you do. In my country they would call you a jester," she says.

"That's what I'm here for...the laughs," I say.

I hand her another gin, though she hasn't finished her first, and her fingers touch my hand with the glass. For a moment she stares into my eyes, piercing through the twenty odd drinks I've built up around myself in defense. In any other situation I would lean in and kiss the girl, but I don't move a muscle. What do I want from life? A frightening thought.

"I want serious," she says.

"Okay, I'll be serious. Let me think."

"No, from life. That's what I want. If you take everything serious, even fun, then you don't miss anything."

"You're funny though."

"I take joking dead serious."

She picks up a knife and points it at me with a murderous stare. But she can't hold it in and starts cracking up.

10:23 PM

On second thought, what I want from life is for Christian to cut the shit. On our walk to the next bar, he is droning on about his latest trip to Mexico again. "Puerto Escondido, a small little beach town that offers the biggest waves on the West Coast." No one cares, bud. Except the two ladies are yucking it up. Marissa's holding on to my arm as we walk and watching her laugh at another man's stories makes me want to kill someone. Not her of course. Her laugh makes my stomach quiver. The way her neck gets taut and her mouth opens wide and her freckles spread and reach for her ears. I'd like to be the man that makes her laugh like this.

At Christian's suggestion, we stop at a little taqueria the size of my apartment. I want to say fuck this place, but it does look cool. The shittier the wallpaper, the better the food and drink. Lou's bar tour has turned into the Christian self-fellating show and somehow, I must get this train back on the track.

Christian runs off an order of drinks and tacos in Spanish but when the waiter asks him for a card to hold, Christian's arms have taken the form of a T-Rex. My sister must pay a shit wage. I wonder if the Instagram version of Christian is just an illusion. He turns around to tap his pockets as if his wallet has grown legs and walked away. The evil part of me wants to leave him out to dry. I get giddy waiting for him to come up with an excuse. Even better would be to watch his card get declined. I am not ashamed to say I'll do anything to make myself look better to Marissa. I wait a half a second and then realize I don't want to taint this night. I can hear my father's voice in my head, which never happens while I'm drinking. It says something along the lines of never doing something you will regret in the morning. I've already broken that rule fifty times tonight, but I stop the counter before it hits fifty-one and hand my card to the waiter. There's another line from my father that pops into my booze-laden head. I try to ignore it but can't. *I proposed to your mother in seven days.*

"Why are you paying?" Marissa whispers to me. "You paid at the last place."

"It's okay. I like paying."

"I'll pay at the next stop."

"Absolutely not," I say.

She throws me a sincere smile. "What do you do?" she asks.

"Nothing important."

"No, I want to know, really."

"You're not gonna like this," I warn her.

"A drug dealer?" she asks.

"Nope."

"Wall Street?"

"Next."

"A sex trafficker?"

"If I was only so lucky. But no."

"Hmmmm…" she ponders.

"It's worse than all of those combined," I say.

"An arms dealer?"

"Close. I market phone apps."

She feigns horror.

"How could you do such a thing?"

"It's a family business. My dad is a partner and I guess I was born to warp the minds of our youth. But it pays enough to handle this sixty-seven dollar bill at this lovely little taqueria, so I'd say corrupting the world with our phone apps is officially worth it."

"What kind of apps?" she asks.

"Let me see your phone, I'll show you."

"I don't have a phone."

"You…what?"

"I *have* a phone, but when I go out with friends I don't bring it," she says.

"I must admit, I'm shocked."

"What's shocking?"

"Now were both phoneless," I say.

"What could go wrong?" she asks.

She smiles, then takes a little nip of her Mexican beer.

The word regal has never entered my mind but there it is, pasted on the inside of my forehead in neon lights. The marquee underneath reads "and intriguing." Don't fuck this up Lou.

11:13 PM

Somehow we've found ourselves in a place with a dancefloor but it feels like we are in an unfinished basement. The piping is visible above and there are little mounds of insulation spray that looks like mold. It feels like drinking in a war zone.

Another round of gin and tonics fuel our corner of the bar that shall remain nameless. No, seriously, the bar's name is Nameless. Ironic isn't it? I couldn't be angrier that this is a place now associated with my bar tour, but Marissa's friend was adamant that it was good.

Christian is off the deep end and has, for all intents and purposes, ditched his own date and is now drunkenly focused on mine. I don't begrudge him. Marissa is not only drop dead gorgeous, she's also fucking hilarious. She's been stealing little glances over Christian's hunched shoulder at me, winking, which keeps me off of suicide watch. It's as if she's entertaining this conversation to get in my head, which only intrigues me more.

Long ago, Professor Lou learned not to show any jealousy. It was around the time those eyes and bangs in the window at the liquor store were attached to a real person. So instead of grabbing Cristian by the arm and escorting him from the premises, I sit next to the friend who still, like this bar, remains nameless. The laidback tactic has always worked for me and, it seems now, is especially working with Christian so intent on embarrassing himself. My talent for hiding my inebriation levels will only increase my standing in Marissa's eyes. The drunker he gets, the better I look. But somehow this thought doesn't cure my dejected position. The friend and I sit on our stools, drinking our drinks, with nothing to say to one another. The bartenders wear overalls. So ironic.

Christian finally loses steam and has to go to the bathroom, thankfully leaving Marissa alone. The two had been speaking in Spanish and their staccato conversation felt like a rambling nightmare. Not learning my mother's native tongue has really come full circle. Christian sneaks behind me and whispers in my ear. "You got any sheet left?"

"What shit?"

"The fucking jyip man. I know jyou hab it."

The man's eyes are crossed and his tongue is hanging out of his mouth like an overheated cow. Do I really need him yapping like a chihuahua sped up with a bump of blow?

"Here," I oblige.

Anything to get him to leave.

A shady high five ensues, which is so obvious it hurts. This maneuver has yet to fail my compadres and I. For half the night, the half with Marissa, I completely forgot about the drug that was keeping me going. Turns out good conversation with a woman is more powerful than any narcotic on the market. And there are always her eyes, those freckles, that could keep a narcoleptic alert.

"Having fun?" Marissa asks.

"Not so much. Your friend isn't as fun as you are," I say.

"Poor Lou," she pinches my cheek like a mother. "Pobrecito."

"If I knew what that meant I would probably be offended."

"It means 'you poor thing,'" she says.

"Is that what I look like?"

"Well, that speech you made at your sister's was poor. And the vodka was worse. And that girl who looked like she was made out of balloons was the worst of all. But to top it off you let me take a, como se dice, ear bashing from your friend."

"Ear beating," I laugh.

"Si, un ear beating," she pretends to smash her ears. "But you do know how to run a good bar tour. I don't know if you're poor or awful, but you are fun. But maybe you're something else or could be. Yo no sé."

"Like what?" I ask.

A house song with a Spanish guitar and an off beat blasts from the speakers, exciting Marissa out of her examination of me. The song has the same rhythm of something my mother would listen to in the house, dancing by herself, while her husband sat in a recliner nodding his head off beat. Life with a gringo. Marissa grabs my hand and pulls me to the dancefloor.

She starts the dance by pushing me out to a safe distance, moving her hips, sundress swaying, feet close together, hands rising above her bare shoulders. She moves closer, inch by tortured inch, until her ass just barely brushes against my belt buckle then backs away with a devilish smile. Her eyes lit with a flirtatious joy. I'm not sure what this dance is or how to even keep the beat, but I try to mimic her moves. Dance apart, creep into one another, barely touch, move away. Each turn we take gets closer, quicker, the distance and time between touches becoming smaller and smaller. Every time we make contact I am afraid she is going to feel what can only be described as a polite boner poking her in the back. Is it not okay to show your appreciation for a woman you find attractive? I am too enamored with the sensualness of this ritual to answer that question.

As she works her way around me and then closer and closer and slower and slower I am filled with a rushing urge of need. I grab her hips, slide my hands down her thighs, as her ass gyrates on my belt buckle. If I was sober there's a chance I wouldn't have lasted even this long.

She turns around, wrapping her hands around my neck, and I have this Cro-Magnon like urge to carry her back to my cave those social science classes were supposed to have helped me crawl out of. But what did they teach me? By this point I would have had to ask one hundred questions of permission. Can I put my hand there? Is it okay if I smell the sweat dripping down your neck? Does it hurt when I grip your thigh like that?

Ignoring any and all rules, I lean in for a kiss. She cranes her neck as far back as it will go, like Neo dodging a bullet, to avoid my lips. She moves a dangling errant wet curl away from my forehead and pats my head like a little boy. I find the whole thing endearing if not the most embarrassing thing that has ever happened to me. At the change of the song, she leads my dejected body through the dead sea of people.

We sit down at the bar alone. Christian and the friend are still out on the dancefloor. In an attempt to avoid Marissa's eyes, I watch them, baffled. Their dancing looks like two people humping with clothes on. It's got a hint of soft-core porn without the smooth jazz. Filthy hip-hop lyrics scream from the speakers. *Ya little stupid ass bitch, I ain't fuckin with you!*

For all of Christian's bodily charm, the long hair, the delts, the jaw line, he moves like a big horny gorilla. His penis is probably the same size as that particular ape's, which is the only proper explanation for his absurd Instagram persona. His dancing is anything but sexual, almost robotic, an agony of the body only. No soul.

"So jyou know Guaguancó?" she asks.

I turn to Marissa, still embarrassed, but her eyes are filled with green delight.

"No, what's that?" I ask.

"The dancing we were doing. Not exactly, but close. It's called Guaguancó. It's a type of Cuban rumba. You're telling me you don't know Spanish *or* Guaguancó? Ay, dios mìo," she laughs, smacking her forehead.

I start to gulp what must be my twelfth gin and tonic, trying to wipe away any and all memory of this night, when she presses my arm down, takes my drink, places it on the bar, and grabs my head. She puts her nose to mine. She stays there, our eyes staring into one another, her breath of gin and mint and heat soaking into my upper lip, noses just barely touching. There is something in that point of contact. Some urge deep inside to stay there yet go forward, to kiss the girl without touching lips.

She finally backs away.

"You see? That's Guaguancó. Getting closer and closer. Teasing and taunting. Building it up. Delaying pleasure."

Christian disturbs the moment by smacking me on the back while sliding the crackling bag back into my pocket. This trick is far less sketchy. No eye contact or an obvious exchange of goods but there is always anxious hesitation; did the bag make it into the pocket?

I'm not sure if it's the exhaustion of the dance, the thirty plus drinks I've had or the denied kiss but I'm starting to feel a little woozy. I can consciously say I am in the middle of a gray out, where the night starts to come in and out of focus. There is only one remedy for this and that's to hit the little bag that's hopefully made it into my pocket.

"I'm going to the bathroom," I announce out of my reverie. "I'll be right back."

"Hurry," she says. "I want to dance more."

I saddle up in a stall and check for the bag. It all hits me. The drinking. The yip. The noise. Marissa. I close my eyes and the black sways up and down like the ocean at night. It's almost impossible to focus on one of the broken white tiles behind the toilet. The only way to power through this is another bump, which I find shaking at the end of my key.

This time it does nothing.

The alcohol has won this cat and mouse game.

Images of the stall begin to flash in and out in real time.

The sounds of flushing toilet stutter.

I take out my phone, which looks like three at the moment. I'm sorry this relationship has started off with a lie, Marissa. Please forgive me. I couldn't just leave it there all alone in the trash. Me and this phone have been through so much together. What if I needed it? What if there was an emergency? What if I thought of something funny to tweet?

Hello?

11:44 PM – April 17th – 2015

Sent.

And then there I am, in the mirror. I'm washing my hands but can't feel the water. My hair is out of control and my eyes look like two glazed donuts. I think the me in the mirror says 'help' but I haven't moved my mouth. Blackout is impending. It's fight or flight, buddy. Fight or flight.

Saturday

10:03 AM

I emerge from chrysalis with no wings to spread, just a dry mouth and a body temp of the sun. Leaning on an elbow, I assess the situation. The room is vaguely familiar but it definitely isn't mine.

For one, it is clean.

For two, it smells fantastic.

That's what's familiar.

It smells like Kristen's room. Very Sexy For Her, a scent by Victoria's Secret, accosts every inch of throw pillow, drape, and couch cushion. I might not be a fragrance expert but whoever named that concoction was right on the money. It may be difficult to tease out this new relationship with the smell of Kristen everywhere. The same part of the brain that handles smells also manages emotions. There was little to no emotion involved on my end with Kristen. Admitting that makes me feel like a pig but isn't that what all of us twenty-something-year-olds want? Sex for the kicks. No strings attached. Never too thirsty. You learn these things in your first class with Professor Lou.

I leave Marissa wrapped in the covers and head to the bathroom.

Either the mirror is distorted or Marissa lives in a funhouse. Don't blame the mirror, kid, you've seen this before. You've prepared for this, you puffy bastard. My face has doubled in size overnight. The bags holding up my eyes seem fragile, as if they were filled with beer.

Submerging my face into a sink full of cold water barely registers. It should reduce the swelling if nothing else. The once glorious waves of powder-induced thoughts now fade away before they begin. There is one errant thought that escapes through the fog. On any normal morning, with any other bed partner, I would groan on in my head about how sleeping with someone is overrated. Not the sex, of course, the actual sleeping. A cocoon of sweat, heat, and hair is brutal enough as is but when your first instinct is to flee, it becomes oppressive. This time I feel different. There is no overflowing dread.

Drying my face I notice the smell hasn't skipped the hand towels. I'm still surprised I can smell anything after last night's antics. There's an odd feeling, the way the towel hangs from the rack with three little pom poms dangling from its edge, that I've been here before.

When I walk out, someone who looks a lot like Kristen is sitting up on the bed, checking her phone. My mind is so mangled it's hard to process what is going on. What would have normally taken two seconds to figure out takes me a whopping ten. I leap back into the bathroom. I shut the door and turn on the lights and there it is, plain as day. Kristen's bathroom in Kristen's apartment.

"Lou?" I hear my name being called by whatever being that's out there.

I turn the light off.

Where the mirror should be there's only a black abyss. I have never been so frightened in my life. I have no idea how I got here. I say Bloody Mary three times. I start to see red writing on the mirror. It's dripping. It says run. Which I do.

"Lou, what the fuck?"

"Hey…Kristen."

"Are you okay?" she asks.

"Yea, why wouldn't I be?"

This is not a drill. I walk towards Kristen with short steps wondering when the evil spirit is going to attack. I cover my dangling cock, a natural instinct for a naked man in the presence of what must be a demon. I stand on the opposite side of the bed, never breaking eye contact, and start feeling around for my phone. Kristen is naked herself but even her dime sized nipples don't distract me. The phone is nowhere in the sheets and the ghost of Kristen present has this look on her face like *she's* the scared one.

"Why are you being weird?" she asks.

"Hungover," I say.

"What are you feeling around for?"

"Nothing? What do you mean?"

"Your phones on the charger. I plugged it in for you last night. You were pretty fucked up. How much did you drink?"

My phone is lying peacefully on her nightstand, charging, just like this spirit said. Aisle may have a point about Kristen. The blond apparition I've been sharing a makeshift womb with all night has no idea she's passed an updated version of the door test. Another Professor Lou insight – if you leave your phone off the charger and she plugs it in for you in the middle of the night, you may have tripped on one of the three good ones. If not…you dump her, and you dump her, fast. Advice co-opted from *A Bronx Tale* should always be followed. This time it has fallen on deaf and drunk ears.

"Too much…clearly," I say.

┌─────────────────────┐
│   10:10 AM   │
└─────────────────────┘

I think about taking my phone and making a run for it, sans clothes. Running around naked in New York City might be frowned upon but not unheard of…

But I don't.

It's not the lack of clothes that make me stay but the confused look on Kristen's face.

10:11 AM

I start to get dressed.

"You're leaving already?" she asks.

She reaches out and touches my leg. Then moves her hand up a bit, and a bit more, until she has a handful of me.

Having a heart is all about action in the tiny moments that make or break your conscience. If my heart says no, my body should follow. It almost does. My hands push her away, my legs squirm, but one part of me does not follow suit. The part with the one-track mind. Going along with this farce infers there is more to this relationship than just sex. If only there was some magical spirit that would allow a cock to deflate in this type of an emergency. This (gasp!) is not the case. The billion years of cock evolution that got my genes to this point take over.

The room is dimly lit through cracks from a shaded window. Ghosts in the white sheets move, solemnly, slowly, rocking up and down like white waves. The whole thing is methodical. I feel like I'm taking stage direction. Put hand here. Slap ass now. Pump. Pump. Pump. It's passionless. Our breath heats the room to a hellish degree. There is no hope for a finish. There is no hope here.

We stop. She walks to the bathroom. A woman doesn't like it when you can't finish. It means there is something defunct with them. In this case, that is not true. Kristen is a shining example of everything a man should want in a sex partner. It's not you, it's me, rings hollow but true.

Sitting gingerly on the bed, I take in the silence. A few moments alone, a few lifetimes alone, could cure me. I check my fully charged phone.

Aisle: Where'd Lou go?

VanNeece: Typical Lou ditch. Sick friend.

Aisle: We're going to Finale if you want to meet us there.

I'd like to clear my good name in the group chat but it is clear, short of a burning building with me inside, I cannot seem to muster up a single care.

I look for a text or a call from Kristen last night, but our latest text conversation has been deleted and there are no calls in the log. What the fuck happened?

Last night is commonly referred to as a blackout—where space, time, and light melt into one incoherent, dark blob. You start at one place, the lights go out, and you end up somewhere else. These time travels are getting old.

Instead of planning my exit, I lie in bed, eyes closed. Distorted images of Marissa pass over a black canvas. Her long eyelashes flutter like crows, freckles spin, her hand in mine crushes into a thousand pieces.

I scroll to the M's in my contact list, hoping, but to no avail. What is usually second nature to drunk me, acquiring a number, has mysteriously been evaded. Though drunk me deserves a good scolding, maybe a few spanks on the ass, I go with the guilt trip. I am extremely disappointed…no, not…not angry…just…disappointed.

With this tremendous opportunity wasted I close my eyes again. The momentary silence is mesmerizing. No cars, no sirens, no talking. A mini blessing bestowed upon my morning.

"What are you doing today?" I hear from the bathroom.

Why do I bother?

```
10:40 AM
```

"I had to leave ten minutes ago," I reply.

She walks out of the bathroom in a robe, ashamed of her unsatisfactory nakedness. I feel ashamed to have made her feel that way. Her nakedness is a blessing to anyone she'll give it to, except me.

"Can I ask you a question?" she says.

These six words, in this exact order, are the scariest in the English language. Personal questions suck, but questions from girls you used to hang out with and were just inside go far passed sucking.

"Sure," I say.

"Did you mean what you said last night?"

What *did* I say?

"Depends on which part."

"That you wanted to see me more," she says.

"Well…we always have fun when we hangout."

"Okay, text me later," she says.

"I will."

I won't.

A sock is missing somewhere as I put my shoes on. I'll have to leave it behind – this isn't the fucking Marines.

```
10:52 AM
```

The PATH train is empty on the ride back to Hoboken and my eyes stare, unfocused and blank, at the empty seat in front of me. Click, click, click. My brain only responds to sounds. No clear thoughts are coming in. No thoughts at all. Just metal, people, metal people, flying by. I vaguely remember a request from Kimberly to check the state of her apartment due to her early flight, but I am too far gone for that. The PATH just keeps on clicking.

10:53 AM

Somehow, in my catatonic state, I remember how it started six months ago. Kristen was 99% perfect. Almost there, but not quite. I don't even blame her for what happened. I should have been prepared for the other shoe to drop. When you are a single man your mind has the tendency to treat women like stocks. A market defines value and the dating market is no different. Some women are bears, both metaphorically and physically, and you short the shit out of them. I was bullish on Kristen. The bob. The bum. The boobs. The fun. All worth dumping your dating capital in. The dating market is always volatile. One day you're infatuated, the next the stock plummets.

I would consider Kristen, in stock terms, to be a crash. Most crashes are precipitated by a speculative bubble and that's what we were creating, twice a week, every week, for 10 weeks. It started too good to be true, as most bubbles do, then burst into a billion pieces with one sentence.

But before the burst, the beginning...

We met at McSwiggan's, my favorite bar. It's a dirty Irish pub that lives up to its name. It's dark, dingy, and you can get lost in there if you aren't careful. To this day I don't know if sunlight has ever entered the place. Blinds shut, TVs on, drinks poured over and over and over. It is a place of wonder and magic.

It was a Tuesday of all nights. The worst night of the week. I had a particularly rough day at the office where I was forced to take part in not one but two whole meetings. You can't imagine the horror.

The only way to forget such a day is to park the car in the garage and head straight to the bar. Do not pass go. Do not collect $200.

I started off with a perfectly poured Guinness that had enough head to drown in and a neat Redbreast in lieu of my normal Jameson shot. I was feeling quite uppity after the two drinks. My pinky was out on the next round. High class drinks for a high class broad. With pinky extended I turned in my barstool to take a lap around the bar and by the grace of God, my finger wound up in the ear of a short young lady. I had inadvertently wet willy-ed the poor girl and I expected to have a drink thrown at me. I wondered if a pinky in the ear was considered sexual assault but even in my wildest porn searches I have yet to see the earhole used as an orifice. This rationale all happened in an instant. Before I could ask for forgiveness, the girl stuck her pointer finger in her mouth, wiggled it around to accumulate as much saliva as possible, and stuck the entire digit into my left ear.

I couldn't have been more enamored with a meet-cute in my life. If I was a regular man with regular feelings I would have dreamed of telling our kids the story. For weeks it felt like this was an actual possibility. I felt the same spark, the same flood of life enter me like I had ten years prior. The ash of Arianna grew like a phoenix in the form of Kristen. A flying blonde bird. For a moment I thought I could finally put the ghost of Arianna to bed. She was no longer needed as a cornerstone in my brain. She had been replaced with a more mature version. An equally wild spirit that could hold a job. The spark was lit and the embers were stoked for eight weeks. Eight glorious weeks.

It had been the first time in years that Arianna failed to make it into my dreams. She no longer held a stranglehold on my subconscious. It was as if I was in some glorious detox. No tremens, no hurt, no pain, just utter release. It was all so easy, which should have set off alarm bells up and down the halls of my mind. Easy come, easy go, in the falsetto of Freddie Mercury should have been playing at full volume in my head. But Kristen played the dating game exquisitely. She was perfect in every way up until the tenth week.

First and foremost, she applied no pressure. This is absolutely crucial to the success of any modern relationship. If a man feels pressure early (or at all) the man will immediately run. Kristen knew this and acted accordingly. The first few weeks of text exchanges went something like this.

Kristen: Me and my friends are going out to "place x"…if you and your boys aren't doing anything come meet us.

Me: Done and done.

There are a few glaring pluses to such an exchange, others more subtle. Professor Lou has an uncanny ability to sift through the details.

1. "If you aren't doing anything."
This verbiage immediately relieves the tension of any would-be relationship. It says she is not expecting anything from me. This is good. Expectations should always be at the lowest level when talking to a man-child.

2. "Me and my friends"
That is a line in the sand that makes it clear this is not a date. Phew. I don't do dates. They are pressure-filled narcissistic tropes that distract from the question at hand – are we going to have sex tonight? I refuse to pay for sex. What else is a date if not upscale prostitution? As much as a woman wants to be independent she will always expect a man to pay. Never, ever forget this, fellas. If you agree to a date it is your wallet on the hook.

3. "You and your boys"
Now this, this is just diabolical. She knows exactly what she is doing here. If I can tell my boys that a girl I want to see has hot friends it kills two birds with one stone. The first bird is that I do not have to ditch my friends to hang out with this girl. It means that the myriad of shit I will get for

abandoning them is avoided. The second bird is that the girl I want to see has transformed into the "cool girl." She is now the girl who not only looks after my physical needs but the physical needs of my nearest and dearest. It cannot be overstated that a girl who attempts to get my friends laid is a keeper. That is of course until that tenth fucking week.

On the nights it was only us we started at a bar. This was non-negotiable. Start at a bar, on barstools, mixed in with a ton of other people on barstools. Never, and I mean never, sit at a high-top table. High-top table equals date and we were not dating. Only fucking. Only having fun.

Another plus about Kristen was her knowledge of the bedroom. The first night at McSwiggan's we made out in a corner and she tugged on my junk for all of five seconds before abruptly leaving. In the midst of her junk grabbing, she slid my phone out of my pocket and put her number in with the eggplant emoji next to her name. It was just the right amount of teasing that can make a man kiss a woman's feet for the rest of her life.

When we finally did fuck she did not disappoint. Her little body contorted into such extreme positions I thought she would snap. She never did. She was pliable and plowable in every way imaginable. Most importantly she knew how to take control. I admit this may be a kink of mine, but when a woman is on top she drives me mad. I'm not for being tied up and ball gagged but a woman who is willing to push you onto the couch and have her way with you is something so fantastic it is hard to find the words. Maybe this little pleasure of mine is an ego trip. This might sound nuts but men want to be wanted too. For every sick-fuck rapist getting jacked up on control there are nine guys who just want a woman to want them. You can call it an ego trip or an ego boost but women want the same fucking thing. We're all just animals here. If I learned anything in *SOC 2200 – Working Women*, it's that men and women aren't so different.

Until they are.

Ten weeks. Eight of them perfect.

Then came week nine. It started like the previous eight. I texted Kristen on a Tuesday, our day now, and received a stunning response.

Me: Hey there, where are we going tonight? I can come to you this time.

Kristen: Hmm…

Me: Just let me know.

Kristen: How about we stay in and I cook dinner?

I gasped at my phone. A night in. Dinner. It was all too much too fast. I felt betrayed. Especially after offering to come to her neck of the woods. I was trapped and she knew it. I felt taken advantage of. There really was no way out of the date and not the fucking. I thought of all the blatant lies I could muster. I'm sick, my family dog died (we don't have a dog), my sister was in a car accident (she doesn't own a car), but I didn't have the guts to pull the trigger. I acquiesced.

Me: Uh, yea sure, what time?

Kristen: Come over after work. Like 6-7?

Six-seven? In an instant I felt older than a retirement home. Six-seven at a bar…fine. Six-seven for a home-cooked meal is…old. Old, old, old, old, old.

Me: I'll be there.

And just like that the pressure was dialed up ten degrees. There's that analogy of turning the heat up on a frog in water so minutely that they don't know until it's too late. Most men are that frog. They don't even realize they are in a relationship until it's too late. Not me. Professor Lou knew exactly what was happening and began to plot his escape. In the meantime, I didn't know what to wear.

What is a date night in? Do I dress up? Throw on a blazer? Or was it a comfy night in? Do I wear pajamas? I couldn't tell what was worse for our relationship but either way I was on edge. Pajamas could mean we are too comfortable with each other. A blazer means not comfortable enough. This is what I hate about dating. The nerve of it all. The balls it has to make me second guess every decision instead of just having fun. If there is one thing dating is not, it is fun.

The trek to New York City was an internal battle. Every stop the PATH train made I mapped my escape. The train would stop, doors would open, and I could see a hole in the crowd only a pro running back could see. My vision of the defense was clear. Cut past the old lady with a cane, follow the block of two small children holding on to their father's hands, use the woman with a shopping cart as my pulling guard, hop over the bum and…touchdown! Instead, I just stood there holding on to a bar as the doors closed. Five stops. Five opportunities to flee and I let each one go. Only an act of God or a suicidal maniac that decided today was the day to end it on the tracks could save me. Neither obliged.

I decided on jeans and a sweatshirt. Jeans to dress it up, sweatshirt to dress it down. Underneath the sweatshirt I had a collared polo shirt, just in case I was walking into a candlelit apartment and Kristen was wearing a dress.

She was actually wearing the exact same attire I had decided on. Jeans and a sweatshirt. It got me to thinking again, maybe she really was a keeper. She clearly was having the same inside freakout I was. Her makeup was lightly applied. No lipstick, a touch of blush, the eye paint was not showy or overdone.

"Thanks for doing this. I couldn't handle another vicious Wednesday hangover. I have this important meeting tomorrow," she said.

"Of course. I like staying in," I lied.

"Do you like Italian food?"

"Love," I said.

"Good, cause I ordered enough to feed a small village."

My sigh of relief was almost audible. If she had cooked a meal for me that would have been cause for concern. Cooking for someone takes time, patience, effort, and love. The latter of which I wanted to avoid. We shared a delicious bottle of wine. I may be an unhinged maniac, but if a woman invites you to her house and offers dinner the least you can do is bring the booze.

When it came down to the question, the real question, the only question – are we fucking – I was concerned when she mentioned there would be none. She was on her period. That didn't stop her from blowing my brains out. Everything about this woman screamed perfect.

But when it was time for me to leave she did the unthinkable.

"Why don't you stay tonight."

There is no question mark there. That's because it wasn't a question, it was a threat.

"Don't you have an important meeting tomorrow?" I asked.

"Yea but you can sleep here…if you want."

This was actual betrayal. I had done everything she asked. I had come over to her apartment, I had donned my date-ish attire, I had eaten her food, I had brought the wine, I had received a biblical blow-job but this…this was too far.

If you want.

She had thrown the ball into my court with no thoughts of my feelings or concerns. She knew what this question would do to us. She knew this meant either we were in a relationship or we weren't. She knew we were at the pinnacle; she wanted it and I…I caved. I always cave.

"Of course, I want to," I said.

I stayed over. I woke up to the morning breath and the breakfast and I watched her get ready and she kissed me goodbye and I felt old and I felt that we were in a relationship. It all happened so fast. So hauntingly fast.

Those ninth week texts transformed completely from the first eight weeks. That was the biggest turn-off of them all. It was like the Kristen I once knew got mounted by an evil succubus.

The texts were filled with solo plans like dinner on a Wednesday (literally the next day), a museum on a Friday night (what in the living fuck), a night in together again the following Tuesday. It was like a switch had flipped in her head. She went from being the cool girl to the annoying girlfriend in the time it took me to say "Of course, I want to."

I succumbed to each text out of a sense of guilt, not a sense of wanting. Each date was surprisingly fun but the cloud above the whole week hung close overhead. The cloud was the messy future. The future of dating, of meeting parents, of marriage, of mortgages, of kids, of life.

The moment of truth happened on a Sunday, the first day of the tenth week. Brunch. She wanted to do fucking brunch. I gagged when I read the text. I'm not much for hollandaise sauce or poached eggs or bellinis or anything involving brunch. Especially on a Sunday. Sundays are a personal day reserved for nursing hangovers and staring at my phone for untold hours. But there I found myself in khakis and a button-down shirt pretending to be a boyfriend. I despised myself. I couldn't tell if she knew how put off I was by the whole experience. She should've guessed after my fourth Bloody Mary that I was doing anything to numb the pain. She even tried, and failed, to stop me from smoking a cigarette. Who was this person?

She couldn't have noticed I was in anguish because she suggested we take a walk in the park after I paid our $180 bill. I wanted to cry but agreed. We sat on a bench and she took a selfie of us. My fake smile was strong. Hers was a genuine sharing of that perfect set of teeth. Then she said what she said and the facades came crumbling down as if a bomb had hit us. The speculative bubble popped. There was a run on the bank. Done. Caput.

"Can I post this?" she asked.

"What?"

"Can I post this picture on Instagram?"

"No," I said.

"Why?"

"Because."

"What? Are you embarrassed of us?" she asked.

"No, just don't."

"Why wouldn't I want to put a picture up with the guy I'm dating?"

"We aren't dating."

"Then what was this last week?" she asked.

The conversation continued like this for an hour until I finally lost my cool. Parents and kids and old ladies were staring at us. They could never understand. Social media makes things official and we were far from official. The guts on this woman. The balls. The gall. We were just fuck buddies. Just good friends that banged twice a week, every week, for ten weeks until we didn't.

┌─────────────────────┐
│   12:07 PM   │
└─────────────────────┘

When my eyes crack open after an hour nap to see a fresh VanNeece glide a rolled-up bill across the windowsill, I feel I must join in. My choice to do this line and go to brunch is as much of a choice as breathing. It's called FOMO. *Fear of missing out.* I'm riddled with the disease. It's in every orifice and pore and organ and bone of my body. No amount of chemo or radiation could get rid of it. Holistic medicine would be useless. I've heard even lobotomies are ineffective.

How VanNeece got into my apartment I'll never know. This is one of the many reasons why you should live in an apartment building with a doorman. Not only do they guard against marauding investment bankers, but if you happen to take a lady home, the pheromones that are kicked up when a door is held open by a man in a Sharper uniform is worth the extra thou on rent. Instead, I live on the fourth floor of a walk up that consists of three rooms: the bedroom, the bathroom, and the everything-else room. I cannot afford the extra thou.

The intruder does drive a hard bargain, though. He deserves every Wall Street dollar he earns. A line, a beer, and a shower are all it takes to push the effects of last night off at least another twelve hours. Rejuvenated and dressed, I plop my ass on my bed, spin my legs over and out the window like a gymnast on a horse. This is what is considered a workout now in my mid-twenties.

It's a clear day, with a slight, fresh breeze blowing through my wet hair. I welcome the chill as my body temperature has possibly reached fever. The small, rusted fire escape is like the bottom of a large bird cage, swaying and shaking with even the slightest movements. There must be some type of code violation here, but who would I complain to? My landlord is a mystery.

Though my life is in danger with every step, I climb all the way to the roof. I have a view that photographers would kill for. Directly across the Hudson, Empire State Building and Freedom Tower in my periphery. The bright lights that held such promise last night now look like cardboard cutouts. It's one big, fake mirage that reminds me of Marissa. I've looked through the M's in my phone five times this morning and can't tell if it's me or the coke doing the searching.

The step with which I stub my cigarette out produces a loud bang. Much too loud to have come from my foot and the splayed butt underneath it. A quick scan of the terrace reveals nothing until the sound comes again, like a gong, beckoning me forth. I walk towards the skylight on the far end of the roof and peek in.

Brown hair. Yellow sundress. A face I cannot quite make out.

I wonder if I'm seeing things.

"You ready Lou?" VanNeece yells.

I walk towards the feeble ladder at the edge of the roof.

"Be down in a minute," I reply.

Back to the skylight, peeking in once more, and nothing. No one.

The scene is all too similar to last night. One moment she's there and the next…poof! Lou the professor and Marissa the magician – a match made for a carnival.

An urge to cannonball through the window rushes over me. I'll make it, scratch-less. Just a couple steps back and one, two, three… jump…tuck the knees…hold the shins…crash land next to a stupefied, and smitten, Marissa…grab her neck…kiss her. Professor Lou, at your service, milady.

But that's just the drugs talking. And, like last night, I hear my father's voice over the substance's obnoxiously loud presence. *I proposed to your mother in seven days. When you know, you know.* I try to ignore it, but it only gets louder. I imagine what Professor Lou would say if I told him that I think I'm in…love? I'm not sure what it is. Infatuation at the very least. There is something in my brain that is tugging me towards this woman. The target is set. Whether the aim is true is another matter. A timer begins to tick in my head.

Instead of swan diving through the window, I walk back down the fire escape.

"What are you doing up there?" VanNeece asks.

"Nothing. This stuff is good. Let me get another one."

"Yeah, it's from a new guy. Hurry."

"A new guy?"

We do another one. My teeth are numb as if they have been cut from their roots.

It's as if last night never ended. Like my night's sleep was just a comma, a short stop before the run-on sentence of my life continues rambling on. There are heavy, fist-like, thumps in my chest, aches in my extremities – a heart attack or just the consequences of last night. There is no time to fiddle with explanations. The show must go on.

1:01 PM

Washington Street looks different in the daylight. A colorful mix of old and young in their spring regalia. The sun's energy has infected the populace. The air is imbued with life again. The temperature has tiptoed above a measly fifty-two. It's as if the dry, cracked, cold earth of winter has been drawn over with lip balm. The difference between the Washington Street from last night and now is alarming. Last night, on our trek to the PATH train, it seemed as if the only places that existed in this miniature city were bars – sucking people in and spitting them out, worse for wear. Now families line the sidewalks. Children hold onto their parents' hands while skipping across the streets. Roving hordes of fresh moms push carriages, with infants sleeping peacefully or screaming as if the world were ending. Small boutiques, barber shops, and bakeries are all filled with a bubbling sect of Hobokenites, thawed out enough to smile.

"There's Carey," VanNeece says, pointing to a table on an outside patio. "And Aisle."

Carey Bresnahan sits with legs crossed. Aisle holds his chin up with a fist. Are his legs crossed too? These poses ooze gossip. These two have gotten used to waiting for VanNeece and I over the years. Punctuality isn't our strong suit.

Carey has been a staple in our lives since the fourth grade. This group – VanNeece, Aisle, Carey, and myself – have attended the same grade school, middle school, and high school. Somehow, we all ended up here after college. Hoboken, New Jersey. Staying friends with the same group of people for such a long time is quite the phenomenon. The only person missing to round out our unit is Brian McAndle.

We sit down, order drinks, and I mistakenly choose the manmosa. A horrible concoction of orange juice, vodka, and Blue Moon beer all in one large glass. My taste buds are reasonably shot so it is not the taste I'm after, it is the result. There really are no other options. This life chose me, albeit through countless bad decisions, so I plod through my shitty cocktail, thinking about a gin and tonic on a balmy night in Spain with Marissa, all while trying to stay in conversation without puking on Carey, who sits across from me. I must find Marissa and this brunch is doing nothing to further that goal.

"How was your sister's party?" she asks the table.

"Fun," I say.

"It was horrible," VanNeece chirps.

"It sucked," Aisle says.

"Aright, aright, aright. Enough. It sucked. That's why I left," I say.

"Same," Aisle and VanNeece say almost in unison.

"Where'd you guys go?" Carey asks them.

"We went to a club," Aisle continues. "I don't know where Louisa went. He just left."

"Another Irish exit huh?" Carey asks. She looks at me, unsurprised by my previous night's antics.

"I met a girl," I say.

"What do you mean you met a girl?" Carey asks, genuinely confused. "I've heard I went back with a girl, I fucked a girl, I took a girl back to my place, I hooked up with a girl, I banged a girl…I have never heard I *met* a girl. What happened?"

"I just met a girl. Nothing to read into."

Carey often takes an interest in my life. Hers has become mundane. She has been in a relationship for five years now and I personally could not imagine such a boring fate. Part of her inquisitions must be our difference in life choices. One can be envious of a life lived on the edge or one can feel bad, obligated to help in any way possible. If I were on the proverbial fence, I'd say Carey leans towards lawn number two. Or maybe she just enjoys the gossip. I assume a relationship can get quite stale while waiting on a ring. A ring that is supposed to satisfy you. A ring that will end all sadness in the world. A ring that injects sweetness back into a soured relationship.

"Really, nothing crazy," I implore. "We were at this random bar and she disappeared out of thin air. One minute she was there and the next, nothing."

I try and picture the night but only pockets of black spots appear, as if I were staring into the sun.

"Then…I ended up at Kristen's," I say.

The table laughs.

"Would you like another man-mosa, sir?"

The waiter stands over me like the grim reaper.

"Sure."

"What was she like?" Carey pushes.

Carey's eyes are big, and wide with curiosity, but they drop at the edges like a sad spaniel. Her cheeks are nonexistent. The skin and bone are one. Her nose, a pointed Roman, is something she has campaigned to change since high school. She has never gone through with it. By itself it would not be a beautiful nose but on her it is dignified. She sips on a bellini under the shadow of a derby hat. A scarf sits on her shoulders like the Pope's. All that is missing is a ring to kiss.

"Same old Kristen I guess? She wants to start hanging out again."

"Oh god," Aisle rolls his eyes, "you idiot. Are you going to start hanging out with her again? Run her down the same road as last time. Build her up…let her down?"

"Really? Buttercup? Whyyy do you build me up?" I begin to sing.

"Build me up," VanNeece echoes.

"Buttercup baby just to let me down."

"Let me down."

"Not Kristen! Not Kristen you morons. I don't care about Kristen. The other girl. What was she like?" Carey breaks up the band.

"Oh, Marissa."

"Marissa, huh?"

"Yes…Marissa. She's Spanish."

"Spanish. Sticking with your own kind, eh? Slick move."

I wouldn't expect Carey to understand the cultural differences between all the Spanish-speaking peoples. She can barely grasp the fact that I am anything but white. Even after a home cooked meal by my mother it didn't register that we had anything but tacos and burritos. We had neither. The difference between a Cuban and a Spaniard is more in tune with the difference between a person from New Jersey and Alabama. I think her brain would melt if I tried to explain the inner workings of the different diasporas of Hispanic communities. Dominicans hate Puerto Ricans. Puerto Ricans hate Dominicans right back. Venezuelans and Colombians have their moments. Mexico and El Salvador are at each other's necks. Everyone hates Cubans.

Cubans hate Argentinians. There are more rivalries in the Hispanic community than SEC football.

"If she looks anything like your mom, you're in business," she continues.

"She's a different type of Spanish. Spain, Spanish," I reply to no one in particular.

Though I've squandered most of the good looks my mother has given me there's still a small hope that I can reverse the damage at some later stage. Aisle smirks at me. We became friends in fourth grade too, bonding over our shared gift and curse of having good-looking moms.

This conversation only exacerbates my longing for bed. Last night's disappointment is gaining on me like a hungry lion and I am just a bleeding, injured gazelle.

1:47 PM

But I don't hightail it to bed. I have a girl to look for. I attempt to gather clues from the previous night and only come up with a yellow sun dress and a pair of arresting green eyes.

"Soooo…thoughts on Brian and Jen?" Carey switches the subject.

Until now, I had erased all memory of the news that Aisle dropped on me at the pregame last night. The fact that Brian and Jen are now Facebook official may be the true reason for my leglessness on the PATH train into the city. What else is there to do when receiving such painful information than to drink your thoughts away?

Unfortunately for this table, mine have come back with a vengeance.

"Fuck her," I reply, no hesitation.

"Hot take, Lou. Tell us how ya' really feel," VanNeece says.

His cologne wafts off him as he turns his chair.

"How does he not see it? Does the poor bastard have eyes? Or ears? A nose? I can smell that girl from a mile away. Physically *and* metaphorically. We all know she's doing something on the side. We've all been to her place of 'business' a few too many times, right? We've told him it's not the best look. We're all reliable sources considering we leave our houses and see what's going on. Has he been back to High Noon since he met her? Or is ignorance now bliss? Put some blinders on like a race pony and pretend the place doesn't exist or that his girl doesn't work there? That's what makes me more mad than anything," I say.

"Madder," Aisle corrects.

I rip him limb from limb with my eyes and continue.

"It's not even that he's with *her* or that she makes him look like a fool. The fact that he doesn't leave his house is infuriating. He won't even answer a text or a phone call unless he has a built-in excuse for why he can't come. Here, look at this," I say.

Texts don't lie.

Me: Yo tryna go grab a beer?

Me: Any plans tonight?

"Those were two texts from last week. No response. Then I tell him about my sister's party and…"

Me: Dude. Answer me. My sister's having a going away party Friday. We're gonna pregame at my apartment then go over there. Come.

Brian: Ahhhh…that sounds fun. I wish I could make it. I'm going to my parent's house Friday though.

"And he left the group chat! Are we that awful to talk to?" I ask.

Out of breath but confident in my case to the jury I feel a tweet coming.

Girlfriends sound fun.

1:50 PM – April 18th – 2015

Sent.

On opposite day.
1:51 PM – April 18th – 2015

Sent.

"She really isn't that bad," I hear from above.

"Shut up Aisle," I say.

"Seriously. The few times we've hung out with her and Brian it's been fun. She's always happy and knows the best bars. And she doesn't strip, she bartends. She has your dream job and you still do not approve. The disrespect to her and her profession is appalling!"

Aisle smiles. His smarmy mug infuriates me.

"Aisle. Let me spell it out for you in plain chapter English. If your girlfriend knows all the best bars, it means she's spending way too much time at bars. How does that not get through your peanut-sized brain?"

He clearly needs to re-take Lou 101.

"But *you* spend all your time at bars…what's the difference?"

Aisle's small frame conjures a mixture of contempt and sympathy. The transition frames he's wearing are stuck in a gray middle phase. He makes a great point but I can't let my fight for Brian end there. I will use every piece of propaganda at my disposal. I will lie, cheat, and steal to get my friend back. By any means necessary.

"Aisle, my son, haven't you ever heard the saying 'you'll never meet your wife at a bar'?"

"No."

Neither have I, I'm making this up on the fly.

"Well, Aisle, you'll never meet your wife at a bar. And I'll even do you one better. You'll never meet your wife at a strip club bar. The longest lasting relationship that has come out of High Noon is someone leaving with herpes. God forbid my friend gets herpes. God forbid…" I trail off.

1:58 PM

Around me is an amphitheater of confusion. A shadowy phalanx of people in the foreground of a blaring sun. "All rise," an ultimate judge has commanded, what is the verdict.

"Are you going to finish that?"

"Let's go."

"C'mon Lou what are you doing?"

Half a beer sits warm in front of me as my eyes adjust to life. I haven't fainted, I just haven't been here. I'm overwhelmed by the sheer amount of Marissa's on Instagram. Where do I even begin? In the time it takes to slug down the dregs, the group is already walking down Washington Street.

We pass a few tempting specials on the way to Green Rock: five-dollar beers until 6 pm, 7 dollar well drinks until 5 pm, a pitcher for ten bucks. These specials would be highway robbery anywhere else. Green Rock is not known for its Saturday specials unless you count the number of females that end up attending. I'm surprised it is not advertised. You'd have to be a mute or a mutant to not end up in conversation with a halfway decent looking girl here.

But women, like all great things, require sacrifice. They are like living gods, but instead of the bull's head or slaves' hearts of yesteryear, you end up sacrificing…

"The fuckin' Gamos. Someone already spilled onna' fucking Gamos," VanNeece says.

Ferragamo's. Fine Italian leather shoes that VanNeece knew not to wear here.

"Remind me to stop frequenting this dump," he adds.

VanNeece sacrifices another pair of designer shoes but I, on the other hand, seem to be sacrificing my sanity. I feel like I've ingested déjà vu. I've been here before but everyone in the bar has a ghost-like quality.

After sliding sideways through a slim front bar, already packed with eager drinkers, we make it to a square, open, back bar. Our unit stands around, waiting for someone to make the first move. I even see Carey cover her yawning mouth with a hand. The next decision can be insidiously costly or propel the day onward. I find that it has come down to me to make the decision.

Professor Lou walks up to the podium:

Men...

Women...

Students...

Soldiers.

Times like these come twice a week if you're employed. The infrequency shall not dilute the importance.

For five days this week they have beaten you down. From nine to five, for forty hours, they have captured your soul and used it for their own greed. Even VanNeece, who enjoys work, would feel the intimacies of his soul being crushed daily if he had one.

But what is forty hours to a lifetime?

Hoo-ra!

My comrades, what is forty hours to a lifetime!?

Hoo-raaaaa!

Men...

Women...

Soldiers.

By the grace of the gods, we are bestowed with this holiest of days. This day shall not be taken lightly, or for granted, and through this day the gods shall speak through us. We, this day drinking crew, are at the precipice of something great and momentous.

No man can be a good day drinker who is not honest in his dealings: so pay your tabs and tip your bartenders and above all else drink your drinks! I believe, if nothing has been neglected, we, the day drinkers, can outlive and outshine our tyrannical bosses and managers! We shall drink in the clubs and we shall drink in the bars. We shall take shots, sip beers, and drink mixaronis. And...in God's good time...

the day drinkers, with all of their power and might, will step forth to the rescue and liberation of this great city.

Though half this speech is plagiarized and all of it is done in my head, it's how I feel when I place our first drink order.

2:16 PM

"Ten pickle-back shots."

"There are only four of us," Aisle says, uninspired.

I hand my card to the bartender.

"Open or close it?"

This question comes as a surprise in the same way a deer is surprised that a car, again, is barreling down on him. Although the subject matter is a tad less serious than a *Hamlet* soliloquy, it still begs the question: to close or not to close?

The Professor's pros and cons to closing one's tab are very complex. But the answer is self-evident.

"Keep it open."

This was never really a choice. What is an all-day drinking performance without a little skin in the game?

After taking three of the ten shots ordered I tug on VanNeece's sleeve, almost unable to speak. He understands my nonverbal cue and slyly hands over the goods to reboot.

For every ten suspect bathrooms there is always one grand version. In New York this ratio is far smaller, because in the 70s and 80s the owners partook with the patrons. Green Rock's main bathroom is as susceptible to intruders as they come. There are three urinals and one stall with a broken hinge. Nowhere to run, nowhere to hide. But, if you continue past the men's on your right and women's on your left and push further into a dark hallway, further than you thought safe or possible, there is the metaphorical light at the end of the tunnel. Metaphorical only because there is no light, just a small iron door. Opening it reveals a haven equipped with a metal toilet, mirror, and sliding lock. The walls are brick and the cold emanates through the cracks. A refreshing change from the hot bodies packing into the bar like sausages. A restart and reboot.

After exiting my cave feeling a little more Cro-Magnon than usual, I somehow slip my way into a serious conversation about the New York Yankees with a random group of known associates. This group is dressed on the fratty side. Each has a pair of faded jeans, a backwards dad hat, and a Patagonia vest, though it is obvious they have never climbed higher than a few mansion floors. The only thing distinguishing one from the other is a different patterned button down and shade of boat shoe.

I view this group with equal parts reverence and disdain. It was a group of these exact types that introduced me to the joys of hard partying in the first place. It took me half a semester to remove the shackles of pressure to attain a 4.0 GPA. Though I never joined a frat, I did graduate with a middling 3.0, a bachelor's in software engineering, and a master's in alcoholism. I wonder if they hate themselves as much as I hate me.

3:01 PM

Half the reason I started smoking cigarettes was to avoid monotony. A bar can become mundane if you end up talking to the wrong crowd and those frat boys were boring me to tears.

The muffled sound of people and music from inside the bar sounds like covering your ears in the shower. Clusters of young men and women roam the streets. We are far from the uppity shops and families of four. The shuffle of wedges on gravel, the echoed clack of high-heeled shoes – these palpable sounds of promise fill my damaged ears. It's a welcome change in scenery.

"Are you almost done with that?" Aisle asks, covering his nose with his shirt.

I raise my eyebrows.

"I hate smoke," he says.

"Then why'd you come out here?" I ask.

"That girl from the other night texted me."

I lean in to look at his phone but a pack of females walk by us into the bar. One in particular catches my attention. A tight dress, heels, and eye contact. I stub my cigarette out and follow them in. The text goes unread.

The music feels louder upon re-entry and the bar more packed than when I left it. The dancing has also escalated. Sweaty couples grind to the four on the floor with little regard for onlookers.

It doesn't take long for the girl in the tight dress to take center stage. She dances with no one, gyrating her ass like a witch hovering over a cauldron. Twerking, the kids call it, but the word barely does the motion justice. It's nothing like a twitch or jerk but a mesmerizing incantation.

She's quickly surrounded by a herd of wild men, as drawn to the spell as I am. They silently bark and howl. Still, she dances, beautifully unfazed. Then the woman on the dancefloor is Marissa. Either Marissa really is endowed with superpowers, or my brain is melting. Marissa grabs my hand and pulls me to the dancefloor. This time some light grinding ensues with a little PDA I am not even ashamed of. No Guaguancò. No temptation. Just action. The yellow dress. The brown hair. It's all there between my hands. Solid and real for a moment. Then it melts like memory. Marissa fades. The yellow dress and brown hair disintegrate into the floor of the bar. The girl is still twerking all alone. With no one, for everyone.

The music thumps, my heart pounds with it, and I am stuck, drunk, alive, and numb.

4:13 PM

On my fourth cigarette break I am seeing two cigarettes below my nose. No amount of the white stuff can get me back on the right track but damn if I haven't tried. Mid puff I take a peek down Hudson Street. I see two yellow sundresses, two sets of brown hair. Two reasons I need to wrangle the crew out of this bar and follow that dress. The rational thought that Marissa would not be wearing the same dress two days in a row doesn't reach my frontal cortex. She is here, in my neck of the woods, and I will track her down. She would probably say that sentence was creepy. It was creepy. But I am a man on a mission.

I stumble back into the bar and corral the crew. Informing them I have closed my tab is a sure-fire way to get their feet out the door. The bar is still hammering out ear-shattering top forty hits and the dancefloor is filled, but this is no time to stay. I have a girl to find.

"Where are we going?" Carey asks.

"I saw her take a right down Newark Street. I think there's a tequila bar down that way," I say.

"Who?" she asks, confused.

"Come on, let's go," I urge.

We walk down a block and take a right towards the water. No signs of a dress, so we all shuffle into the Tequila & Taco's joint. From what I can remember, Marissa enjoyed tacos.

The vibe is quieter here and our raucous voices turn heads. It might be too early for some to be belligerent but not our group. Things were just starting to heat up and I reopen my tab for five tequila shots. Even with the salt and lime this shot goes down like acid.

I feign an excuse to go to the bathroom and take a look around the place. It is a squat room with low ceilings and bright Mexican colors splashed on the walls. Frida Kahlo's painted eyebrow is resting above a table of ten. There's a margarita pitcher in the middle, a smorgasbord of tacos around the edges, but no Marissa. The people at the table look at me as if I was shaking a change cup in their face.

The next two booths seem to be dates. Though these random people haven't heeded my warnings on the pitfalls of dating, I walk past each one and turn back to see the hidden person on the opposite side of the booth. No Marissa. Thank god. If she were on a date I might collapse. I finally make it to the bathroom with nothing better to do than hit the little bag of white wonder. Maybe a little more will light the way. Maybe a little more will reveal Marissa. Maybe a little more...

4:43 PM

"What the fuck is up with you man? You seem off," VanNeece asks.

"Agreed," Aisle chirps. "First your sister's party, now pulling us out of Green Rock. What is going on?"

"Has Lou lost his touch?" Carey asks.

Maybe I have lost my touch, or my mind. But most importantly, I've lost Marissa. I continue to careen my neck around my group of friends to check any window willing to give me a glimpse of what I'm looking for.

The view outside one particular window puts me into a trance. There is a light glare off a fire hydrant. The air glows and vibrates around it. Every five seconds the brightness is disturbed by a couple. Two people walking hand in hand, smiling, laughing. They come in all different shapes and sizes and orientations. After the fifth couple, the faces turn into mine and Marissa's. We are happy. Glare. We are deep in conversation. Glare. We are belly laughing. Glare. I don't know how long this goes on for.

"Aren't you going to eat?" Carey asks. "This is your people's food and you haven't touched a thing."

Besides the blatantly hilarious racism, I ignore their pleas. I want to say Cuban food is not spicy. Cuban food is different. Spanish influenced. French influenced. Taino influenced. African influenced. We drink rum, not tequila. Chili peppers or jalapenos don't frequent a Cuban's plate. You don't need all that spice to mask the heavenly goodness of ropa vieja or a Cuban sandwich. Explaining all this would take time and effort that I can't waste on educating the uninitiated. They've already heard this diatribe and have chosen to ignore it.

I refocus my attention outside, my peripheral vision of the booths and tables flung around this establishment. Any last vestige of my five senses is concentrating on the color yellow with a swaying brown. Marissa. Marissa. Marissa. And besides, after this many drinks, which are now in the mid-teens, eating is futile. No number of tacos could mop up this mess. A burrito would go down the hatch only to come back up with a fiery vengeance. Once the drinking has started the eating takes a back seat.

"Try this." VanNeece shoves a margarita in my hand.

It tastes like tequila with a splash of lime but the salt on the rim feels like a meal, adding needed electrolytes to my deteriorating system. I feel like one of those marathon runners who keeps little packages of salt in their hip pockets for hydration. The Mexicans might not be Cubans, but they still have some good ideas.

After the crew finishes their food they seem sluggish. Another reason to stay off the food when you are trying to have a good time. The immediate release of dopamine from the food comes crashing down and all you want to do is sleep. It's called a food coma, much different from the booze and yip coma I am currently inducing myself into. I hear mumbled excuses to leave, to go take a nap, to meet back out in a couple of hours when I see it. It's fleeting, just passing the door, a little wisp of yellow dress in the wind, the end of a platformed wedge.

"Let's go somewhere else," I suggest. "It's dead here."

Without waiting for an answer, I'm out the door and there it is again. Down on Sinatra Blvd. heading due north. I begin to walk as the dress disappears behind a Retro Fitness club that I am a member of but have never been to. The $5 a month is inconsequential and the peace of mind knowing I could go if I wanted to is priceless. One day I will hit the gym. One day I will quit the booze. One day I will shun the yip. One day...I will find Marissa. Today is that day. I walk as quickly as possible in the direction she has disappeared, not waiting for the rest of my comrades. I hear one of them yelling to slow down but I can't. My life hangs in the balance.

Turning the corner on to Sinatra I cannot make out anything in the sea of people. Pier A is packed with picnickers, frisbee-ers, hacky-sackers, a conglomerate of boring people doing boring things. Marissa is nowhere to be seen in this group. Thank God. My infatuation with this woman would plummet if I found her hula-hooping with her gal pals. On the left side of Sinatra Blvd, past the Retro, there are seven or eight bars looking out onto the Hudson River. The scene is as pretty as a line of Parisan café's looking out onto the Seine. There are round wrought-iron tables under canopies, colored umbrellas with little flaps waving breathless, drinks, people, laughter. The sounds of the river lapping against the dock, the smell of salt, the squawk of gulls, almost calm my nerves. This picturesque view is ruined when I realize I don't know which establishment Marissa has ventured in. I decide we will hit every one. Start to finish. We will find her. We will succeed. We shall overcome.

6:07 PM

I lost the crew around bar number four. I don't know where they went and don't care. The sun recedes quickly between buildings and I am going down with it. As soon as that hum, that natural glow, sinks into its final resting place it will be impossible for me to carry on.

The cigarette I am currently smoking has lost its value. Where it once gave me energy, it now just makes me dizzy. I've imbibed a shot and a beer at seven of the eight bars in my search. One more to go.

On second thought, I do care that all my friends have disappeared. It is eerily similar to the way Marissa disappeared. I light another cigarette. Something isn't right. The pit in my stomach has grown into a small shrub. The answer could merely be physical. Drinking and drugging with little to no food has been known to cause a certain amount of pain. But I am used to that. What I am not used to is this anxious foliage growing in my gut. Something is afoot. In lieu of checking bar number eight I let angst urge my legs towards home.

It's a long and arduous trek. The sun is officially down and the streets are filled with bars and people, like bugs to shining light. With every breath the smell of coming rain fills my left nostril and propane my right. A light breeze passes through the noise. There's a ghoulish nature to the faces I can make out. Eyes are not quite symmetrical. Mouths morph into swallowing black holes. Buildings creep inward like bending trees, surrounding me in a tunnel. Everything around me has gone dark. Everything inside me has gone dark too. There is an impending sense of dread.

About a half a mile into my walk through Halloween Town, I pass the police station. It feels like the only place that is correctly proportioned. The cops outside have the faces of welcoming grandmothers. Their uniforms have a calming quality. Serve and protect. It hadn't occurred to me until now that these disappearances are something that the police should be notified of. My mind is not working correctly but any warmth my body can feel on this cold dark walk is emanating from the yellow sign that reads: Hoboken Police Station.

Before entering this haven, I take a detour down an alley a block away. It smells like old, soaked peanuts with a hint of shit. With the swiftness of a bear trying to open a jar of peanut butter, I tug the little bag out of my pocket and snort a few bumps off the end of my key.

"Ehhhhh!"

I jump back at the sound of a loogie being hawked from the shadows.

"Hello?" I ask.

"Ehhh!"

As my eyes finally adjust to the pitch black I see a homeless man with his head resting against a plastic garbage can. He's holding a sign that says, "*Just need some help.*" You and me both bud. Instead of the typical dollar bill, I make this guy's day with a package of two cigarettes and the rest of the bag. I can't go into a police station like this.

"Thank you," the guy says. His voice sounds like a woodchipper.

"Make good use of it. I sure know I was," I say.

"You'll find her," he says.

"What?"

"You'll find her," he repeats.

"What do you mean I'll find her? Do you know where she is?"

He clears his throat.

"My spine hurts!" he yells, placing his nose directly in the bag and inhaling.

I hightail it out of there, afraid for all passersby who encounter this man once the drugs kick in.

6:23 PM

I'm out of breath. A lady police officer looks at me impatiently. She's the size of two normal ladies, but it fits her. Her sedentary life has widened her. A desk job will do that. I've seen people grow as wide as they are tall in the cubicles. It's like a time traveling device. You walk in the office, get fat for twenty years, and squeeze out the other end. I'm reminded I need to quit my job before it happens to me, when the woman speaks. Her face is that of a mother with over ten kids.

She cares for them all equally but can't tell them apart. She stays seated, a hen nesting.

"Can I help you?"

"Yes," I take a gulping breath. "I'd like to report a missing person."

"Okay, son. Take a seat and I'll get the form and we'll fill it out. Is this person under the age of eighteen?" she asks.

"No mam."

Relief stretches over the woman's face. I guess when the person missing is of an adult age there is less urgency because it takes her about twenty minutes to get her ass up, into the back to find the form, and finally into the seat next to me. Her ass can barely fit in it. Her hips squeeze at the sides and she looks at me in extreme discomfort.

"Okay, let's start with the basics."

"So I met this woman and…"

"Hold on there, cowboy. Before you get to the story I need some information. Does this woman have a disability?"

"Not that I know of."

If anything she is the opposite of disabled. In all facets she is more than able. Looks, brains, personality, humor. She's got it all and then some.

"Is she endangered in anyway?"

"I don't know. That's why I'm here."

"Okay, so we'll put a maybe for endangered. Was the disappearance involuntary?"

Involuntary from my perspective. But she could have seen the writing on the wall. That poor little Lou wasn't worth it.

"I don't know. But for arguments sake let's say yes. One minute she was there and the next she wasn't."

"Okay…"

I want to scream.

"Did the person become missing during a catastrophe?"

"I don't even know what that means. Isn't it a catastrophe when someone goes missing?"

"A catastrophe could mean a fire or a flood or a…"

"Her being missing is a catastrophe to me," I finally blurt out.

"Okay, so no catastrophe. Now let's get some bio information. Name?"

"Marissa."

"Marissa what?"

Shit.

"I don't know."

"You don't know the missing person's last name?"

"We never got to that stage," I say.

"The stage of knowing the missing person's last name?"

"That's right."

She's now looking at me out of the side of her eye. She increases the volume of her walkie talkie at her side as a precaution for the psychopath she now sees herself next to.

"Sex?"

"Female."

"Race?"

"Spanish."

"That's not a race sir. You mean to say she is Hispanic or Latina?"

"Sure. She's from Spain."

"Okay, so she's not an American citizen?"

"I don't know. She was born here."

"Son, if you don't mind me asking, what *do* you know about this missing person?"

"I know that her hair is the same brown as good leather. And that her eyes are a green that would make the Irish jealous. And across her nose are all these freckles that look like they tickle, they're so light and beautiful. And she wanted me to throw my phone in the garbage. And I went to the bathroom, woke up, and she was gone."

"And this was in Hoboken?"

"No, New York City."

"And where did you wake up?"

"In another woman's bed."

She stands up in slow motion and starts talking in code into the walkie talkie. The numbers she says mean nothing to me but the way she says them makes me think I need to get the hell out of here. She finally sits in her own comfortable chair, which I am hoping will change her mood. It doesn't.

"Okay, first, this is the Hoboken Police Station. If you want to report a missing person in New York you have to go to New York. Second, I can't add a missing person to the NCIC database with no last name or no record of them being an American citizen. And third, what's your name?"

I don't even hesitate. The last thing I hear is "we've got a runner" before I am out the door and down two blocks in a matter of seconds.

7:01 PM

I haven't stopped running back to where I came from when I bump into a harmless shoulder that goes flailing, almost crashing to the pavement.

"What the fuck!"

Hey, I know the sound of that moan.

"Lou? Where have you been?"

It's Kyle Aisle.

"Uh, I was…"

"Lou!" I hear Carey form behind me. "Where have you been? We're about to go to the club at the W Hotel."

"I called you five times," VanNeece says. He's chewing on his bottom lip. I cannot tell him what I did with the bag he gave me.

"Let's go then!" I say.

Let's go home is what I mean.

10:33 PM

"You better not leave," Aisle yells.

The music is pumping out of speakers the size of Easter Island statues. Synths and bass drums and wild percussion are battering my ears from every angle. It's so loud that it isn't.

"Why would I leave?" I yell back.

"Your eyes look like glazed donuts," Aisle yells.

Aisle puts his hands around his eyes like binoculars and walks away.

Carey is sitting on a couch near me, sipping a drink the color of blood. She's talking to two girls I don't know. They are both pretty in the "anything will do at this point" sense. I watch as she taps one and then points back to me.

The girl approaches me. I can smell the faint hint of perfume, sweat, and the sharpness of smoke from a set of sparklers that were just walked by.

"I'm taken," I say.

"What?" the girl yells.

"I'm taken," I scream.

"That's great. Do you have any blow?" she asks.

"I gave it to a bum," I yell.

The girl walks back to Carey, perturbed.

Carey looks at me like a mother who has caught her child doing something bad from far away. She mouths *what the fuck*. I wave her over.

"What the fuck was that? I set you up," she says.

"I...I don't want her," I admit.

"What do you mean you don't want her?"

Just as I'm about to let it all out, bare my soul, reveal the buried truth, a band of three come jolting out of a hidden back room. One guy has bongos, another has a trumpet, and the third has a violin. I don't know what hell we've walked into but this entire scene feels fake.

They start playing their instruments over a kick drum that matches the speed of my pounding heart. Somehow it's gotten even louder.

"I think I really like this girl," I yell to Carey.

Carey just nods her head, smiling. She has no idea what I've said due to an ear shattering trumpet solo. It's for the best. I sound naïve. I sound moronic. I sound like someone who needs to go to bed.

But the night continues. Just as the day continued. Just as the night before continued. Just as the weekend before continued. Just as it always continues…

TIME UNKNOWN

A red door appears in front of me. A tilted number 9 stares back, as confused as me. Either it's crooked or I am. My apartment is number 7, this much I know. The only image in my head is that of the sky window and a yellow dress. Maybe if I had actually cannonballed into it this morning I wouldn't be here right now. Maybe Marissa has been living one floor above me this entire time. Maybe I am just blacked out drunk.

I watch my hand move to knock, knowing it has ceased all communication with my brain.

Don't knock. Don't knock, you idiot.

"Marissa?" I ask it.

I haven't made a good decision in a decade and this will only add to the list.

I knock.

I wait for an answer.

No one's home. Behind the door or behind my eyes.

My head finally hits pillow, thrilled to be alone. Too many trips to the bathroom leave me wide eyed with no rest in sight. My heart shakes, jerking from left to right like a trapped animal.

I really haven't made a good decision in
a decade.

Sent.

I scroll, searching through the blinding light of my phone. I have gotten through 800 Marissas. Mercifully, my brain finally shuts off.

Black.

No fade.

Just black.

Sunday

[11:03 AM]

There is no happiness like waking up in your own bed. That happiness becomes meaningless when you realize you are drastically hungover. This is not something sunglasses and Advil can fix.

To the most hungover, more hangover shall be given.

This is Professor Lou's principle.

Most people *think* they have had a hangover, but they are just masters of self-pity. My current feeling of debilitation is reserved for only the few, the proud, the degenerates. It only adds to the pain when someone describes a simple headache or some tummy pain with the same diagnosis of "hangover". I'm sure in the future there will be some type of algorithm to accurately assess one's hangover type and level. In the meantime, we will just have to trust Professor Lou's peer-reviewed papers on the different types of hangovers he has encountered. I can assure you; the firsthand accounts are horrific.

11:05 AM

"I'm never drinking again," I actually say out loud.

This is easier said than done.

At this point, if you think I'm a drug addict-alcoholic-womanizing-all-around-piece-of-shit you wouldn't be wrong, just remember one thing: I pay for it dearly. The only way to mitigate the pain is by remaining motionless. I plan to stay this way for as long as possible, staring into the abyss of guilt and embarrassing thoughts, until it's time for a Sunday trip home.

Usually, in this state, I would cancel. Not because I feel like shit but because of the endless questions about why I look like shit. They've seen me like this before. Red eyes resting on black bags, a less than stellar appetite, dazed and confused. It will barely phase them. The problem with this Sunday is that Kimberly won't be joining.

Most children are aware that there is only so much attention parents can bestow on them. Like a colonizing nation they begin to plunder the natural resource. Me? I yearn for as little attention as possible. I am the Switzerland of siblings which inserts me into a precarious situation. My parents will actually want to know how *my* life is without Kimberly present.

How are you Lou? Awful. *How's your ex-girlfriend?* She never was my girlfriend. *How's the new girlfriend?* I don't have one. *There isn't a new girlfriend?* I stop answering. *We were married when we were 20. You're 25. We'd already had you by now. Do you even want to get married? How's your job? When are you going to stop drinking every weekend? When we were your age we never went out like this.*

The ceiling I've been staring at begins to spin and whether that's a result of the hangover or in preparation for 21 questions, I'll never know.

11:39 AM

When your mom is dressed up as a mime you should have a clear notion that you're not in reality. This, I hope, is universal. In the gray wasteland that I am currently engulfed in, her once-olive face is painted white. My small, child-like hands hold on steady to a grocery cart. Looking down at my baby legs dangling through the cart holes is startling but understandable. This is a dream.

The why never seems to reach the surface.

Like, why is my mom in her mime Halloween costume circa 1995? And why am I an infant? And why is there no color in this place?

The only thing that changes here in this reoccurring hell is the background noise.

It feels a tad claustrophobic in this grocery cart because part of me still feels like a six-foot-tall 25-year-old. This is only the beginning…

As my mom pushes the cart, she begins singing La Linda Manita:

Qué linda manita
qué tiene el bebé
qué linda, qué bella
qué bonita es.

It's a song Hispanic mothers sing to their infants.

When she finishes, I look down and my hands have doubled in size. I can feel someone sneaking in the shadows. She starts again.

Qué linda manita
qué tiene el bebé
qué linda, qué bella
qué bonita es.

Singing mimes are more terrifying than their silent counterparts. This time it's my chest puffed out like a bodybuilder. As I continue to grow I can see a yellow flap of cloth in the distance of this colorless wasteland.

> Qué linda manita
> qué tiene el bebé
> qué linda, qué bella
> qué bonita es.

Please don't let my legs be next. I'm begging her to stop with no words. My head begins to grow and there is pressure on all sides like a bad sinus infection.

> Qué linda manita
> qué tiene el bebé
> qué linda, qué bella
> qué bonita es.

It's the legs this time. The cold bars clamp onto my thighs. What breaks first, the metal or my femurs?

And there's a floating yellow dress, waving brown hair…

> Pon, Pon
> El dedito en el pilòn.

12:05 PM

Waking up is a short relief. As the pain comes crashing down the gray place doesn't seem so bad. Sitting naked on the side of the bed with the sheets acting as a shawl is a look I am not proud of. There's a rom-com on the TV. I don't change the channel. Although I refuse to tolerate corniness from friends and foe alike, when I'm alone and barely coherent it is the only type of interaction I can handle. If ever there was a time I needed to feel some tears on my cheek, this is it.

Somehow, out of the depths, I'm able to muster up a tweet.

> There is no way the government hasn't found a hangover cure.
>
> 12:10 PM – April 19th – 2015

Sent.

And another.

> We can shoot people to a moving rock in space but I'm crippled from a few too many tequila shots?
>
> 12:11 PM – April 19th – 2015

Sent.

You would think I'd have deleted Arianna's number by now but there it is, first in the contact list. If only she could have been named Zoe. Swipe left. Delete. It'd be that easy. But I can't muster up the courage. Instead, it stays there. Public Enemy Number One. I scroll down to the M's again and still, there is no Marissa.

Moving from my contacts to peruse the different socials feels like minutes but turns into hours. There are searches for Marissa mixed with reruns of last night's depraved episode. Guilt and shame at the latter. Hopelessness at the former. There are too many Marissas in this world.

I take a porn break hoping to drum up some sort of dopamine in my desert of a brain. I am halted in my tracks before completion when an actress in one of the videos is wearing a yellow sun dress. I've never stopped mid-onanism before and somehow this makes me feel good. Better than a finish would. I cannot rid myself of the few memories of Friday night. The yellow sundress against her tanned arms. Her eyes, curious. Flashes of the side of her neck. Guaguancó. How have I never heard of Guaguancó? Marissa has more sex appeal than any porn star can provide.

Then my phone vibrates.

Kristen: Hey

3:28 PM

I ignore the text and throw my phone under the covers. There is now a documentary that has followed the rom-com on my television about a man who murdered his wife. The antithesis of rom and com. I'm not sure what I'm watching but either this channel is schizophrenic or I am. According to the husband he doesn't remember smashing his wife's head in with a hammer, burying the body, and then moving to Texas under a new name. I call bullshit, but some doctor with the same hair thickness as Donald Trump seems to think that the husband has a rare disease called dissociative amnesia. The husband does not remember his wife, his name, or even his adult children. A shiver runs down my spine. That could either be my hangover turning into actual illness or a recognition that I too am forgetting a lot lately.

I remind myself to look into this dissociative amnesia further when my phone rings.

Mom calling.

"Louis, when are you coming here?"

"Whenever dinner is going to be ready."

"It will be ready at five," she says.

"Five? You guys aren't AARP members yet, are you? I'm going to have to call that home I've contemplated throwing you in," I reply.

"Very funny Lou. Very funny. If you ever put me in a home… Estaras muerto también."

"I don't know what that means mom. You never taught me remember?"

"Ya ya ya…never taught you this, never did that. I gave birth to you, didn't I? That should be enough. Did you go to church this morning?"

I almost laugh. She asks me this question every Sunday and hasn't gotten an affirmative once. God helps those that help themselves and I've done nothing on my account. There's also that confusing bit of the Cuban diaspora that I still don't understand. My mother has a small shrine in a downstairs closet to the orisha Yemaya– the Santería goddess of water. How this has anything to do with the Catholic Church still confounds me. Though she is able to synchronize both in her head, I'm unable to believe in either.

"What time is it?" I ask.

"3:30."

"I have to get up then."

"You are still in bed? Ay dios mio."

"See you soon, Mom."

I shuffle my way to the shower as if my feet were in shackles. While normal people stand in the shower, this afternoon I have been reduced to the fetal position. I even plug the drain in hopes of the water rising enough for me to drown. The water smacks at places that I didn't know could ache and the warmth only exacerbates my pounding temples. When I finally decide to stand up, water tickling my shins, vertigo attacks. Black and white dust fills my eyes. It takes a few moments to pass as I grasp the slippery walls for dear life.

Before putting on sweatpants and a sweatshirt, an outfit that is sure to send my father into a tailspin, I lie naked in bed, shivering under the covers. There is only one thing worse than feeling this way, knowing it all could have been avoided.

Is this hell or a hangover?
3:33 PM – April 19th – 2015

Sent.

5:31 PM

Tweet. Favorite.
Scroll.

.

.

.

Scroll.
Retweet.
Scroll.

.

.

Switch.
Scroll.

.

.

Instagram search Marissa's name for the third time.
Scroll.

.

.

.

Scroll.

.

.

.

.

Scroll.

.

"Dinner's ready," I hear from the kitchen.

It is dark outside when I finally look up. The TV groans out an episode of *60 Minutes*. I can hear the last splatters and bubbles of the simmering meal and the smell has filled every corner of the house. The glorious incense of a home cooked meal that once invigorated my soul is now making me queasy.

The house I pulled up to an hour ago is the one I grew up in. It's two stories, tan with big white coins, landscaping, a pool in the back, and a small broken fountain in the front. It's one of twelve exact models in a neighborhood where each family has .7 acres, 2.5 kids, a dog, a backyard, and a two-car garage. I am rich to poor friends and poor to rich friends. Another limbo I must dance.

Slugging my way off of the couch and over to the dinner table is a larger affair than I had hoped. My parents seem to be well underway on their own dinner plates.

"You want wine with your dinner mi hijo?" my mom asks.

It is terribly endearing that she has no idea how I currently feel. My hand covers the glass she is about to pour the red liquid into. There's a chance that if she pours it, I will drink. A mother doesn't choose to be blind, she just is.

"Absolutely not," I say.

This simple refusal of wine with dinner is like a gun going off to start a race. This race will be one of condescending conversation, even judgement, all under the noble cloak of caring. The first person to raise their voice will lose the race but win the battle in this long war that has been raging on for the better half of the last decade. I can barely keep track of the wins and losses, or what game we are even playing anymore. I am pulled into another match when my father asks how my weekend was without so much as pretending to look away from the TV.

"Fun," I reply.

"Did you sleep in your contacts again?" he asks.

He continues his staring match with the TV. Eye contact between us is avoided at all costs during battle. If eye contact is made, it is an automatic loss for either side because the consequence is actually having to mean what you say.

"What is that supposed to mean?" I ask.

"Unless you want to come up with a new excuse for your eyes being so bloodshot, then you know exactly what I mean."

"Do we have to do this tonight? Huh? Can't we just eat in peace?" my mom says.

She directs this anger toward my father, which will only serve to increase his hostility towards me.

"I'm surprised the boy even came, Carmen!"

Still no eye contact, but behind the frames of his glasses I can see his disappointed blue eyes. His skin is so white that it's pink. The stubble growing from his face, which will be gone come morning, makes him look exhausted. That, along with his salt and pepper hair, makes it quite obvious that my life has taken a toll on his.

"It's not like he eats anymore," he continues. "He used to come home and throw three plates down his throat like a glutton. Now he just pushes his food around the plate like he's shoveling snow. He's a mess. And you still serve him first, Carmen! A mess..." he trails off.

He has a point. I've barely picked at the rabo on my plate. It was once a favorite dish of mine. The transcendence of cow tail, browned and soaked in a red sauce, can be life changing. It is also one of the last tethers I have to my roots, the only proof that I have Hispanic blood inside of me. But my antics have rendered my stomach useless. The ghosts of my ancestors shake their heads in disapproval.

"And you used to get mad about me eating all the food," I respond in kind. "There is no winning with you."

"You were such a good kid. I don't get it."

"I'm not a kid anymore," I say.

"No, you aren't. You are a mess," he says, finally looking directly at me.

Again, this point is taken. I could just agree, for my mom's sake. It's in these moments where Kimberly's services are needed.

"I'm not a fucking mess."

"Don't curse at the table," he says.

"I'm not a mess," I say.

"Look at you. Look in the mirror and tell yourself you aren't a mess."

I've already tried that.

"I'm fine," I say.

"You're a mess," he says.

"Let me just guess what comes next. You never did this when *you* were young. You never drank, you never went out. That's why you are *so* successful. That's why we have food on the table. Blah, blaah, blaaaah. I've heard this a million times. Don't give me another speech because you didn't get to do what I get to do. You met mom when you were twenty for God's sake. Of course you didn't do what I do. Good for you. Lucky you. But I don't have that. I go out because I have friends. Mom is your only friend."

I let these words out with immediate regret.

"You're right. Your mother is my only friend. My best friend. Maybe you should go out and find a woman like her. I proposed to her in seven days."

I regret my regret.

"Here we fucking go again," I say.

"Don't curse at the table."

"Here we go *again*."

"What? All I'm saying is that finding a good girl will make you stop all this bullshit and get you to focus. Focus on being a productive human being," he says.

"Don't curse at the table," I fire back.

"I own the fucking table!"

"How am I not productive? I work five days a week and only drink two. Now, I'm no math genius like yourself Pop, but that's a pretty solid ratio."

His thick lips crack open. His earnest jaw loosens, lightening the rest of his serious face. A smile followed by a chuckle and then a full-blown laugh. Even his metal-rimmed glasses dance at the bridge of his nose. I laugh with him. It isn't until my mom joins in, loudest of all, relief in her eyes, that I lay down my weapons.

My mother's eyebrows finally drop from their scared position around her hairline. She can now enjoy her meal in peace. She is one of those mixed Cubans. Her mother was dark as a shadow, her father an off-white. A frowned upon relationship resulting in a frowned upon child. A mulatto. All the talk about racism in America makes me giggle when hearing stories about the harassment my mother faced in her native country. There were rocks thrown at her from the poor dark girls and sneers from the rich light ones. The attention from boys didn't help her standing in the Cuban girl community but when you are as beautiful as my mother, when your amber eyes could cure disease, when your skin is the color of sandalwood, when your body is one that drives Latino men into a wild fury, you tend to attract jealousy. She must have chosen my father because he is the antithesis of your typical Latino male. A nice gringo boy.

Dinner continues peacefully. We enter into the potentially poisonous subject of work but it is better than going over my weekend habits. It is also something that we have in common. To say I am low on my father's company totem pole would be a vast understatement. Though he is part owner, there is only so much he is willing to do for an employee that doesn't give a shit. This is what kills him, the underlying fire that lights him up when he sees me. I'm no Billy Madison but a part of me knows that the only reason I still have a job is my father's good name.

"How is Doug?" he asks.

Doug is the loud to dad's silent partner. He's also the father of one ghost-like mirage in a liquor store window. Arianna couldn't have fallen further from a tree.

"I don't know, I don't really see him much. He's always at meetings or lunches or dinners or events. You know him," I say.

"Yeah, all the shit I can't stand. I always just wanted to sit in a room or in my car and program until your mother got home," he says.

Though it was mean and uncalled for, I wasn't lying about my mom being his only friend.

"So…you still like the position you're in?" he asks.

"It's fine."

"Fine?"

"Yeah, it's fine. I'm good at it."

"Lou, you know you *are* better than fine. You *are* smarter than settling. I just don't get it. You graduate from college without trying. You start working at one of the best app developers around and you aren't even trying to move up. Or at least move out of this ridiculous marketing department. Apps market themselves these days."

"Exactly, so I don't have to do much," I reply, smiling like an idiot.

He smirks. Then laughs with his head in his hands. This laugh goes against his fervent seriousness. Goes against everything he ever stood for. Goes against the days he worked in his father's bakery for free at the age of ten. Goes against him graduating college in three years. Goes against him working in an accounting firm 60 hours a week and designing computer programs on the side. Goes against him taking a risk and starting a software business. Goes against every story he told me that confirmed the adage of getting anything you want if you work hard enough. I am convinced the humor gene comes from somewhere deep in my father. Because, despite himself and all of his beliefs, he does laugh.

7:12 PM

Dinner ends abruptly for no other reason than my father's internal clock has gone off. *Early to bed, early to rise, makes a man healthy, wealthy, and wise.*

> Late to bed, late to rise, makes a man ill, broke, and dumb.
>
> 7:13 PM – April 19th – 2015

Sent.

On the couch, digesting nothing except last night, I scroll through my phone in a light daze. The clanking of dishes should be my cue to help clean up, but I don't hear anything over the deafening light of my phone.

Through my haze I see a fragment of a yellow dress in one of Carey's Snapchats from last night. The scene looks to have taken place near Wicked Wolf, a bar in Hoboken hugging the Hudson River. If Marissa was there I must return to the scene. Or...it was nothing. I'm seeing things. I can't rewatch the video due to the nature of Snapchat's disappearing act, so the words *I proposed to your mother in seven days* replay in my head instead. That gives me five days left. The thought alone is comical. If I proposed to Marissa she'd most certainly laugh her way back to Barcelona. We don't live in times where proposing on a whim is romantic.

7:20 PM

My mom sits next to me and begins parting my hair to one side. Her hands smell like Mr. Clean's dish soap, a product she has never strayed from. She's holding a picture of me and my sister at a playground. My sister's about a foot taller than me and my skin, my smile, my eyes look innocent and untainted.

"What do you think about Craig?" she asks me.

"At least she's not with that schmuck anymore," I respond.

"Si. Odiaba a ese idiota."

"Idiota indeed," I say.

The night I punched said idiot in the face was one I can still remember with vivid pride. He was her college boyfriend and his father had just donated enough money to get a wing named after him. But all the money in the world couldn't stop idiota from putting his hands on my big sister. The charges were magically dropped when I explained to the father that his adoring son had given my sister a shiner the size of a computer mouse. I gave him three in kind.

"Pero, why does she have to go to England?" she asks.

"Because she loves him, Ma. That's what people do. Right?"

My mother nods her head.

"I'm just worried for her. Like your father is worried about you, mi lindo. And, I know I don't usually say anything to you pero, I'm worried," she says.

It hadn't occurred to me that my mom was getting older too. Up close, she looks more defined than I remember. Her energetic golden-brown eyes are tethered by crow's feet. A potent nest of curly black hair, tied in a loose bun, holds streaks of gray. Even the palms of her hands feel old as they rub against my forehead.

"I know mom. I'm not oblivious. It's just…I'm not getting any younger. Who knows how long I have left to do this. Next thing you know I'll have a baby, a wife, a life, and then…poof," I say.

"Is that what you think happens?" she asks. "Poof? Aye, mi hijo, that's when life finally starts."

"I know what I'm doing," I say.

"Do you though?" she asks.

I nod my head, not totally convinced.

She leans over me and takes another picture from a small wooden accent table next to the couch. It's an old one. It's muted, as if there was an in-between stage from black and white to full color. There are three boys, two older ones with patchy beards and big curly afros and the young one in the middle, my dad. She rubs my dad's cheeks through the frame.

"Now, I already know what *you* are going to say," she says. "'We all die anyway, might as well have fun, right? Life is too short to not go out and party, man!' You are like a badly written mystery. This craziness runs in your blood and at the end of it you'll only end up ugly and hurt or dead. If only you could have met your father's brothers, then you would know."

"He doesn't talk about them," I protest.

"They died at a very bad time for your father. He was sixteen. Right at the time you need someone to look up to."

She crosses herself.

Even through the thick fog surrounding me I finally feel a pang of something like emotion.

"I know."

"Maybe next Sunday you go to church, mi hijo. Talk to a priest. You need it."

Before I can say no, I hear my father call my mother from the bedroom upstairs.

"Ma, one question. What's Guaguancó?"

Her eyes look like they're going to burst out of her skull.

"Oye, mi hijo. Es un dance. Very sexual. Cuban. You don't ask your mother about these things," she says laughing.

"But what's the dance like?" I ask.

She covers her face, rubs her temples.

"Okay a man and a woman dance rumba side by side and the point is the man..." she looks around as if her own mother were watching her. "the man tries to grab the woman's..."

"Vagina?" I ask.

"Si, pero, don't say that. I'm your mother."

"Okay, then what?"

"The woman is supposed to block him. To protect herself. Never…letting it go to easily. You understand? Si? Okay, that's all I'm telling you. Goodnight my boy. Sleep in the guest room if you like. You could use the rest."

It is a tempting offer. An unperturbed night of sleep is exactly what the doctor ordered. No cars, no horns, no bars – just the sweet and boring silence of the suburbs.

My mom disappears into a closet next to my dad's office downstairs for a minute and then scurries upstairs. I see little plumes of dying blue smoke creep under the cracks in the door.

7:25 PM

I can't remember the last time I was in this room. A pantry is supposed to be used for canned food, boxes of treats, mac n' cheese, bags of salty snacks, maybe a shelf dedicated to cleaning products – not for prayer to an unknown deity. But this isn't a normal pantry in a normal house. This is a house run by a Cuban immigrant.

The shelves have been removed and there is only a waist-high tabletop with a clean white cloth draped over it. There are seven blue and white mother Mary candles, long and tall, that have just recently been extinguished. There are seven cigarettes evenly separated in an ashtray. There are seven miniature conch shells, seven miniature star fish, and seven miniature anchors strewn around the table. Yemaya's number is seven and these chachkies are her offerings.

There is no reason why any red-blooded American should have ever heard the name Yemaya or know what the fuck I am currently looking at. This is called an altar and this particular altar is dedicated to the goddess, or orisha, Yemaya. She is the orisha of the ocean and fertility, and my mother's patron saint. Santeria is the child of the West African Yoruba religion and Catholicism. The slaves brought Yoruba to Cuba and smuggled their beliefs under the guise of pretending they were Catholic. Oddly, the religions match up. Orishas in Yoruba are the equivalent to saints in Catholicism. They map so succinctly that my mother can believe in both with no existential confusion. Church on Sundays. Babalawo on Saturdays.

I did one of those online quizzes a while back to find out who my orisha is. Turns out I am Elegua, lord of the crossroads. He can be represented as a child or as an old man. He is known as the trickster of all the orisha's. He represents the beginning and the end of life, the opening and closing of paths. Remembering this now seems odd. Limbo is the gist of my existence and the online quiz hit the nail on the fucking head.

Speaking of tricks, I think about stealing a cigarette, or all seven. I could use one now more than ever. When I go to snag one, probably cursing my mother for good, I see a card under the ashtray. I take it. It says, in simple font, all lowercase, *find what you are looking for.* I turn the card over and there is a number and address for her babalawo on the back.

A babalawo *is* a priest, of sorts.

My mother did recommend I talk to one…

┌─────────────────────┐
│   7:46 PM   │
└─────────────────────┘

I want to call it a night. I don't have the energy or proper brain function to visit with a spiritual lunatic. But just as I am about to leave, I hear my parents from their bedroom.

"I don't get it Carmen. I really don't get it. He is surrounded by idiots except Brian. Brian's the only one who's got his shit together.

I talked to his mother last week and she said he's settled down with a nice girl. I forgot her name. Joanne, Janine, something with a 'J'."

Jen, dad. It's Jen and she's a stripper. Or was a stripper. She claims to be a bartender paying her way through college but if you saw her the first night they met, you would have been hard pressed to discover a difference between her and the women on stage. She was wearing a leotard barely covering her nipples that descended into a thong. It looked like one of those outfits Olympic gymnasts wear but three sizes too small. Technically she was pouring out drinks that night, but her real job was to flirt with the customers. To drain them of their money in hopes that the more drinks they bought the better chance they had of sleeping with her. Brian fell into the trap. Now look at him. Facebook official. And little does he know all strippers start behind the bar. Bartending is just the minor leagues until you get called up to the show.

"He es going to figure it out honey. Don't worry. He es a good boy."

"He was," Dad says.

"He still is pero he's just going through something," she pleads.

"Going through something? He's twenty-fucking-five."

"Don't curse papi, let's sleep."

Papi? I'll fucking yak.

My phone weakly vibrates.

Kristen: Sunday Funday? Wicked Wolf? We just got here.

Of course Kristen is back in Hoboken tonight. A loud, obnoxious bar is what is being offered here. What would I get out of this? The answer is nothing except compounding interest on my hangover. I don't want to go anywhere near Hoboken. I'm looking for answers and all I've got is more questions.

"Fuck it," I say.

The babalawo beckons.

8:05 PM

The babalawo is located in the Bronx. Not a place I want to go but it doesn't seem like I have much of a choice. The card says it all – I need to find what I'm looking for. My situation is desperate. Crossing the George Washington Bridge on a Sunday night was not on my bingo card.

I stop at an ATM before crossing the bridge to acquire as much money as I have left. That's one thing I know about Santeria, it ain't free. Even if this is my mother's babalawo, no life advice will be given without some cold hard cash. I might not get any guidance at all considering I've never done any of the prerequisites. My mother says in order to make saint, to be officially indoctrinated, you have to wear only white for an entire year. For that reason alone, I could never be a full believer. I wouldn't make it out of the first week with any clothes left.

I wish the GPS was wrong, but I know it's not. I cross over the Alexander Hamilton Bridge into the Bronx and head south on 87 towards Yankee Stadium. Even the nice parts of the Bronx are terrifying to my yuppy ass. Before and after the beautiful Colosseum that my beloved Yankees play in are chop shops and motels and other buildings that look like they were built for the sole purpose of trafficking humans.

87 does this big circular roundabout of the Bronx's perimeter, riding south next to the Harlem River, then curving around the East River. Think of the Bronx as a big knee joint connecting the thigh of New York State to the shin bone of Manhattan. I'm at the bottom of the joint, starting to make my way back up onto 278.

I can feel Rikers Island from here, which has to be an omen. That's another thing Santeria believers are always going on about. Signs, omens, warnings, prophecies. If you thought Italians were superstitious, you have no idea how deep Cubans who practice Santeria can get. My mom made fourteen pieces of oxtail tonight, of which I ate half of one. That's because fourteen is divisible by seven, her saint's number. No matter what day of the week or time of the month, my mother wears some combination of white and blue, Yemaya's colors. If my mom were to make duck, she can only make it on a Saturday, Yemaya's day. On September 7th my mother is out of commission, as that is Yemaya's feast day. Though there are no processions with the Virgin Regla around the suburbs of New Jersey like there are in Havana, she can be heard, locked in her room, listening to Celia Cruz and doing chants. If Cuba was anywhere close to a first world country and they were livestreaming the procession, she would be watching it as intently as the Super Bowl. There are probably a hundred more mini superstitions my mom does that I don't even know about. I'm not sure how my dad feels about it all, but he knows this is a hill she will surely die on and avoids it like the plague.

When I finally arrive at the destination, I don't really believe it. The address is near P.S. 62 Inocensio Casanova. I'm not sure if the school is named after *the* Casanova but this omen, rather than the Rikers Island one, is something I can get behind. A life filled with debauchery and fornicating didn't turn out so bad for Casanova. He died at the old age of seventy-three, peacefully in his bed, with a life full of stories. Doesn't seem so bad for a man who was on the run for the majority of his life. I tip my cap to the original fuck boy and knock on the ominous apartment door.

8:39 PM

A large black woman with her hair wrapped in a black scarf answers the door. Her eyes are as big as half-dollars and the whites are a mix between yellowed jaundice and sharp red veins. They look like mine after a bender. Have you slept in your contacts, Ms. Babalawo?

Regardless, they are calming. She's wearing a loose white dress that looks like a pillowcase. It barely covers her large breasts and even larger stomach. There are layers of bracelets on her wrists. She looks like she gives good hugs, and that's exactly what she does. I embrace her. I don't know why I expected the babalawo to be a man but I am pleasantly surprised that this woman knows what I need.

"I knew you would be coming," she says.

Of course you did.

8:47 PM

"Your mother has come to me on your behalf before. She is very worried about you. She says you have a spirit inside you that is dangerous and needs to come out. It looks like nothing I've done has worked, so I am glad you've come to see me," the babalawo says.

"My mother?" I ask.

"Carmen, of course."

Her accent is thick with the Caribbean, though I'm not sure which island. How she knows that Carmen is my mother makes my asshole pucker.

"What have you already done?" I ask.

She ignores the question and starts preparing some concoction in a bowl on the altar that takes up half of her living room. There is a large cross on the altar which touches the ceiling. It has chicken feathers draped over it. Two bottles of half-drunk rum man the corners like rooks on a chessboard. There are small seraphs floating on ceramic white clouds, an unknown animal skull, a box of cigars, a black baby doll, and an unlit menorah. I hadn't realized that Santeria moved towards Judaism but I'm sure there's a reason for it. There is also a plethora of beaded necklaces with different sizes and shapes for any type of sick pleasure. I know it's not good to be thinking of ass play at a time like this but I've got time to kill. I'm sitting in a musty antique chair that moans if I move an ass cheek. The apartment smells like it has been painted with stale smoke. It's dark in here, which is probably a good thing. Candles of varying length burn atop tables that line the room, line the one small hallway, line the walls.

As the woman turns around she blows a heap of white powder on to my face with no warning. I probably look like I did on Friday night, except this isn't coke. I'm afraid to ask what it is so I lick my finger and swipe a little off my eyebrow, but before I can taste it she smacks my hand.

"Don't touch. Your orisha is Elegua. I can tell boy. The jester has a hold on you."

The jester line stops me dead.

"Marissa?" I ask the woman.

"That is who you are looking for, but Elegua has other plans for you."

She turns towards the altar, grabs one of the bottles of rum, and slugs about a quarter of it. She takes another sip, spits into her hands, and starts rubbing it on her face. My eyes start to water just imagining what she's feeling. I have no idea what's going on but I know this lady is the real deal.

"You...you...you..."

With each successive "you" the woman's voice changes. First it's a young girl, then an old man, and last, a little boy.

"You remember you," the little boy in the big black woman's body says.

"I what?" I ask.

The woman puts her face right up to mine. Her eyes are no longer jaundice and the veins have disappeared. They have taken on an innocent look.

"You remember you, Lou."

It sounds like a nursery rhyme.

"You remember you, Lou, and you find who."

The voice changes again. This time to a gruff old man.

"You are at a crossroads. I am Elegua and I am your dead uncles and I am your grandfathers and grandmothers and I am Elegua. If you seek to find what you are looking for you must choose."

In a single woosh all the candles are blown out and I am in complete darkness. Everything is still and silent and I am praying to Elegua or God or Jesus Christ that the next part of the ritual doesn't involve any animal slaughter.

"There are rules you must follow if Elegua is to lead you through the crossroads," the babalawo says. She is back to speaking in her normal Caribbean voice, and for that I am thankful. "On Mondays, you must wear white. All other days you must wear red, black, and white. Here are four masks of Elegua. You must place these over the doorways in your home. That is where Elegua lives, in the passages from room to room. Crossroads. I know there are three doors. Always keep one in your pocket. You cannot whistle in the house. Ever. Do you understand? Never. And do not say a word of this to anyone."

In the darkness she takes my palm and places the four miniature masks. I can barely see her eyes and as mine start to adjust I can make out a small stream of light under the crack of the front door.

"Where can I find Marissa?" I ask.

"If you choose correctly, you will find her."

"Choose what exactly?"

"Only Elegua knows that," she says.

"And how can I get in touch with this Elegua?"

"Listen," she says.

The babalawo disappears into the blackness of the room. I'm not sure where she went. One single candle relights with no one in sight to have lit it. It's a tall candle on the altar and it is shining a mini spotlight on one of the half-filled bottles of rum. I walk up to the bottle, taking it as a sign, and swallow a nice hefty swig. For the first time in my life, I am actually scared at what I just drank. It feels like I've swallowed fire.

9:13 PM

All of the lights in the apartment turn on at once. Another odd coincidence I can't fathom. Either this place is booby-trapped to make for the creepiest, most otherworldly experience, or the otherworldly actually lives here. I'm not sure what to believe but I have the urge to get the fuck out. I was hoping that Santeria would provide me answers and instead I'm left with a bag full of questions, heartburn, and masks of Elegua.

The babalawo comes out of the hallway with a white plate in one hand and a dripping coffee filter in the other.

"Sit back down," she says.

She has a commanding voice. I sit.

"Would you be able to tell me if someone is dead or not?" I ask.

I'm not sure where this question comes from but it could be that twisted documentary I watched earlier. Wife dead, husband gone mad. It's just occurred to me that this may be the only place on the planet that I can commune with the dead and if Marissa is now deceased I would like to know. Then I can end this search and get back to my life.

"Is this the person you are looking for?"

She dumps the filter of coffee grinds on the porcelain plate, smashes her fist on the pile, and removes her hand.

And there she is.

Made out of coffee grinds, but there she is.

Her eyes are shaped like perfect circles with pinches at the end. Somehow, the brown grinds and the white plate make them glow green. Freckles don her nose. Her wild hair almost moves about the plate. Moisture from the coffee drips down the plate and when I finally realize it, I can't look away. The plate has a yellow mark on it right where Marissa's dress would be. I'm either seeing things or I'm a believer.

I gulp, nod at the babalawo, and want to weep.

"Then she is still alive. You must find her within the next five days. If you don't then she is gone forever."

I reach out and hug the babalawo. It's better than the first one. "Go now, and don't forget the rules. And the money…"

I almost forgot that this little ceremony was gonna cost me. I drop all the cash I have left in a bowl on the altar and leave.

10:00 PM

In the rearview mirror, my face is still white with the powder. I look like a calavera. If I get pulled over there is no doubt I will be going directly to jail. Superstition stops me from wiping it off. This Santeria stuff has already got to me and I realize why my mother is so intent on following it. I have a feeling I want to keep the spirits alive. So…

I snag a bottle of rum from my favorite liquor store, which stays open until midnight against code. Just one of the many reasons I love Hoboken. They also take credit cards, thank Elegua, because I'm all out of cash. I'm not usually a rum guy but the fire in my stomach has receded to coals and it needs to be stoked. Elegua said listen, and I am.

As I enter my apartment I get another text from Kristen, urging me to come to the bar. Sunday Funday is a ritual only the truly die hard can participate in. I try to ignore the text, pour a big glass of the rum over the two ice cubes I have left in my freezer, and begin to pray. I'm not really sure how this works as I haven't done it in quite some time. I'm not sure what to say to Elegua but it goes something like this:

Please, just let me fucking find her.

After my lengthy prayer, I nail in the three masks. One over my bedroom, one over my bathroom, and one over the door to my apartment. The fourth stays in my pocket.

Between my mother and father's seven-day engagement and now my own five-day countdown, all the signs are pointing to this week being crucial. I should relax. I should get a good night's sleep. I should clean my room. I should make some calls. I should pray.

Please, just let me fucking find her.

Two more texts come in from Kristen mid-prayer. I'm not sure what that means, but it has to mean something.

The babalawo said listen…

11:33 PM

Elegua or God or Jesus are not here at Wicked Wolf. Neither is Marissa. I took Kristen's urging as a sign that maybe, just maybe, I was being led to where I needed to be. To where Marissa is. It was that big glass of rum that let my guard down.

In between Kristen yapping in my ear and the blasting 90s rap music, I am keeping my eye out for a yellow dress. If she's *still* wearing the same dress two days after meeting her we have a whole other set of hygiene issues, but that doesn't occur to my semi-comatose brain.

I stick with the rum, this time mixing it with Coke. Not the white kind. The capital C kind. The night turns into an unnecessary blur. I have work in 8 hours but that doesn't seem to deter me from pounding down these shitty cocktails and keeping my eyes peeled for more signs. I have five days to find Marissa according to the babalawo and I'm wasting them at Wicked Fucking Wolf. My blood alcohol level is probably somewhere in the mid-teens. My aches and pains need healing. Open wounds need solace. I could have just said no.

But I didn't.

I can't.

Monday

APRIL 20TH, 2015

7:31 AM

"I gotta go to work. Text me later."

Kristen's voice is groggy and defeated. I pretend I'm still asleep until I hear the relieving click of the door.

I deserve a little credit here. We did not have sex. The evidence of this is that I am fully clothed in the same jeans and t-shirt I went out in. There isn't even a zipper undone or a condom wrapper in site. Good job, Lou. Good fucking job.

With one eye, I check the clock. 7:31 AM feels like midnight. An hour and a half before work is plenty of time, even with the pain currently crashing in from all sides. Still fully clothed and muddle-brained, I attempt my gymnastics routine out the window for a cigarette. I can't feel any worse.

It's a cold morning. The air is crisp and fall-like with none of the latent mugginess of spring. The wind off of the Hudson travels between buildings, gaining momentum until it smacks me in the face. There are no sounds yet except the hollow wind and a cat which sounds like it's uttering the name of a Chinese dictator. The facades and sky meld together in hues of gray and concrete as I puff at this dreadful fire between my fingers.

There are a thousand things I could worry about at this moment but at the top of the list is my lack of white pants. I'm a straight man. I don't own white pants. The babalawo was very precise. All white on Monday. There are two options, both of which suck. I can wear white joggers which could lead me to getting fired or I can rock a pair of white long johns underneath a pair of normal blue chinos. Option number two feels like a shortcut, but with the very real possibility that it could cause sweating to the point of dehydration. And if Elegua is watching, he'll know. I don't know enough about Santeria to understand how I can or cannot wear white, so I decide to risk it all. White sweatpants, a white long sleeve t-shirt with a pocket to spruce it up, and white sneakers. I'm going to stick out like a snowflake in hell. Add to my prayer list the hymn of hoping Doug is out of office.

As I dress for work, I try to call my sister in London. It goes straight to voicemail. Part of me wants to check in, exchange pleasantries, make sure she landed and that she didn't walk in on Creag with some British slag. But if I'm being honest, I need to know if she has ever met Marissa. More to the point, if Kimberly has met her, then why hasn't she ever introduced us? I call four times, think about leaving a voicemail, and suddenly remember this is the 21st century.

The idea to call my sister occurred last night, during a spell of what could only be described as insanity. In the midst of Kristen's mildly amusing stories from her trip to Vegas, I thought I was hearing a voice speak to me in Spanish. At first I thought Kristen was talking about a farm animal that had ventured onto the strip, but when I closed my eyes and listened, the voice kept saying "llamame". Llamame, llammame, llamame. I thought maybe my eardrums had ruptured due to the voices of Ja Rule and DMX blasting at insane levels, but the voice was clear and precise.

When a voice in your head repeats call me, call me, call me, you start getting funny ideas. The first idea was scrolling through my phone to find some hint of having wrongly saved Marissa's number. Maybe I saved it under hot spanish woman, or yellow dress, or future wife, or accidentally put a space in front of the name. There are thousands of ways you can mess up adding a contact. Kristen continued to drone on about slot machines and famous DJs while I went through my entire contact list, line by line. I found no clues and Kristen didn't seem to notice I had my head buried in my phone for the better part of an hour.

When I finally came up for air, nodding and smiling as if I'd enjoyed whatever Kristen was saying, a rando walked up to us and asked me if I was Kim Kennedy's brother. It was kind of surreal and the Spanish voice saying llamame stopped abruptly. I looked around for help, wondering if the random person in front of me was a stalker. Kim has a pretty rabid following on Instagram but how they would know her close family members is next level.

"I saw you on one of her posts, I think. She made a piece for you. A lampshade was it?"

I almost spit my drink out laughing. This was a true fan. Three years ago my sister *had* made me a lampshade. It was after she visited my apartment for the first and only time. She was mortified that her baby brother could live in such squalor. The insta-famous Kim Kennedy could not fathom one of her own having little to no furniture in an apartment with a bareback bedside lamp. I don't know what ever happened to that lampshade, because the lamp next to my bed is still shadeless. But I do remember it was pale white with pictures of different types of house phones. There was a fiddleback, a picture frame, a two box, rotaries, all in jest at my making fun of her house phone. And that's when it hit me. All the signs coming together. Kimberly Kennedy would have to know Marissa, and I had to call her.

So I guess you can say that Elegua was right to lead me to Wicked Wolf. It may have cost me recovery, and it certainly didn't help with the Kristen situation, but at least I have a plan.

8:45 AM

For a half hour now I've been walking aimlessly in the parking garage off 2nd and Sinatra. On Sunday, in sheer excitement, it never occurred to me to take a picture of where I parked or to pay attention to anything other than getting home and hanging those little Eleguas. Instead of counting the number of winding turns up, or staircases traversed down, I had an eye out for signs.

> **Been looking for my car for a half hour. I think it's a sign not to go to work.**
> 8:45 AM – April 20th – 2015

Sent.

As the aimless search continues, the echo of a pair of high heels moving with purpose reaches my ears. When I look up, I can't believe what I see.

The woman continues up a stairwell and I decide to follow at a safe distance. The hurried clack slide of heels on concrete is just barely audible. It is not the business attire she is wearing that has led to this move. Nor is it the brown hair, swaying at the lapel of her gray jacket, or the confidence of her walk. It is not even the siren sound of her heels. What has driven me to this level of creepiness is a short glimpse of yellow stuffed under her right arm.

Three floors up and out of breath, all sound except my wheezing has disappeared. I take a few steps out onto the parking deck, stop, and listen. This is repeated around the entire floor with no results. My version of echolocation has failed. But suddenly, right in front of my eyes, appears my car. The old Honda Accord, embarrassed of its owner as if we were both donning dunce caps. The door creaks some sort of insult as I get in the car.

I try and find music that will whisk my head away from its current, dangerous place. I am hanging on the edge of normalcy. Even my fingers are exhausted. There is a heavy space in my head, a black hole of negativity into which everything seems to be falling. A drunk's regret.

┌─────────────────────┐
│   9:10 AM   │
└─────────────────────┘

Late for work.

This is not a new phenomenon.

For a company that makes phone apps, our offices resemble an insurance company's. There are no amenities. Nothing is here that doesn't need to be. It's a far cry from Google's campus. When I imagine Googleplex, I see a stark antithesis to Avalanche Apps. Google's building must be exotic, something out of a futuristic Mesopotamia. Bouquets of indigenous flowers hanging from the walls of curved buildings, and a gondola ride to one's cubicle through trickling waterfalls. Meanwhile, our building is a gray rectangle made of concrete. We have a fax machine. I repeat, we have a fax machine. The only vegetation is two small strips of grass between the sidewalk and the entrance. The only missing piece is a chain-link fence around the perimeter with spirals of barbed wire on top and a basketball court. Even prisons have basketball courts.

Half of the building is subleased by a small CPA firm. The lack of difference between us and them is staggering. If you are of the mindset that environments shape people, then look no further than 3022 Business Way. A gray box that breeds gray boxes. If you are of the group that believes genes shape who we are, then this is one stunted gene pool. Number crunchers who couldn't hack it at one of the big three. Ones and zeros pushers who couldn't cut it at any other software company in the world. If someone decides to date in-office their procreation should be illegal. The amount of mediocrity trapped here should never be allowed to spring forth new and average life.

Sometimes, I wish we actually were half prison, half office. At least then one side would be interesting.

At my desk, a corner cubicle facing a depressing window, I take a moment of silence for the weekend that was. This moment turns into a half hour blank stare, caught in the abyss of a black computer screen. It isn't until I come out of the depths of this thick brain fog that I realize I am very, very nauseous. I turn the computer on and its light flashes in vertical tunnels, then a blue screen, then a black screen, and then more light racing from top to bottom. I shut my eyes, unable to handle the frenzied mess.

With eyes shut, head heavy, it is quite possible that I fall asleep.

Okay, I fall asleep.

The rude awakening comes at an undetermined time in my nap's first cycle.

"Lou, how was your weekend, my man?" A thick-handed slap thumps down on my shoulder.

There is no need to wake up, or turn around, to know who this buffoon is. If the voice, fat and jolly as Santa, does not give it away then the crumbs and oil smeared on my shoulder sure do. It is the office manager, Jim.

"If I knew, I'd tell ya Jim! I wasn't really there for much of it. From what I'm told, it was great, you corny fat fuck!"

All of this I think.

"Good, Jim," I say.

My eyes remain closed in prayer, hoping he'll move on to another victim. But the heavy gut breathing is still cemented behind me. If Jim wants my attention, he'll have to understand that it comes at a cost. Today it is the possibility of puking on his penny loafers.

"Good to hear Lou! Gah-ha-hud to hear! I actually went to this crazy club on the L-E-S," he says.

Jim is ignorant of the current state I am in, even though I am in this state every Monday. He is also ignorant of the fact that I clearly said, "Good Jim" not "Good Jim, you?" This blind and willful ignorance must be what makes him so terrific in his office manager role. The only part of his little speech that is worth a reply, or a slap on the mouth, is his abbreviation of the Lower East Side. It is only a matter of time before he starts saying things like FIDI or U-E-S or L-O-L.

"So, we left this FIDI happy hour…" he begins his story.

I can't retain much. I finally open my eyes and watch as he balances his lopsided weight between the outsides of his loafers. His mouth fumbles under a thin mustache and the constant grasping of his scraggly beard is almost as vomit-inducing as his attempt to convince me his weekend was awesome. He whips out his phone and tries to show me a picture of some new club. I try my best not to look but when he shoves it in my face I see a grainy picture of yet another club.

"…we got bottles," I hear him say. "…one of the bottle girls wanted me…"

I turn away and close my eyes, unable to cope.

"Hey Doug. Didn't think you were coming in today?"

In any other state or any other clothes, I don't fall for such an obvious ruse. The excitement in Jim's voice is the dead giveaway. If Doug were actually in the office Jim would have assumed his role as office bitch, nipping at Doug's oversized pant leg. This fat and obnoxious fool a mere sniff away from Doug becomes a brown-nosing bulldog. None of this registers fast enough as I shoot up from my reclined position. My left-hand lands on the keyboard, my right on the mouse – a perfectly executed dismount. But Doug is nowhere in sight.

"Ha! Got ya! LOL!" Jim says. He is very pleased with himself.

As Jim walks away he mentions he's going to have to write me up for my attire. I imagine doing awful things to Jim but am too hungover to go through with them. In fact, I'm too hungover to care.

┌─────────────────┐
│   10:47 AM   │
└─────────────────┘

I can fuck off an entire day of work by looking up nonsense online, but today my search is specific: the documentary I watched on Sunday. The one where a man murders his wife, moves away under a new identity, and has no recollection of his wife, her murder, or the children they had together. I hate to say this, but I can't help but laugh. Imagine pulling the excuse that you don't remember twenty years of marriage? I knew marriage wasn't for me but fuck, can it get *that* bad?

I skip past all of the garbage clinical links and go straight to Wikipedia for the definition. Dissociative amnesia is a memory disorder where you completely forget chunks of time, place, and personal information. This inability to recall information often happens during times of high stress or trauma. Does drinking upwards of twenty alcoholic beverages count as traumatic? Because this sounds exactly like what happened to me. One second I am enjoying a night out with someone I want to be with and the next thing you know I am in bed with someone I don't. There's a hyperlink for the term "dissociative fugue", which sounds interesting, so I click it.

Now this, this is more me. "A fugue state is a reversible amnesia that is directly tied to unexpected wandering or traveling." When you start at one place and wake up at another, not understanding fully why or how you got there, you have gone full fugue. I'm not even sure how to pronounce the word but I just assume it sounds like fugazi and begin to say the word in a Brooklyn Italian accent. Foo-goo, bao.

When I get to the signs and symptoms page of the fugue disease I am freaked out.

Symptoms of a dissociative fugue include mild confusion and once the fugue ends, possible depression, grief, shame, and discomfort. People have also experienced a post-fugue anger. Another symptom of the fugue state can consist of loss of one's identity.

Depression, grief, shame, discomfort. I don't think four words have better encapsulated how I feel every Sunday. The fugue is the hangover. The hangover is the fugue. And yes, I am extremely angry that I didn't get Marissa's number. But now I wonder if Marissa ever happened in the first place. Had meeting her just been the start of my fugue?

11:08 AM

When I finally scroll to a list of famous fugue cases I am petrified. I was expecting this Monday to be another wasted day, full of self-loathing and minimal work. But I have done enough digging to be convinced I am one of these fugue freaks. For example, one woman who had a fugue back in '08 for twenty days ended up being rescued from the Hudson River. That was just one of three more fugues, each lasting longer and longer, until she had a fugue in St. Thomas during a hurricane. Supposedly she was in one of these fugue states and decided to go for a swim. Talk about bad luck. They're still looking for this poor girl.

Then there is the case of Doug Bruce. He is the defacto star of the documentary *Unknown White Male*. I'll have to watch that tonight to see if I can find any similarities to my case, but the summary is enough to give me douche chills. Doug "awakened" on a subway in New York City and had no clue who he was. When he got off the train he had been wiped clean of all his previous life – experiences, family, friends, even his own name. With no clue of who he was he went to the police who checked him into a psych ward under the name of "unknown white male". The only clue they found was a phone number written on a piece of paper inside of a Spanish phrase book. Of all the links, I click the one where the clue is in a Spanish fucking phrase book. Doug Bruce has still not regained his memory.

I'll admit I am not at this point yet. I am aware of my family, my friends, and who I am. I am Lou Kennedy, I say to myself. I am Lou Kennedy. But it wouldn't surprise me if one day I woke up from a long bender and found myself married to Kristen Birdock with kids, in-laws, and no recollection of where my life went. This is what I am trying to avoid. This is why I need to find Marissa.

2:01 PM

After a long lunch and an even longer clock dump, a ritual where you sit on the toilet for as long as possible whether you have to go or not, I'm back at my desk. Slumped in for the long haul, I attempt my first email. These last three hours of the day are the most excruciating, slower than any Turnpike traffic. Even if I were to actually work until 5:00 PM, these hours are twice as long as the first five. In my mind, I'm putting in 14-hour days.

Scrolling through my emails, up and down, side to side, I somehow get a year back. I scroll up to the present day, and down again, this time two years back. This takes three minutes and is repeated for the next three hours until it's time for my miserable, traffic-filled drive back to Hoboken.

5:31 PM

I'm melted into the couch like a D.A.R.E. commercial watching *Unknown White Male* when my phone vibrates from the kitchen counter. Though tempting, there is no chance of movement for the

Monday crowd. This may be a shocking revelation to the uninitiated. Monday through Wednesday is for the industry. Bartenders, waiters, chefs, and bouncers finally get their chance to enact some revenge for the hurt we normal people have caused them all weekend. I am friends with these fine people and if needed, can binge on a weeknight. But on this Monday there is absolutely no chance of me getting off my couch or out of my white sweats. I ignore it.

But the phone doesn't quit. It vibrates again.

By not looking at it I can avoid the guilt of not answering. More importantly, I can avoid whatever the person calling wants me to do. Purposeless calls ended in middle school. Since then, there hasn't been a single phone call dedicated to the art of conversation. Any call you now get is one of persuasion. How are you doing is now what are you doing.

The phone doesn't care.

For the third time, it begins vibrating.

Maybe it's an emergency? Maybe it's Marissa?

At this thought I sprint to the phone, barely answering it in time.

"What's up?" I answer, out of breath.

"Were you jerking off?" a woman asks.

"What? No? Just leaving the gym."

"Yeah right. You haven't been to the gym in years."

It's Carey. I'm dejected and in severe pain from my quick movements.

"New year, new me."

"That was supposed to start in January."

"Whatever, what do you want?" I ask.

"Come get a drink," she says.

No.

Two letters.

Two simple letters.

N-O.

The hardest syllable in the English language.

I'm in no shape to leave the house. And what good would it do for me to go hangout with Carey? It would be worse than going to a strip club. Getting laid is not an option and I'll still end up paying for the drinks. This is an easy, rational decision. N-O. No.

"I need someone to talk to," she says after a long pause.

5:55 PM

"Sure, where do you want to meet?"

"Tom's Bar," she says.

"Why all the way uptown?"

"Just come, I'll call you an Uber. I don't want to drink alone."

I take a moment.

"Call me when it's here."

Five minutes later the driver is waiting in front of my building. He seems annoyed at the 25-second ride up Washington Street, but that's his problem. I could have walked, maybe even should have walked, but my body has turned soft since college. Like a nice Merlot, I've smoothed with age. The edges I once had – hard forearms, cut calves, even small ridges where my little paunch now resides – have all but disappeared. I'm like a cliff that's been perpetually beaten by the ocean, leaving nothing but a sandy beach.

6:01 PM

Tom's is made of two long rectangular windows, one down Washington Street, the other West on 14th Street. From the outside it looks like a jovial version of *Nighthawks*. The bar runs long and parallel opposite the 14th Street window and at the end of the glowing mahogany is Carey, sitting alone. The crowd is distinctly older, a mix of business types, weathered drinkers, professionals. Sprinkled in are some industry standards like the bouncer at 1 Republik and a particularly good-looking bartender from Green Rock. I wave at both, receiving waves in return, which relieves me of any anxiety I had over my behavior this past weekend.

"What can I get ya?" the bartender asks.

"He'll have a glass of pinot noir," Carrey intrudes.

I raise my eyes at the bartender letting him know the choice is not mine.

"You'll have two glasses of wine with me and then you'll go home."

"Why would I do such a thing?" I ask.

"This isn't going to turn into a wild night. I just wanted someone to talk to who actually gets it," she says.

"Actually gets what?" I take a sip of my wine and to my utter disgust, I enjoy it.

"My situation."

"What would I get about your situation? I've never been in a stable relationship. I know absolutely nothing about keeping a woman happy. I can come here and make you laugh but I couldn't even scratch the surface of what Matt is thinking. If I, by the unlucky grace of God, find myself with a woman for over five years, I'm either marrying her or killing her. There's no coming back from a five-year relationship."

She laughs.

"See, you might not think you get it, but you do," she says.

Lou Kennedy started a twitter poll: Marriage or suicide?

6:06 PM – April 20th – 2015

"From what I've just said, how do you conclude that I get what it takes to be in a relationship?" I ask.

"Well, at least you understand romance," she says. "I mean, the gist of the whole thing is that you want to be with a person, and you're willing to do just about anything to be with that person. And if you can't be with them, then murdering them is in the realm of possibility. That's romance. And I'll kill Matt if he doesn't propose to me within six months."

"Rational," I conclude.

But my little spat with today's research has me thinking. Is what I'm saying to Carey what I actually believe? Could I kill Marissa if her love was unrequited? I motion to the bartender for another drink and try to signal that I want a big one. Preferably the rest of the bottle.

I look at my phone. Marriage comes fast out of the gates:

Marriage: 100% – 2 votes
Suicide: 0% – 0 votes

6:12 PM

"How should I do it?" Carey snaps her head towards me. "If he doesn't propose, how do I go about this?"

Carey's wet eyes shimmer under the dim bar light. A smirk with evil intent spreads across her face. Her majestic nose has seen murder, it knows deceit.

"Poison. Do people even check for that anymore?" I ask.

"Poison it is," she says as we clash our glasses together.

She's kidding, of course, and so am I, but I can't get the guy who murdered his wife and forgot his own identity out of my head.

"Wouldn't it be easier to hire someone though?" I ask.

I'm not sure what depths of hell this question has gurgled up from. Murder for hire seems like one of the more cowardly ways to go about killing a spouse. If you're mad enough to think about killing someone you love you might as well take all the risk and reap all the reward. Regardless, I think it, I say it, and now my mind is on another tangent. I'm worried.

The whole thing with dissociative amnesia is that your brain attempts to block out trauma. If the trauma is heavy enough you can forget who you are entirely. It's a form of protection. A way that your brain allows you to continue surviving. If your brain knows that something you've seen or done is going to kill you, it erases it. It's pure survival. There must be a reason Marissa was there, right in front of me, and then poof, gone. My brain is protecting me from some horrid scenario I witnessed or took part in. I try my best to piece together what happened before I woke up in Kristen's bed but I only see a black hole.

"Easier, sure," Carey says. "We live in New Jersey. I'm sure there are about fifty murderers for hire in the nearest square mile. I could probably throw a rock at a window and the chance that there is a murderer for hire in the window I hit is at least 10%. I don't care how much Hoboken has been gentrified. This place is still crawling with the mob."

"You think so?"

"I know so."

"Have you met one?" I ask.

"Well, there was this one time. I met a work friend over in Union City for a drink and..."

"Why would you ever do that? I'm Cuban and I don't go to Union City," I say.

"It's up and coming. We were at this place called Cuba Libre and there was a suave looking guy sitting at the end of the bar. He was wearing one of those suits with wide lapels, smoking a thin cigar inside, a little glass of whiskey. He had a mustache the thickness of four-point font. He kept eyeing my friend and before he left the bar he slid her his card. It just said 'Mr. J' on it with a number."

"So you think he was a murderer?"

"Well, the bartender told her that she should throw that card in the trash. So of course she didn't. It wasn't until we got up to leave and I went to the bathroom and saw him in the kitchen holding up a chicken by its feet and a knife to its throat," she says.

"Santeria," I whisper.

"What?"

"Nothing."

"Well, after I told my friend she threw the card out. But I think she's still mad she did. The whole intrigue of it. Women are weird. We assume a man's a killer and it doesn't send us running for the hills."

"I bet you wish you had that card right now," I laugh.

"You're right. Mr. J looked more lethal than poison," she said.

This seems like a story Carey would have told me a long time ago considering I'm Cuban, but she probably thought the place was just your run of the mill Mexican. Timing is everything and hearing this story now has my ears perked up to the signs. If I'm going to believe in this Santeria stuff then I must remember, there are signs everywhere. Numbers to notice, animals to keep an eye out for, color patterns that will illuminate some fate. It's the practitioner's job to pay attention.

"Do you remember what street the restaurant was on?"

"Uh, no. Why?"

"Just want to check out the food one day."

"You sure you don't need someone killed, Lou?"

Need someone killed? I need someone found.

6:47 PM

"What about Jen?" she asks.

I'm thrown by the question. Would I have Jen bumped off to get my friend back? Possibly.

"Maybe a little poison. Not enough to kill her. Just enough to get her sick for a while so that Brian is sufficiently grossed out by her.

Then he'll have to break up with her. You can't watch a woman shuke and still be attracted to her."

"Shuke?" Carey asks.

"You know, shit and puke at the same time," I say.

"I just gagged."

"See. Just thinking of that grosses you out."

"I gagged because Matt did that once. It was…awful."

"And you still want him to propose to you? Please, enlighten me."

"It was after he got injured in college. He was so distraught he chugged 12 beers in under an hour and he was already on painkillers. He's lucky he shuked and didn't die. I sat by him on the toilet for the entire night just making sure he was alive. And the fucker still hasn't proposed to me," Carey says.

My phone lets me know that marriage is out to a big lead, but suicide is on the board.

Marriage: 88% – 8 votes
Suicide: 12% – 1 vote

"All I'm saying is that I've done my time, don't you think?" Carey continues. "Five years with Matt. Five years! I just want to know he's committed, knock me up and call it a day. Am I asking that much?"

This diatribe has me staring at the bartender, attempting to telepathically order something stronger. Carey continues, undisturbed.

"Anyone in a relationship understands the expectations. Ring, wedding, baby. In that order would be ideal but I'll take what I can get at this point. It's just frustrating to be the girl that has to push. I don't want to push. I want him to be like Eric Decker," she states.

"Oh, god."

If my eyes could roll any further into the back of my head I'd be looking into the depths of my own sluggish brain.

"What do you mean *oh, god?* Eric Decker is the perfect man. Jessie James Decker is the perfect woman. And all he does is constantly knock her up. She's popping out babies left and right. I mean look at this."

She shoves her phone in my face.

At first glance, Matt and Eric Decker have more in common than I'd previously realized. Mr. Decker has his hair quaffed with a slim line part and is wearing a pair of Ray-Bans. He looks like the NFL's version of JFK. His shorts are somehow cut above his entire quad and there's a slight bulge under the drawstrings. He is wearing a tight gray Jets shirt which could rip open at the biceps at any moment. None of this distracts you from his wide, white smile and the woman who is wrapped in his arms, Jessie James Decker, country singer extraordinaire.

Like Mr. Decker, Matt also has it all. A similar quaff extends an already 6'5" frame to an off-putting 6'7". White teeth shimmer between his lips as if he's never had coffee or a cigarette. Matt's physique is leaner than the NFL star's but this we can chalk up to a different choice of sport. Matt played college basketball, destined for greatness (an NBA bench player) at Rhode Island University. He could do no wrong on the court except blow out his knee, thus ending his career and causing the shuke incident. Even though his career was cut short Matt remains a good-looking man with his arms around a beautiful woman.

"So, this is your perfect life? The life you always wanted?"

"Pretty much," Carey says, snatching back her phone. "Ughhh… look how happy they are. You can't fake this type of happiness."

"Oh, yeah?"

On my own phone I browse Carey's Instagram account for some rival material. She has posted plenty of picket-fence fodder for me to choose from. One catches my eye. Carey and Matt dressed in all white, surrounded by Matt's family. The only thing standing out more than their outfits is the collection of blinding smiles. This affinity for abstaining from anything brown seems genetic. Everyone in the picture is tanned and taut but more importantly, happy.

"You see a difference?" I ask, feigning ignorance.

"I do," she said. "That night we were at his family's house in the Keys. We got into a fight talking about how soon we wanted to get married. He said he wanted to wait until we were living together for at least two years to make sure. Who says, 'to make sure'? I left the house and stayed at…wait. You know this story. You think these two had that problem?"

She pushes the Decker's at my head again.

"Yeah, probably. Everyone has problems."

I pull up a Decker family photo. Professor Lou has the ability to tell a real from a fake. It's taken years of devout study in the arts of Instagram to decipher such hidden mysteries but I've put in the long hours.

"Take this one for example…"

The picture shows a bedroom smothered in rose petals. In the middle of said bed is a Ferrero Rocher the size of a bowling ball. The caption reads: Best Valentine's Day Ever.

"For starters, no man could design such a beautiful spread," I say.

I wait for it to click. Carey's eyes have gone dreamy. She's now floating in the fake world of her imagination, the world where a man lays rose petals on her bed, instead of seeing the point.

"Huhhhhha," She lets out a sigh.

"I'm saying he didn't do this. No real man could. It's too perfect. Not a petal out of place. She did this. She woke up early, her kids were screaming in her ears while daddy Decker stayed blissfully asleep, unaware it was even Valentine's Day. After she got the kids out the door to school she woke the comatose Eric, who had a few too many beers the night before, and kicked him out of the house for the day. He obliged. Why would he stay in that nagging home all day? Then she went to work. She sprinkled the petals on the bed and the floor, inspected and reinspected the lighting of their bedroom. She put all the dirty clothes away that once covered the floor. Then she whipped out her Valentine's Day gift to herself, the vaunted human-head-size Ferrero Rocher. Her favorite chocolate, which Eric seems to forget every year. In conclusion, she took it upon herself to make her own Valentine's Day glory that her husband could never provide."

"No."

"Yes."

"No…"

Professor Lou has just told his pupil that the moon landing was, in fact, a hoax.

I look at my phone: You smell that? I smell it. Suicide's making a comeback.

Marriage: 58% – 14 votes
Suicide: 42% – 10 votes

"When's the last time you looked like this?" she asks.

She pulls up a picture of the Deckers at a winery. Their eyes are glazed with what appears to be joy, but it is far from joy. It's the numbing effects of the third glass of shitty cabernet. They are smiling. They are beautiful. But there is a fight in their future. Professor Lou can see it through his professional lens. The way Mrs. Decker's jaw is taught, just a touch tighter than a regular smile. One wrong look from Mr. Decker in the direction of a hot little waitress and this entire scene is going to explode into a full-blown domestic abuse scandal.

"I've never looked like that. Christ, look at his arms. Even when I played football I had more chest than biceps."

I roll up my sleeve and attempt to make a muscle. Where my arm once contracted at will, it now droops at wont.

"Not the looks, you moron. I mean happy. When's the last time you felt as happy as they look."

"Never," I say, confidently. "Never, because it is an illusion."

7:01 PM

"You're a real asshole, you know that?"

I nod. I do know this.

Carey places her phone face down on the bar and folds her arms. In my plums I can feel either a slap or a lecture, and I'm not sure which one will hurt more.

"Since you're mister miserable tonight, I want your take on Brian and Jen. Not the cool cliché take, not the nonchalant take, and not that take at brunch on Saturday. What do you really think?"

I will admit the take from Saturday was not great. Attacking my ex-best friend and his woman? Not the best look. That morning I was in no shape for any human interaction. But those feelings, in some way, are exactly how I feel. It may have come out poorly but the sentiment was real.

"First, it's not *my* life. I can have an opinion all I want but it won't change the fact that he's going to have to live with his decisions. The only thing I know is that being young is the most important attribute you have. Time, Carey. Time. Yesterday we were in elementary school, tomorrow we'll be in our graves. That's the way it works. He'll have years to play this game. The find a wife, live happily ever after, have two annoying kids you want to punch in the face but are forced to love all while holding down a meaningless job that pays for changes on the house your wife wants game. He's 25! The best age there is. The age of every girl in the bar being in your wheelhouse. The world is at his fingertips and all he has to do is pocket that shit. Instead, he's lightly tossing it in the air and smashing it with a baseball bat. She works at a strip club, Carey. There has to be something a little off, no?"

Carey finishes off her glass of wine in one gulp. My immediate thought is that this might turn into a party. Maybe we'll both get hopped up and make some bad decisions. As she takes a deep breath, I understand that this isn't going to be one of those nights. I've seen my mother make this same face and it never ended well for me.

7:11 PM

"You need to grow up," Carey says.

"What?"

"All of that young stuff is bullshit. You're young for less than half of your life. You're going to be that guy who's 35 and still at the bar trying to pick up chicks. And by the looks of it you're going to be a bag of pulp with wrinkles at 35 too. No one likes that guy, Lou. You remember Tucker? The 25-year-old who came to all our high school parties. Have you seen him on Instagram lately? The guy is wearing highlighter shirts and a bandana at music festivals. He's almost 40. Don't be that fucking guy."

"Don't compare me to Tucker. I'm not Tucker. God forbid I look out for my friend," I say.

"You aren't looking out for him. You're jealous of him."

"How am I not looking out? He's making the one mistake you don't make. You can make a thousand mistakes in this life but wifing up a girl is one you can't get back. It's the most important decision. Fuck a house, fuck a car, fuck a job. The only important decision is the person you decide to spend *all* your time with for the rest of time. And he's spending *all* of his time with a glorified bartender, possible dancer, and definite question mark," I say.

"And you want that person to be you. You can't impose on people. There are only so many things you can do. You have to pick. And your time is running out, Lou. Before you know it you're going to be 40 and alone, and the next time you blink you'll be drooling on yourself in some retirement home with no one to come visit."

I've had enough of this ear beating and head to the bathroom.

I check my phone and the results may surprise you.

Marriage: 48% – 24 votes.
Suicide: 52% – 26 votes.

Remember, these are *my* loyal followers.

┌─────────────────────┐
│   7:16 PM   │
└─────────────────────┘

The signs really are everywhere. I changed out of my white pants in fear of looking like a lunatic at a bar I frequent often. To my delight, a special surprise is waiting for me in the back pocket of the ones I now don – a leftover bag of VanNeece's secret stuff. I take a bump to muster up enough courage to tell Carey more about Marissa, but when I return to the bar, she's gone. Her wine glass is nowhere to be found and if she's in the bathroom she brought her bag with her. I have to admit, one of the many reasons I am happy to be a guy is that my entire life fits into pants pockets.

"You want to close out?" the bartender asks.

I'm confused by the question. The place is filled and there's this jovial atmosphere of being out on a day you're not supposed to be. Keep em' coming boss.

"I'll have a double bourbon, please."

The bartender nods and pours the syrup-colored liquor. I'm trying to get as much drinking in as I can before Carey comes back to scold me some more.

┌─────────────────────┐
│   8:01 PM   │
└─────────────────────┘

Three bourbons in I find myself still waiting for her. I've texted her twice already and decide the third time is the charm, but a reply never comes. The text goes green, which is even weirder considering Carey has an iPhone.

VanNeece mentioned he got this stuff from a new guy and I wonder if I'm amnesiac, drunk, or hopped up on some new illicit product. The bartender begins to look a little grainy, like a hologram, and I can't feel the fourth bourbon going down my throat. I was supposed to take it easy tonight and now I'm in la-la land.

When I look out the long window I feel like I'm actually sitting in the *Nighthawks* painting. My vision has a gooey quality to it. People pass by the mirror like mirages, faces are blurred out, each body leaves a trail of light in its wake that lingers. It's like the shutters in my eyes are set to slow motion and bits of the past are staying put in the present. I turn back to the bartender who now looks like a ghoul, and I'm sufficiently freaked out.

In the mirror behind the bar I notice flashing blue and white lights. They smear across the mirror as if they've been painted by a long brush and when I turn around there is a cop car pulling someone over. I try and stare at a tray of peanuts, focusing on one in particular, when I realize I haven't eaten since lunch.

8:53 PM

The cab ride feels like science fiction. I decided on a cab because one-eyeing an Uber on my phone proved difficult. There was also the little issue of speed. It was the cop's flashing lights that reminded me of my little run-in with the law on Saturday. I'd almost forgot about it but now I feel like a man on the run. Instead of waiting for the other shoe to drop I am headed due north, following the signs to a little Cuban restaurant that may or may not employ a Santeria hitman.

9:02 PM

Memory on drugs is a funny thing. The last time I was in Union City was the last time I went to church with my mother. I can feel her sitting next to me.

"Estas bien?" she asks.

"Sí."

"No estas bien."

"I'm fine mom."

I wasn't fine. I was viciously hungover after a little Easter-themed college party that went down on a Friday night and ran into Saturday morning before returning home for Easter. She would've been appalled at the girls in their Playboy bunny outfits. The only thing that rose from the dead that night was the little guy in my pants.

I remember trying to erase those blasphemous thoughts from my head on our approach to the church, but it's hardly a competition between scantily dressed girls and women in their Sunday best to a college boy.

The priest did his best to put the fear of God in me that day and failed miserably. The Latin went right over my head as I stared at the bleeding man upon the cross. I was so hungover I couldn't take my eyes off of his. He was more hurt than I'd ever be. I was awoken from my reverie when the priest screamed at an octave higher than ears are meant for.

"Idleness is the devil's workshop!"

The priest had a point, I guess. I didn't really have much to do before embarking on this search for Marissa.

I knew that going to Easter mass would require a couple of hours of sacrifice for eternal glory. That glory was a cookout at my mom's friend's house where they were roasting an entire pig.

In a way I was finally at, and am currently heading to, a personal church. Cuban food has serious restorative properties. The smells are like incense. The tastes are like the body and blood of Christ. Actually, they're *better* than the body and blood of Christ. Who needs a fake and tasteless wafer when you can bite into an empanada filled with beef and olives and raisins? What's the use of non-alcoholic blessed wine when you can sip on a fine mojito?

The cab driver's swerve and horn shake me from my little reverie. If he hit the jay walker I'd have no choice but to get out of the cab and run for it before the police showed up. This night is becoming scarier by the second.

If you're scared, go to church.
9:05 PM – April 20th – 2015

Sent.

I'm not entirely sure why I find these Ice Cube lyrics so comical. Maybe it's because I am currently terrified. Reality is slipping from my fingers fast. The past and the present are melding. Texting Carey for the seventh time with no answer just heightens my fear.

9:22 PM

The front of Cuba Libre is the same as almost every Cuban restaurant I've ever been to. There is a thatched roof resting under the glowing lights of the restaurant sign. In between the Cuba and the Libre is a neon palm tree beckoning you inside. The streets are lively in Union City for a Monday. If you closed your eyes you'd be hard pressed to know you were in America. The staccato beauty of the Spanish language is interspersed with a couple English verbs like "okay" and "fuck off" – three words there are really no translations for. It's times like these that I find it inexcusable that my mother never taught me her native tongue. Fluency could have helped me navigate this little slice of New Jersey, but more importantly, it could have helped me with Marissa.

When I think of Marissa I am reminded why I am even here in the first place. The signs. They all point to this place.

┌─────────────────────────┐
│   9:25 PM   │
└─────────────────────────┘

The restaurant is thin and long and filled with rattan everywhere you look. There are rattan chairs and rattan tables and rattan fans in the shape of palm leaves, slowly spinning. The bar is made of wood with rattan edging and the barstools are tall and…rattan. When I sit down at the bar I can feel the thatching stretch and the thick-string joinery give way. It's surprising that the bartender doesn't have anything rattan on him. He's wearing a short sleeved guayabera shirt with the customary four pockets.

"Que puedo conseguirte?"

I assume he's asking what I want to drink so I answer.

"A mojito, please."

"Okay. Comeras con nosotros?"

The only word I can make out is the 'okay'. He can tell I am confused.

"I'm sorry sir. Are jyou going to be eating with us?"

"Yes, please."

"Okay, perfecto."

Joining me at the bar are a typical cast of late-night Jersey Hispanic characters. There are two men laced in gold chains and gold watches and big gold crosses around their necks. They speak with heavy accents marred by years of cigar smoke. If you plugged your ears you would think they were Italian. With them, but not speaking to them, are two gorgeous women. They are made up as if they were attending a ball except their clothes are so tight against their bodies it's hard to tell the difference between dress and skin. I am wary of making eye contact with either one as it might incur a broken appendage or limb, but it's hard not to stare. I think it's safe to say that Cubans rule the roost when it comes to genetics, as well as food. It's only fitting that such a gene pool with such a cuisine would be mired in consistent political and societal upheaval. You can't have it all.

After my first sip of mojito, I finally feel at ease. Though I am here on a mission I might as well enjoy it. I notice a band setting up on a miniature stage behind tables that are now being cleared to make way for a dancefloor. I keep my eyes peeled for the murderer but continuously get distracted. There are the two gorgeous women, the hard-looking men, the diners, the bartenders, the waiters, and then my empanadas. There is a healthy debate of what is to be put in an empanada and the only right answer is meat, olives, and raisins, which these have plenty of. There is a reddish sauce in a small dish that I would usually skip but I decide to give it a whirl. I'm glad I do. I ignore my stomach's warning that I've drunk too much and devour three of them in what feels like seconds. After another mojito down the hatch, I am still hankering for more food and there's only one choice: a Cuban sandwich.

I'm not sure about the weed intake on the island of Cuba but whoever invented the Cuban sandwich must have been baked. Ham, pork, swiss, pickles, and mustard sounds like a combination only the highest of the high could come up with but somehow it works. It's like a smorgasbord of leftovers from the fridge thrown together between a pressed roll, but voila, perfection. In the middle of my third bite, I'm scared shitless by a blast of horns, drums, and congas. In an instant, the bar is cleared, the tables are empty, and everyone is up on the dancefloor except me and a man at the far end of the bar near the kitchen.

He fits Carey's description. Suave looking. Suit with wide lapels. Thin mustache. An unlit cigar between his teeth. He looks like he's been dropped here from Havana in the 20s. We make eye contact and I look away before getting put on his list.

I decide to indulge in a few more bites of my sandwich, possibly the last I will ever taste.

When I look up he's sitting in the stool next to me.

10:01 PM

"Oye, mi hijo. Estas comiendo ese sándwich como si fuera el último sándwich del mundo. ¿Te gusta?"

"Huh?" I reply. I feel a piece of pickle fall from my lip.

"Tu no espeak Spanish?"

"No. Not really, no."

"I should have guessed. What is a good-looking white boy doing at a Cuban restaurant in Union City so late on a Monday?"

He says this with a devilish smirk. The pencil mustache perks up at an odd angle. The man looks like one of those villains in a silent movie.

"Fleeing," I say.

"Que es fleeing?"

"Running away."

"Oh yea? From what?"

"The cops," I say, hoping this reveal will endear me to this terrifying man.

"Aye. Maybe you should leave here then? We don't want any trouble."

Hmmm…

This man is supposed to court trouble. Someone running away from the cops could owe him a debt. Real mafia shit. *I do you this favor, and someday, and that day may never come, I may ask you for a favor in return.* He should, at the very least, feign interest in *why* I'm running from the cops. But he doesn't. He looks at me and then at the door.

"I'm just kidding," I say. "I'm hungry and there is nothing in the world like Cuban food."

"You know what I said in Spanish before? I said you looked like you were making love to that sandwich man. And a white boy. I am impressed."

"I'm not all white," I say, taking minor offense. "It's just the skin. My mom is from Cuba."

"Really? And you don't know how to speak Spanish? That's a shame."

"You don't know the half of it."

"What did you like better? The empanadas or the Cuban sandwich?"

I have a feeling there is something underlying this question. He is looking for some special answer, some secret code that will get me back into his good graces.

"What was that sauce for the empanadas? I usually don't like the sauce they give you with empanadas but this one was good," I say.

"Come on, I'll show you."

10:30 PM

I follow the man into the kitchen. My toes feel numb and my left arm is throbbing. It's either a heart attack or just your run of the mill nerves when finding yourself face to face with a killer.

"Is your name Mr. J?" I blurt out.

"So you have heard of me?"

I thought the kitchen would be louder but it looks like my meal was the last one served. The line cooks are putting their knives away, drinking beer out of tupperware, laughing, folding up their aprons.

I am not sure I have ever seen a group of people so happy at work and I am infinitely jealous.

"My friend said you gave her your card."

"And did this friend ever use said card?" he laughs, then winks.

"Well, no. She threw it out. She said the bartender warned her and then she saw you beheading a chicken."

"The bartender huh? Pendejo. He's just mad my face looks like this and his looks like a shovel hit it," Mr. J says.

"I have to come clean. The bartender told my friend you were bad news. She thinks you are a hitman. That's why I came here," I say.

He picks at his thin mustache. Contemplating what? I don't know, but I hold onto one of the lowboys hoping I don't pass out.

"You need someone killed?" he asks. He is sincere.

"No, I need someone found."

"Who?"

"A woman I met. She's disappeared."

"It's always a woman, isn't it?"

I explain my predicament. The whole thing from start to finish. Marissa, Kristen, the cops. It feels like a confessional. Me and Mr. J, the murderer priest. He grabs us two Hatuey's and cracks them open. I hadn't noticed that my mouth felt like sandpaper until taking a sip. Maybe he'll take the job, but I'm sure he now won't kill me.

"My friend, that is one crazy story. But I have to tell you I am not who you think I am."

"Who are you?"

"The owner."

If I wasn't fortified with just around eight drinks and a bump I would feel utter embarrassment. Instead, I start to laugh, relieved that I am not involved in a sinister plot with a possible murderer.

"You are a crazy white boy," he says, laughing.

"I told you, not all white."

"It's funny, you know, your friend said she saw me cutting up a chicken. That's exactly what's in that empanada sauce. Chicken blood.

You gotta get it fresh or it curdles. I was showing one of my guys how to do it properly you know? It's not exactly up to code but who cares? If there is a choice between a rule and doing a thing right, always go with doing a thing right. You know what I mean?"

"So, you weren't sacrificing the chicken?"

"Sacrificing? What?"

"You know, like Santeria."

"Santeria? Are you crazy? I'm a Catholic man. None of that booga booga shit here. Jesus Christ only."

He crosses himself thrice and says a little prayer and I wonder if I've chosen the wrong religion to guide me on my path towards Marissa.

"You want to see how the sauce is made?"

"Absolutely," I say.

I watch the man pour a blood mix, mojo criollo sauce, and different spices into a dish and am mesmerized by the deftness of it all. He takes a finger to it, licks it, and adds a little more of what I think is pimentón. He seems pleased and asks me to taste. Delicious.

"My friend," he says. "Consider your bill taken care of, and if you ever are looking for a job I can always use people who look at my food the way you do. Especially ones who know English."

He laughs maniacally.

It's the laugh of a hitman.

11:41 PM

When I get home I tap the three Eleguas on each doorway. Then I check the rooms for private investigators that must be assigned to my case. The guy who tried to report a missing person and then ran is clearly guilty of something.

The coast is clear.

I lay on my bed and think of the food I just ate, the food on that Easter Sunday, the food that has tethered me to any real sense of who I am. I can see my mom dancing in that backyard on Easter Sunday, smiling, waving at me, her teeth like chicklets surrounded by dark skin, the smell of pork and beer, the crack of pig skin in my mouth. I begin to whistle the tune that was playing from the two loudspeakers on stands in that backyard. "Candela" by Buena Vista Social Club.

After a minute I hear a loud bang coming from the floor above. When I look outside of my room, I can see that all three miniature Eleguas are on the floor.

I forgot about the whistling rule.

I'm fucked.

Tuesday

APRIL 21ST, 2015

8:55 AM

Getting to work on time after a rather tame wake up feels like a miracle. Ten drinks and Cuban food turn out to be just the right amount of hair for this dog. With no debilitating headache or toxic fumes releasing from my gut I should be in a great mood, but calls to my sister and Carey on the ride in have both gone to voicemail. It's never been this hard to get a woman to talk to me.

Well, that's not entirely true. Every boy has at least one experience of denial that they would rather forget. Unfortunately, I'm reminded of mine every Tuesday morning during a meeting with the programming team, marketing team, and Doug. It's Doug's taut, muscular face and evil brown eyes that do the reminding. Arianna has those eyes.

The meeting is held at 9 AM in the basement of our office building where the ones and zeros pushers are kept away from other human life. This is a requirement for focus. There are no windows or social interaction down here, only cubicles and a small conference room. You could strut through the aisles naked, walking a leashed tiger, and no programmer would notice. They are glued to their screens with headphones in. It's just the way they like it, and the way my father designed it. But on Tuesday mornings they are forced to interact with other living beings. An hour a week shouldn't kill them but by the looks on their faces, the programmers are dreading it.

The main agenda for the meeting regards a task management app, one of our top sellers. The meeting is fairly boring. I bring nothing to the table as far as insights go and anytime Doug begins to talk, I am forced to actively suppress harrowing memories of the inciting incident with his daughter that occurred ten years ago on a family vacation. Instead of listening to anything he says, I try and distract myself by counting the number of dots poked in the ceiling panels. Occasionally I throw in a fake laugh, which is one skill worth my salary.

My fake laugh is so perfect that I may actually be laughing.
9:33 AM – April 21st – 2015

Sent.

9:52 AM

Three hundred and twenty-five...three hundred and twenty-six...three hundred and...

"And I don't care how it needs to be done, but these usernames need to be saved. I don't care what social media platform they are coming from either. I want any username that has ever clicked on one of our ads," Doug is saying.

He strikes an intimidating figure, built like a marine and pacing the front of the room like a general preparing troops for battle. Only the real sickos who enjoy this job find him inspirational.

"We can already do that," one programmer says.

"What? I can't hear you. Speak up young man, speak up!" Doug shouts.

"We can already do that," the programmer repeats himself, "but there are privacy concerns."

"We can? Good. Print me a report daily then. I want to know exact usernames, email addresses, first names, last names, pet's names, ANYTHING that will help market these god damn apps. Because remember, if we can't sell it, none of you have jobs. Meeting adjourned," Doug says, ignoring the latter half of the programmer's statement.

He leaves the conference room with the rest of the marketing team trailing behind him. I lag behind. I try to make eye contact with the programmer that had enough balls to speak up. He's got a black bowl cut, suspicious eyes, and he's wearing dress clothes that are two sizes too large for him. If I'm not mistaken, he's got Velcro shoes on. None of him seems to belong.

"Hey man, what's your name?" I ask.

"Steven," he says. His eyes shift from my chest to the floor at a rapid rate.

"So, you're telling me we already track all of that information? Like, for example, you could tell me anyone with the name 'Steven' who has clicked on one of our apps?"

"That's correct," he says. "It's just legally some users have requested their privacy. It's meaningless though. More of a suggestion than a law."

Steven looks squeamish admitting this to me. Maybe it's the dubious smile on my face.

"Steven, can you do me a favor?"

9:57 AM

"M-A-R-I-S-S-A."

"I'm only seeing ten Marissa's that have clicked on the task manager app," Steven says.

"What about all the apps we sell?" I ask.

"Give me a minute."

Steven types at a furious pace. The words per minute must be astronomical, though I can't decipher if what he's typing are words or hieroglyphics. When he finishes and taps enter, there are thousands of records pulled up with different Marissa's from different social media, all of which have clicked on an Avalanche app in the past five years.

"Can you send this to me?" I ask.

"Legally, it's a little dicey, like I mentioned. Why do you need this information anyway?" he asks.

"I'm trying to find a girl, Steve."

"Steven," he corrects me. "What do you mean 'find a girl'?"

I try to explain my situation. One moment she's there and the next she's gone, but Steven has this confused look written across his face. It's not merely confusion, but shock. Waking up in a woman's bed is possibly something he's never done before and he's definitely never woken up in the wrong woman's bed. I'd be stunned if he's ever been so much as overserved. Mortified would be the only proper way to describe the ruddiness spreading across Steven's bleached cheeks.

"She's like a bug," he finally says.

"Excuse me? She's nothing like a bug. She's got two legs and beautiful freckles and when she speaks I can't stop smiling and she doesn't bring a cell phone out with her and do bugs wear yellow dresses?"

"Not a real bug, a programming bug. When a program doesn't work and we can't figure out why, we call it a lost bug," he says.

"Hmm…what do you do when you've lost a bug?" I ask.

"Retrace our steps. Start at the beginning and run decoder line by line. It's a pain, but it works."

"Interesting. Okay Steven, get me that report," I say, doing my best Doug impression.

"You mean *trade* the report," he says.

Now Steven is the one with the naughty look on his face.

"What kind of *trade*?"

11:04 AM

Me: You females wanna grab a beer tonight?

This text message is so loaded that my friends will have no choice but to go out. The idea of retracing my steps seems like a plan worth following, and if it doesn't pan out I refuse to be stuck with Steven all alone.

The trade was simple – a report for a night out on the town. Turns out Steven doesn't have many friends and my little sob story has him thinking he'd like to have the same problems I have. I assured him these were not problems worth having. In fact, I admitted that I was possibly losing my mind. That didn't seem to faze him.

Aisle: I'm in.

VanNeece: Same. Can we get drinks in the city though? I get out of work at like 6:30 and know a poppin happy hour.

These two play right into my hands.

Me: It better not be one of those finance bars.

VanNeece: I stand by my theory…chicks like money.

Aisle: Which only helps one of us three.

VanNeece: Not my problem you majored in communications Aisle.

Me: As long as the rich guy buys the drinks.

VanNeece: Deal.

Aisle: Fine.

As much as I try to convince myself that I am going out tonight simply to do a job, the evil pre-game jitters have already weaved their way inside my head. The problem with knowing plans so early is that it only leads down one rabbit hole: getting drunker, quicker. It's a phenomenon that I have not been able to explain but, according to accounts of other degenerates, it's a real thing. You know the plans, the place, even the drink you're going to order. You wait and wish the clock forward and suddenly you wake up the next day with little to no memory of what happened. It's as if your brain had been getting drunk on anticipation and the first sip of alcohol is just flipping a switch. Immediately, fully, and heavily drunk.

6:42 PM

Here we are. Rooftop bar. Poppin' happy hour. And I am immediately, fully, and heavily drunk.

I stare out at the city with heavy lids. There are little leprechauns hanging at my temples, trying with all their might to drag me down. The titillating conversation between Aisle and Steven is just not enough to keep my eyes from shutting. Even though we're almost 80 stories up with a solid April breeze, my face feels like it's been inches away from a fire. I'm only halfway through my second whiskey and ginger ale. I shouldn't be feeling this way. My eyes fill with tears at random. This is stage three of being drunk. Unfiltered emotion. In the distance the Freedom Tower looks like a miracle, or a mirage, I'm not sure which.

"Where's VanNeece?" I ask.

"He's supposed to get out at 6:30. He works 15 minutes from here. You know how those Wall Street guys love coming out in their work unis. I'm pretty sure VanNeece bought a new watch he wants to show off.

A Peter Luger? A Philip Luger? I don't know, something expensive."

"Who's VanNeece?" Steven asks.

"Jeez. I'll be passed out by then…" I say out loud to myself.

"What?" Aisle asks.

"Nothing."

Aisle is unaware that I have been mentally drunk all day. He's also unaware of the trade I've made to bring Steven out with us. The excuse that my boss forced this upon me doesn't compute. When have I ever listened to my boss? Worst of all, Aisle's unaware that if I am to retrace my steps I must start with matching my alcohol intake from Friday.

6:50 PM

According to VanNeece, this is where the "scene" is. The word sends chills down my vertebrae. But there is an immediate recognition of the scene in which VanNeece speaks so highly. The fuss is not about the view, or the never-ending unintended beauty of staged brick and mortar, but an angelic group of twenty-somethings that just approached the barman.

It's hard to focus on the phone Aisle insists on shoving in my face. Text messages from the girl he cried with are blurry. It's impossible to focus with the surrounding distractions.

"There is some serious talent here," I say.

Steven nods, sipping his drink out of a miniature straw. He is wearing a different outfit than the one he donned at work, thank God. A flannel that fits his meek shoulders, a graphic t-shirt underneath, dark glasses, jeans. He's even changed out his Velcro shoes for a pair of Vans. He looks, dare I say, cool. This is not the same guy from the basement of Avalanche Apps.

"This is far past talent boys. This is like getting the call up from the minor leagues. We're in the majors now. If you're not on your game you'll be sent right back down into baseball obscurity. No guts, no glory. Heroes get remembered, but legends never die," I say.

"Are you hammered already?" Aisle asks.

"Na, I'm good," I reply, looking through him.

Slowing my intake would be the preferred move at this point but it seems an unlikely occurrence and after my third whiskey ginger I have passed the emotional stage and proceed to gawk openly at the beautiful women amassing at this rooftop bar.

VanNeece, my personal BALCO rep, finally shows up, takes one look at my drooling eyes, and slyly hands me a bag before saying a word. With a sigh of relief, I head to the dugout. Yip is no different than steroids. As I walk away I hear him say, "Whodafuck is this guy?"

7:01 PM

My triumphant return from the bathroom feels like a batter making his way to the on-deck circle and this particular batter has wisely applied the cream and the clear. Like I've said, luck is when hard work meets performance enhancers. Ask McGuire. Ask Sosa. Ask Bonds for God's sake.

VanNeece is already talking to a group of women as I approach the batter's box, ready to swing for the fences. I tell Steven to follow my lead.

"...so you're from Texas?" I ask one girl, interrupting conversation.

"Yes. Austin," she says.

"Bats," I say

"Lots," she says, before moving on with her life.

I'm not entirely sure what's just happened. No smile? No smirk? Bats, honey! Bats! The double entendre, the cream and the clear, bats, at bat!

Some girls just don't get it.
6:58 PM – April 21st – 2015

Sent.

When I look up I see two flowers sticking out of Steven's hands. It doesn't seem real. As quickly as the flowers appear, they disappear. They go on like this for minutes before I realize Steven has started a magic show. I'm filled with rage. I want to stop this madness as quickly as it starts until I realize the girls are yucking it up. They are giggling, laughing, trying to touch the flowers until Steven deftly David Blaine's them away again. First one rose, then two, then three. Each appearing and disappearing. VanNeece is as mortified as me until he too realizes this shit is working. I am all but bumped out of the circle forming around Steven, hanging on the edge of the group, hanging on the edge of normalcy, hanging on the edge…

7:07 PM

I'm alone at the bar for good reason. I've struck out on every at bat but am doing my teammates more harm than good. Quarantine is the responsible decision for everyone's health and safety. I cannot be trusted to speak out loud.

I didn't think getting *this* fucked up would benefit my original plan, but it has. An Irish exit was always in the cards and my friends have taken to Steven as their new leader. I can't leave just yet but when I do, it will be with no guilt on my conscience.

Another plus about being drunk is that small moments from Friday are returning to my frontal cortex. Christian for one. I pull up his Instagram. His profile is as infuriating as ever. He's currently on some far-flung island in an infinity pool, #livingthedream.

I'm living a fucking nightmare, Christian.

I DM him.

Me: We need to talk.

I'd usually be overcome with embarrassment as I hit send, but in this state I do not give a flying fuck.

I order another beer. With one eye closed, re-reading my message to Christian is a breeze. Impatiently waiting for a response leads to another shot, another beer. After ten minutes I go on a pretend search for my friends. When tomorrow comes along and they ask me where I went I will tell them I looked for them. I will tell them *they* left *me*. It will be a sham, because tonight I am on the hunt.

7:17 PM

The elevator plummets down, floor after floor. Leaning in the corner, watching strangers glide in and out, is drunk old me. The disdain of said strangers is palpable. I wink and wave. Or was it a blink and burp?

My phone vibrates.

Kristen: Hi

At this point I should have known that a text from Kristen was inevitable. Of course she would text me right before I enact my plan. I ignore it and try to concentrate.

An Irish pub somewhere near 23rd Street is my goal. New York is filled with Irish pubs. You can walk a block and hit three. Though I feel about a thousand blocks away from 23rd Street, I begin to walk north hoping the fresh air will give me time to regroup. My goal is to find the nameless Irish pub Marissa and I sat at, enjoying our first Irish Car Bomb together.

I wonder if the Irish in Ireland get offended by the term when I spot one of those ridiculous scooters leaning against a fire hydrant.

I don't think this is the proper place to park one of these vehicles but I consider it a sign from Jesus or Elegua or whatever deity is willing to help. My plan, if I am not drunk enough to accept it, is to retrace the steps of our bar crawl. Finding Marissa will be similar to prayer. If I repeat it enough, she will show up.

The scooter works without me having to swipe my card. Even though there is the name of a bank plastered on the side of it, I wonder if I've just stolen someone's personal mode of transportation. A problem for another day. I'm enroute.

7:20 PM

By the time I pass Union Square Park at a brisk seventeen miles per hour, things begin to look familiar. People flash by, windows flicker past, I dodge garbage and humans alike, and the next thing I know my equilibrium is assaulted by a building that is somehow 2D and 3D at once. I feel like I'm going to puke. I try and train my gaze from the Flatiron Building to the street. Next thing I know, I am confronted with the blackness I am most familiar with.

When I open my eyes I see miniature pieces of gravel as big as mountains. The sidewalk smells like shit. I am being laughed at by a group of teens with identical hair – poofy tops and skinned sides. Their bangs shake in front of their eyes as they belly laugh at the old man who's fallen off his scooter. I notice a homeless man curled up under a jacket with a cane sticking out halfway into the sidewalk. He's holding a sign that says: "You won't find it here". Why do the homeless have a way of speaking to me? This is one of those signs, literally and figuratively, that I should go home. But when I look up an Irish pub is smiling at me from across the street. It's the one. It has to be the one. I ignore the jeering of the small crowd that has formed around me, leave the shattered scooter near a storm drain, and enter.

The pub is quiet. It is a Tuesday after all. There is a mixture of dark mahogany, bright brass, old beer advertisements, and mirrors giving off the ambience of the old country. I recognize the same corner of the bar we originally donned and take a seat.

The bartender looks at me with a quick raise of eyebrows and then nonchalance.

"A Car Bomb please," I say.

"You sure about that?"

"Of course."

It's not in a bartender's nature to question someone's drink order so I walk to a long mirror that hangs above a shuffleboard table. My hair is pointing in all sorts of directions and there is gravel stuck in the side of my cheek. I need to clean myself up if I'm going to meet the girl of my dreams.

The girl of my dreams…

Just the saying makes me shiver.

Not in a romantic way. In a scared way. Seeing myself, dirtied and disheveled, does nothing to put off my worry that I'm not even here, that I am making this all up, that I have drunken and drugged myself into a fugue. Regardless, I am going to follow this through.

As I return to my seat there are two Irish Car Bombs, locked and loaded. I don't remember if I ordered two. I don't think I did. It's a sign. I wait for all of three seconds before taking mine down and then I wait some more. I wait for her laugh. I wait for her smile. I wait for her voice.

A belch comes from the corner.

"Marissa?" I turn and ask.

No. Just an old man who's drunk beyond measure. I think he's pissed himself.

My resolve does not waiver.

Any minute now she's going to come in and order me a gin and tonic, a mint for my stomach. Any minute now she'll come and give me a mint for my life. A fresh start. A new beginning. Something to care about. Any minute now...

┌─────────────────┐
│   7:31 PM   │
└─────────────────┘

It doesn't take long for me to take down her Irish Car Bomb. You really don't want to let the Baileys curdle. Any minute now turns into ten. A third Car Bomb before leaving puts me on skates.

If I am really attempting to reenact the night we met, then I am doing a pretty good job as far as booze intake goes. I was drunk then. I'm drunk now. And the drunkenness actually makes for an easier time remembering where to go next. That's what's weird about drinking. You might not have the best memory or the best motor skills but somehow previous drunk moments start to become clear. Awash in this clarity I head north-east towards a no-named Mexican place that I feel just might be this way.

If I knew a prayer to Elegua, I would be chanting it right now. It is starting to worry me that I have invested all my mental and physical capital in believing my mom's babalawo when I don't really know shit about the religion. You could say I am appropriating my own culture. Here I am in my blue slacks and my white button down and I have a little figure of Elegua in my pocket that I can't stop rubbing. But that's about all I've got. The rest is faith. Which in a weird way makes me more religious than a whole lot of yahoos out there. I am just hoping, above all, that I will be led to Marissa.

There's also been this other countdown in my head, just nipping away at my sanity. The babalawo said five days. My father proposed to my mother in seven. If, in this moment of clarity, I can admit that I look up to what my parents have then the true counter of seven days since meeting Marissa coincides with the babalawo's five. When you look for the signs they always appear.

I'm not asking for a lot. I don't need to be betrothed to Marissa by end of day Friday. I just want to find her. To talk to her again. To hear her. To grab her thigh. To smell her skin.

7:47 PM

Yikes, that sounded creepy.

I'm not always this creepy, Marissa.

But that's what infatuation can do to a man.

Creepiness is like a virus. Once it's in the blood you can't suppress it without antibiotics. My creepiness started when we met and now it's seeped into every action. What happened to cool Lou? Where has the professor gone? Professor Lou would smack any student's hand with a ruler if he admitted he wanted to smell a woman's skin. Even if it smells like wood with a hint of light flowers and a dash of fried cooking oil. And her hair, her hair is like…oh Professor, please make it stop. It's like I can't help myself.

I am pulled out of my internal softness by the sounds of a Mexican corrido leaking into the street. I follow the sounds of the polka like music. Stop number two.

It's smaller than I remember. But I don't remember much except staring at Marissa. I don't even remember my drink order. The only thing I know for sure is I didn't touch the food. Which is a shame because the menu looks astounding. I'm not hungry but the cachete de res tacos are screaming my name. Most places are scared shitless to put weird meat on their menus but when you've grown up eating calves' liver and oxtail, it's the weird meats that make your mouth water. I order a beer that comes out in a miniature stein and wait for my tacos (and Marissa).

The tacos come out.

Marissa is still nowhere to be found.

After my first bite I'm inclined to see if I can get in the back of this kitchen and ask how they've taken the face of a cow and made it so god-damned delicious. They bring out a small two-piece elote, free of charge, and I devour it along with another beer to keep my tongue from burning off.

Alone and filled to the brim, I'm not sure what my next move is, or what I expected.

Show up to each spot on the bar crawl and then what? Maybe she is out doing the same thing? She could be anywhere. One stop ahead or one stop behind. Or alone in her room. Or with another man. Or in Spain.

The thought of another man angers me down to the molecule. Somewhere deep inside gurgles. Or is that the spicy sauce on the tacos?

I decide to do something different. Something drastic. Something I've never done before.

The last time I was in the place I paid the entire bill. Showing off monetarily isn't usually my style but neither is dining and dashing. Einstein said doing the same thing again and expecting the same results is insanity. Professor Lou says *run*.

┌─────────────────────┐
│   8:09 PM   │
└─────────────────────┘

"I'm not insane. I'm not insane. I'm not insane."

Running down the street repeating this doesn't prove my point.

When I get ten blocks away and find that there is no Mexican with a machete chasing me I take a seat on the curb and try to catch my breath. My lungs are making the sounds of a scuba tank. Cigarettes might not be *great* for your health, according to Marissa, but I think she would agree that tobacco has been a part of religious traditions since agriculture. I am reminded that the babalawo was consistently blowing tobacco smoke on her shrine. There must be some type of communion going on between the smoke and the gods, so I light one up, suck it down, and light up another.

The cigarettes don't seem to be working when it comes to communing with the Orishas, but they do make me feel dizzy and disgusted all at once. I'm either going to hurl or pass out.

The last stop on the bar crawl is somewhat of a blur. I remember a dancefloor and Marissa's body. I can almost conjure the feeling of the way she moved. The flutter of her ass. The wave of her dress. Nose touching nose.

Eyes shut, puffing the cigarette, watching wave after wave of yellow dress, I begin to recite the St. Anthony prayer. This I am more familiar with than the Elegua in my pocket.

Dear Saint Anthony, please come around. Something is lost and can't be found. Dear Saint Anthony, please come around. *Someone* is lost and can't be found.

8:22 PM

Nothing.

Except when I open my eyes there is a pizzeria in front of me named Marissa's. That's right. Marissa's Fucking Pizzeria. I couldn't make that up.

Or maybe I could.

Following the signs has led me here, but the signs could all just be tricks of the mind. The universe is either talking to me or I am falsely projecting my desires onto the universe. Amnesia is one helluva drug.

8:27 PM

The pizzeria is like any other in Manhattan. There are slices behind a glass counter and a fella with gangly arm hair and a thick unibrow wrapped in a stained white apron that asks "whatayawant?".

I order a slice to be polite and take a seat at a thin bar pressing up against the front window. I see my reflection mixed in with the outside world. I'm simultaneously chewing on pizza and a fire hydrant. I'm not sure if I'm hallucinating. I mean to text VanNeece and ask him what that stuff was he gave me but get lost along the way. I begin to type Marissa's name into the Instagram search bar again, as if that's going to help my situation, when the window begins to shake.

BAWONG. BAWONG. BAWONG.

The window rattles and echoes like a crash cymbal. Both my hands hit the counter, stuck like a scared squirrel, until I look up. My heart, my poor weak heart, plummets into my nether region.

It's almost too easy. Too coincidental to believe. An overload of synchronicities.

Because there she is, standing there like she has been summoned. Marissa, waving. In my mind I wave back, but in reality nothing moves. Both hands are still glued to the table as I struggle with reality. Just wave, I tell myself. A look of aloof confusion emanates from her green eyes, maybe even a hint of concern, but after a minute-long stare down she walks away.

A sudden cosmic jolt knocks me off my chair and out the door. Faintly, I hear the manager yelling about something I've done. Whatever it is, he'll understand. This is Marissa we're chasing after here.

"Hey!" I scream. "What are you doing?"

"Walking," she says. She is unphased. "What are *you* doing?"

She hasn't turned around to see me desperately running after her like a clown in big rubber red shoes.

"Nothing, nothing. You caught me off guard back there."

"No keeding? Your eyes went cross," she says.

An unintended laugh escapes me.

She finally stops and turns around. Disdain makes her freckles look like a cheetah's.

"I thought I'd never see you again," I say, shamelessly.

"Yet here I am.'

"Did you see the name of that pizza place?"

"No."

"Marissa's. Marissa's Pizza."

"What are the odds?" she rolls her eyes. "Usually when a guy disappears on me I take it as a sign. Not some sign from the heavens or a magical foreshadowing. I take it at as an actual sign. Like one that says stop or go. A man who wants me makes it happen."

She turns abruptly like a soldier and continues walking. Her heels sound like the angry march of thousands and I'm like a mutt, begging for scraps. Professor Lou would be appalled at this behavior.

"I don't know what happened," I say. Or do I plead? "I think I blacked out. One second I was with you and the next I woke up. Warm vodka shots will get ya every time."

"That's convenient for you."

"Not in the slightest," I say.

"Why are you following me? You can just disappear like you did Friday and pretend like this never happened."

I'm tempted to reveal all but I just can't push myself to tell the truth. The stalker-esque adventure I've been on sounds more like the beginning of a *Law and Order* episode than a romantic quest. I've chased a yellow dress, reported a missing person, been to a babalawo, had dinner at a murderer's restaurant, and spent countless hours on my phone trying to find you, Marissa. And that was all before I decided to retrace our steps, bar for bar. I find myself frozen with embarrassment.

"I haven't stopped thinking about you," is all I can come up with. It's a form of the truth.

"That's unfortunate," she says.

"Why?"

"I decided I'd never think about you again," she says.

"What about a second chance?"

She walks away again. I should let her go. She's said her piece, I've said mine, and it's done. Over. I've blown it. This whole act she's putting on should be the ultimate turn off. I'm surprised she didn't snap her fingers three times and crick her neck to the side while telling me I wasn't worth her thoughts. But she's walking away slowly this time. There's no machine gun patter of her heels. I decide to walk next to her for as long as it takes. The line of romance and rapey is fine and I'm balancing it like fucking Philippe Petit.

"What are you doing?" she asks.

"Going this way."

"Which way?"

I look up at a sign and say, "East on 26th."

Her stoney demeanor crumbles into a suppressed smile. Her mouth doesn't move but the freckles seem to be lifting like a bunch of released balloons.

"And then where?"

"I'm not sure yet."

She lets out a deep breath.

"Fine."

She walks ahead of me as we squeeze through an aluminum awning. Her slim, black, trench coat dances to the same beat of her black heels clicking down the street. The brown waves of hair skip on her back. Though she isn't wearing yellow, she is awash in the glow of streetlights.

The streets are empty and only getting worse. But it's hard to notice a possible mugger when Marissa's jawline is in your peripheral. Her quick turn into a dilapidated doorway snaps me awake from a daydream where I grab her neck and kiss her.

8:41 PM

She hasn't said a word to me as we enter a dark tunnel. Either I'm blacking out again or she's leading me to my doom. At the end of the tunnel is a raspy voice that matches the older Spanish madam behind a lamp-lit desk. Her nose is pointed, black hair pulled into a tight bun, and her lips are blood copper. She looks like a woman who has seen things from this random corner, down a random alley, in a random building in New York City. A beautiful time traveler. A seer and knower. Her cigarette burns slowly in an ashtray.

"Where are we?" I ask.

She ignores my question.

"Hola!"

"Bale, bale."

There is a cacophony of Spanish and laughter and kisses. I keep my ears peeled for any drops of the name Lou but get nothing in the tornado of words I can't understand. The madam looks at me with raised eyebrows and Marissa begins to walk down a set of steps. The madam points me to follow. For a moment I feel flattered and then set up. A small nightmare flutters through my head. Armed men emerge from the dark tunnel to rob me for all I've got. They won't get much. I don't know if it's Marissa, the fugu, the drink, or the drugs that have me on edge but here I am, teetering on the brink.

We end up at a sketchy door. Behind the door are rumblings and as it's opened, music bursts out as if it were holding a long-held secret. Tambourines, trumpets, horns, and drums being banged and blown at such a furious pace my heart skips to the beat. To my surprise and relief, the place is packed. Sweaty noses and cheeks shimmer in this dimly lit Cuban palace. It has to be Cuban. The band, visible under blue lights, are all wearing the same guayabera shirts and thin straw hats with forearms and feet pumping.

Marissa grabs my hand, thankfully pulling me down a thin strip next to the dancefloor. Behind and above the sweating mass are tables filled with shadows of men and women under a cloud of smoke. Though their eyes are nowhere to be seen, I can feel them follow me. What is he doing with her? these eyes ask. It's a fair question.

"Gringo. Stupido gringo," I hear a man whisper under a cumulus cloud.

"Mama, leab hing," another pile of smoke says.

I imagine the comments continue until we seat ourselves at a crescent-shaped booth far enough away from the dancing and heckling to put me at ease for all of two seconds. A man, who looks like he is part of the band, seats himself next to Marissa. Not sure who this man is, or what he is doing kissing Marissa's cheeks, leaves me motionless, mouth agape. Though he is a much older man, he seems capable of convincing a beauty like Marissa to cheat on her own age bracket.

"Hola. Me llamo Alfredo," the man says.

"Hi, I'm Lou," I say, cautiously shaking the offered hand.

His hands feel hard and calloused. His face is mean. It isn't an intellectual leap to assume *I'm* being taken, not my wallet. Marissa laughs, yet to say a word, which only fuels my panicked mind. Alfredo, what is your next move? A quick survey of the room yields no clear exit signs, but there is a door, with a bouncer securely stationed in front of it. One of Alfredo's men, I presume. The babalawo said I had five days but never mentioned I'd be kidnapped in the process.

My attention turns back to Alfredo. A traitor's name. You broke my heart Fredo. You too Marissa.

"Would you like a drink?" the waitress interrupts my *Godfather* zone out.

"Si. Uno reposado," Fredo says.

He sips tequila. Only psychos sip tequila. I can feel saliva build under my molars.

"Una rioja," she says.

Spanish red wine, an undeniably sexy choice for someone who is facilitating a kidnapping.

"Whiskey," I say, staring at the waitress, begging for mercy.

"Do you like the music?" Marissa asks. Her bottom lip briskly touches my ear. In an act of utter self-control, my eyes stay trained on my man Fredo. He's watching the band with a keen eye, surveying what I now assume is his establishment.

"Ah, yeah. Can I ask you something?"

"Si que?"

"Can you stop speaking Spanish?"

"Why?

"It turns me on."

And I don't understand it.

She laughs, which catches the attention of Fredo. He interrupts our banter, asking Marissa a question that I can't hear over the blaring music. The only question I can imagine him asking is, "What did this gringo joker say to make my woman laugh? Where I come from, homes, we punish those who make another man's woman laugh." Fredo has now become a parody of a Mexican gangster in my mind and this train doesn't seem like it's getting back on the tracks anytime soon. Marissa's response, though inaudible, must be something like, "don't kill him yet, he's so entertaining." On cue, she rubs my head and pinches my cheeks. They both begin to laugh diabolically.

The waitress interrupts their murderous plot and places the drinks on the table. I take mine down in one and ask for another. If I'm going down, I am going down how I want. They both look at me worried, as if maybe I am a man that is not to be fucked with. A man that is on to their plans to kidnap and graft the gringo.

"What are you doing?" she asks.

"Going down how I want."

The confused look on her face makes me think my prediction is somewhat premature.

"Lou," she says softly over the music somehow, soothing me into an easy lapse of judgement. Then she drops the hammer.

"This is my father. He's an artist and my boss. He's why I am in New York."

Father?

I don't do fathers.

Fredo's features soften and smooth. His arms in his shirt seem to shrink, and I imagine fewer tattoos underneath. His mustache morphs from bandido to bushy. But still, I'm cautious. One second you're getting kidnapped and the next you're in the presence of an artist. A man of significance and soul. An ar-teeeest. I don't think so. I watch him as he watches the band.

"This is his favorite spot in the city whenever we visit. He knows the owner. He was commissioned to do some paintings here years ago and they stayed friends."

"Oh yeah? Where are these paintings?" I ask, unconvinced. *Knows the owner* is code. I've seen all the movies, know all the endings. The paranoia continues to creep in as the potency of whatever VanNeece gave me starts wearing off. My hands start to shake and my gut wants something I can't give it. If only I still had the bag...

"Upstairs in the dining area. Do you want to see them?"

"One more," I say as the waiter brings me my last shot on this earth. I take it down in one again, savoring it this time, not knowing if it will be my last taste of the holy water. She stares, still confused at the rush I'm in.

Even if she were telling the truth, I repeat, I don't do fathers. My record for meeting parents is flawless. Meaning I haven't done it yet. All it does is imply something that isn't there. These parents will not be seeing me often. They will not be paying for our wedding. If you plan on meeting parents you plan on getting married. That *is* the implication. There is no earthly reason to shake a father's hand or bring a mother flowers if you don't intend on bending a knee. Avoid such a situation at all costs. Professor knows best.

She pushes me out of the booth, giving me no choice but to follow her lead. Either we are going to see her father's work or I am about to be stuffed into the trunk of a car.

As we make our way back up the stairs, for an instant, I forget everything. Marissa's frayed tank top rides up her back, revealing a set of back dimples that drive steam out of my ears. How glorious can one woman be? The thoughts of how to beg for my life with dignity are driven far, far away.

We make it, still unharmed, to the top of the steps, wave at the hostess, and walk through a set of curtains into a long hallway. I can hear people cooking, knives chopping, fires blazing, oil sizzling in pans. But the sound is far away, and I could easily be mistaking it for the sound of *people* being chopped up, pieces of ankle and thigh and calf strewn around the "kitchen". I shouldn't have come up here. I should have stayed in front of all those people. Even if they are his people, her "father's people," maybe one would have had some sympathy for me. Maybe one would report this obvious set up.

As we get to the end of the hallway, before going through another set of curtains I grab her hand.

"Do you know why I was at that pizza place?" I ask.

"No. Why would I know that?"

"Because of your name. Marissa's Pizza."

"So you *are* creepy then…." she says.

"No. I'm not creepy. I just…." I pause. Do I really want to admit this? She raises her eyebrows, waiting. "I thought I'd never see you again so I had this idea that I'd stop at every place on our bar tour and just ask the sky or God or something for you to appear. It didn't work until that pizza place and then there you were. Out of nowhere."

I can see her mind parsing through this batshit story. Has she invited a crazy person or the most romantic son of a bitch into her life? I don't even know the answer to that.

She grabs my face and kisses me. It's one of those kisses where you both try to mash your lips as close as they can get without chipping a tooth. One of those where you attempt to go deeper than skin and saliva. She pulls my hand off her cheek and leads me through the curtain.

9:17 PM

Even after such a glorious kiss I still hesitate as we push through the curtains. My eyes squint in preparation for a punch in the face or a gun butt to the back of the head, both of which would be less humane than a simple bullet to put me out of my misery. On the other side lies no such pain. Just ten tables filled with guests eating, unaware of the night that these eyes have seen.

In between each table hangs a painting under a shaded lamp, seven in total. Yemaya's number. They are not what one would expect to be hanging at a restaurant. From a distance, I cannot quite put my finger on what they are depicting, but one theme is consistent throughout: dark. Blacks and reds run moodily from frame to frame, like a hellish lazy river. Not your usual Cuban decor.

Marissa takes my hand, pulling me to each one. After close inspection I see they are filled with fury. The real beauty lies in how Marissa looks at them, talks about them, revels in her father's work.

"Beautiful, no?" she asks.

"Yes. Scary too."

"Sometimes scary and beautiful are closer than you realize."

This is something I am keenly aware of.

I am not a devoted patron of the visual arts and as Marissa drags me from picture to picture I end up staring at the food on the guests' plates. Food I understand. Food that keeps me in communication with my culture. I can't speak the language, don't know the gods, am not even allowed to visit my mother's country of origin, but the food I know.

"In this painting," she points.

"Moro."

"Que?"

"Look at that moro," I say.

"Morose?" she asks.

"No, the rice mixed with the black beans on that woman's plate. My mom makes a great moro. And then over there, back at the second table we passed. There was lechon asado with skin on it you could die for. And look at these," I take her by her hand to another table. People are nervous now but I can't help it. "Tostones and maduro. Two types of plantains. One has to be very green and the other very ripe. Black ripe. If it's in the middle you can make mofongo which is actually Puerto Rican. It's delicious."

"Tell me what this is," she says, pointing down to a dish.

"That is the legendary ropa vieja. I know those words in Spanish. Old clothes. It's flank steak slow cooked in a red sauce with onions, peppers, and olives then shredded. Delicious."

"Mmmm. Can you cook?" she asks.

"Decently."

"Would you cook for me?"

"Get me an apron and I'll go make something right now," I say. She laughs.

"Maybe you should cook for a living instead of marketing phone apps. Then maybe I could move from hating you to respecting you," she laughs.

It's not a terrible idea.

"Can we eat now?" she asks.

"Please."

9:31 PM

If my steps were heavy and timid coming up the stairs, they are quite the opposite heading back down. I even ask the woman at the front desk for one of her cigarettes, and she gladly obliges. The only downside to the remainder of the evening is that the stimulants that Van-Neece supplied are quickly wearing off, while the alcohol is beginning to reestablish itself as the dominant force. My personal bar tour is certainly going to backfire. I know it's bad when I go right up to her father, give him a hug, and plant a double-cheek kiss on his unsuspecting face. Being alive and kicking has overtaken my adherence to the Professor's rulebook.

The food menu is a murderer's row of Cuban delicacies. I decide to order for the table without asking anyone what they want. As I place the last item, chicharrones de puerco, I can feel Marissa's hand on the inside of my thigh. She looks at me like I've cured cancer. I make a mental note that ordering for the table should be added to Professor Lou's shortlist of actions that impress a woman. It's not magic, but it does the trick.

Marissa's father is smiling at me and her hand is two centimeters away from the head of my dick. If this was any other night with any other woman I might revel in the dirtiness of it all. But tonight, I decide to change the subject. A subject that has been ruling every decision in my life for the past five years.

"So what do you do for your father?" I ask.

"A better question is what don't I do," she says, removing her hand from my nether region and allowing me to breathe again. Her father is still smiling at us, unable to understand a word. "I keep him organized, on time, whatever else he needs. Sometimes I think he'd just float away if I didn't tie him to the earth. Before I started working for him he'd just give paintings away. He doesn't understand money. Actually, that's a lie. He understands it when he doesn't have any."

"Sounds like I should hire you too," I say.

"What do you mean?"

"Sometimes I feel the same way. Like I'm just watching my life float by and I have nothing to do with it."

"You work for your dad so you must know how it feels?"

"How it feels?"

"You know, the extra responsibility. It's your father. You have to do right by him after all he's done for you," she says.

"I feel quite the opposite," I laugh.

"Have you ever seen a baby?"

I don't know where this is going but I hope she doesn't ask if I want one. That's a step too far. I shudder to think that a yes would come out of my mouth if she did ask.

"Yes, I've seen a baby."

"Have you had to take care of one?"

"Hell no," I say.

"Then you don't really know what he's done for you."

"He's made me an app marketer. Isn't that enough?" I ask.

She laughs as the first appetizer arrives.

10:43 PM

We look like three disheveled messes when the meal is over but their satiated faces and the empty glasses and plates strewn around the table are signs of a job well done. This would be as good a time as any to ask Marissa to leave, when her father starts speaking to me in Spanish.

"Que te gusta hacer?"

Te gusta rings a dim bell, so I am able to pick up what poppa is putting down.

"I like your daughter very much," I yell over the music.

"Que?" he asks.

"I said, tu hija is muy bonita. Me gusta your hija." I glance at Marissa for reassurance but only get an array of teeth and freckles.

"QUE?" he asks again.

Marissa intercepts her father and his anger. I order another drink hoping it will remind me how to say sorry in Spanish.

After a minute of back and forth, Marissa pats my head and pinches my cheeks again, like an animal who has just peed in the house.

"What did I say?" I ask her. "Did I say something wrong?" I turn back to him. "Lo, siento. Lo siento."

"Lou, he asked you what you like to do…and you said me."

"Shit, lo siento, lo siento, I'm so sorry. I thought you asked if I liked your daughter. And I do. I like your daughter. I don't like to do your daughter. But I like her. Just her. Not like to do her. We haven't even done it yet…umm…" These words spill out, like watching something fall and being just out of reach, not able to catch it.

"Que nada. Hay es no problema." He smiles, also patting me on the head.

"He doesn't really understand any English," she tells me.

I make a note never to attempt a conversation in anything but English ever again. Or learn Spanish.

"When did you start painting?" I ask him.

"He says when he was very young," Marissa translates. "My grandmother used to teach him how to paint in watercolors. They would go down to the Manzanares, a river in Madrid where he was born, and she would have him paint trees hanging over the river, or houses, or people enjoying lunch. This was all before he turned 10. Then they moved to El Masnou, near Barcelona. And his mind was in shock, but not in a bad way. He says that Barcelona is still very inspiring to him."

"What was inspiring?"

As she asks her father it occurs to me that no word in the English language could make a mouth move as beautifully as hers.

"Dali," I hear him yell, breaking my trance.

"Dali?" I look at Marissa with a quizzical look.

"Yes, Dali," she answers.

"Like the real Dali?"

"Yes, the real one. He was his favorite artist and one of his mentors. Dali taught a small class in Figueres. He would make the long drive there with a friend. No one knows about the class, it's not in any history books, it was never really talked about. Dali didn't like teaching that much but enjoyed my father's company. He taught him more about how to think than how to paint. But then," she continues, "he was all for the money, at a certain point. He didn't care for the art anymore, he just wanted to make money. Avida dollars. I guess that's how it goes sometimes. You put all your trust and hope into one person and they disappear. Not physically, just their ideals, their perfection in your eyes."

"Let's do a shot," I tell the old man, attempting to cheer him up. Three tequilas go down between us, and the old man wants another. Finally, something we have in common. It is possible I have stirred up something dormant inside of him.

"Que te gusta hacer?" he asks again.

"I like to cook. And I used to like to read," I say.

"Why used to?" she asks me, ignoring any translation.

"I don't have much time for reading anymore. I work and I go out. That's about it."

"That's a shame," she says.

"I'd read your writing though," I say

"How'd you remember that?" she asks.

"I'm about the same level of drunk," I say.

She laughs, then gets serious.

"You know, language is not as old as humans are, but somehow you can still convey ancient things with words. They are mesmerizing. It's like my father's art. When you write something beautiful you don't have to tell the reader what to feel, they just know it. Writing and reading are very intuitive."

"What are you writing now?"

"I'm working on a novel."

"About?"

"It's about us. Our time. A novel about how time has completely shrunk for us. A year means a minute now."

"So you're a professor too?"

"Huh?"

"Una professora of the times," I try to say.

She laughs and concurs.

Marissa translates the last ramble of conversation to her father.

"Quienes son tus autores favoritas?"

"He's asking who your favorite writers are."

"Jim Harrison, John D. Macdonald, Zora Neale Hurston, Dostoevsky, Oscar Hijuelos, Gabriel Garcia Marq…"

Before I can get the name out her father throws his hands in the air and screams. He goes off on a tangent of quick Spanish that I can't even recognize as Spanish. He gets out of his side of the booth and pushes me in further to sit. He kisses my cheek and rubs my head as if I were his only son. I am guessing he is also a fan of Gabriel Garcia Marquez.

He orders another round of shots while Marissa attempts to translate his erratic thoughts about *100 Years of Solitude*.

"It's like reading the Bible," she translates. "Like a Spanish bible."

"It's almost as unbelievable as the Bible," I say.

Marissa translates and again he throws up his hands in agreement. He hugs me, pulling me into his chest as if to break me. He smells like oud and those lavender candies Hispanic guys love so much.

"Me gustas," he says.

"He says he likes you," Marissa says, smiling at me.

He orders a fourth round. I am not sure who's going to quit first but I'm determined it won't be me. The fourth one does him in. The tequila catches in his throat and he makes an Aisle face that looks less grotesque on an old Spanish man.

"He's going to get sentimental now," Marissa whispers.

A one-time prominent gangster now stares into an empty glass, reminiscing about a fairytale he once lived. He has gone from gunman to sad painter. I can't even see his arms in his shirt as he slumps into the booth.

10:59 PM

Her father is asleep. Even with the blaring music his mouth is open and his breathing tickles the wisps of his mustache. I am envious of a man who can shut it off at the drop of a hat. He is conked the fuck out.

"Let him sleep it off," she says. "He'll be fine."

"He looks like bliss," I say.

"I like that," she says.

"Like what?"

"That line. He looks like bliss. Very nice. I swear my father could be a writer. Maybe that's where I got it from. He once told me that you must live selfishly in your twenties so that you can give your all to your family. He says that's the problem with our generation. We don't get the selfish out of us. We hold it in or wait too long until it hurts people. Everyone is selfish in some way but it's better to get it out of your system while you're young. Not to hold on to it. That's the book I want to write. Maybe you could be a writer too, huh?"

"I don't think so," I laugh. The poignancy of her father's insight hits me in my numb chest.

"Why not? How about this. You tell me a little about your life and I'll tell you if you're a writer."

"How would you do that?"

"Just tell me. Start with your friends."

I start with the necessary descriptions. Aisle looks like a blonde handsome rat, VanNeece resembles a dog in a suit. Brian gets no description or mention. This night is too good to be dragged down by a traitor. If I speak his name I will be pulled down a rabbit hole of negativity that I won't be able to dig myself out of. So why do I feel guilty not telling this woman about my best friend? I want to tell this woman everything.

Instead, I mention a few stories about the good times we've had. Like the one where Aisle's leather jacket got stuck in a woman's purse zipper in Atlantic City at the blackjack table, or the one where Van-Neece got locked out of his apartment in just boxers because he sleep-walks when he drinks too much.

"You guys sound like the wild things."

"The wild things?"

"Like the children's book, *Where the Wild Things Are*. I learned English by reading kids' books. You all sound nuts. That's the expression? Nuts?"

I laugh and nod. It's been twenty years since I read the book and don't know whether to take it as a compliment or a diss.

"What about Christian?" she asks.

"What about him?"

"What's he like."

"He's not my friend," I say.

Jealousy. An abhorrent trait in a guy. Is there anything less attractive? I feel myself forming into Mr. Hyde right here in front of her. The other shoe dropping sounds like an anvil in a cartoon. I can hear it whistling down onto me from 30,000 feet.

"Do I sense..." she starts.

"No. No you don't. I'll tell you all about him. What do you want to know?"

"Nothing. I got my answer," she smirks.

I think I've just broken the good Professor's rulebook and it worked.

Out of habit, I reach into my pocket and take out my phone. *It's 11 PM, do you know where Lou is?* I am about to tweet this but she interrupts.

"Who's so important?"

"My students," I say, staring at the three tweet boxes where there should only be one.

"Quien?"

There is a tinge of jealousy in *her* voice now. Her left eyebrow is raised as if to say tread carefully. As afraid as I am of a Latin woman's wrath I am filled with a joy I can't describe. I want her to question me. I crave her inquiries.

"No one," I put the phone down without sending off this brilliant tweet. I look into her eyes and there are not six pairs. Just two eyes in a storm of freckles. "No one more important than you."

"Now that's what every woman wants to hear. No one more important than me, Mr. Lou."

Her smile spreads like the Cheshire Cat's.

"Let's dance," she says.

11:05 PM

Around song number three my arms are high on the waist of a woman in her fifties. She moves beautifully, lithe, and leads this dumb, half gringo with grace. She's done this before. A partner switch is common on a Cuban dancefloor yet this particular switch is leaving me with a crick in my neck. We're dancing bachata, a simple rhythm I actually know. Even hammered drunk my feet catch on. I take baby steps, move my hips more than my arms, but each time the woman changes direction I must readjust to keep my eyes on Marissa. She's currently partnered with a man in his fifties, his hands high on her hips, and it's driving me looney. The jealousy bug has bit me. Infection ensues.

When the song ends the woman still has one hand on my shoulder, the other tucked into my sweaty palm. The band barely skips a beat and begins to pound the same off-beat rhythm I'd heard the night I met Marissa. My memory is jarred for a second. I am in the bathroom, then walking out, then looking for Marissa, then…

The memory vanishes when the fifty-year-old woman's backside lightly touches between my legs. She moves away with a smirk. The sensual mating ritual has begun. She moves away, bent knees, dancing in a sort of stomping, hip-shaking twerk and I try and follow the movements. Just over the woman's left shoulder is Marissa and the man doing the same dance except the man has made a move that I find unfathomable. Hearing it from your mother is one thing, but seeing it performed on a woman you've become obsessed with is another matter.

When Marissa gets close to him he creeps his hand out to grab her pussy. Just before he makes contact she moves away. This goes on once, twice, and before the third time I have his wrist in the grip of my hand. Knuckles white. Anger red.

I pull his arm up which knocks his fedora off, leaving a half balding head shining under the blue lights of the dancefloor. His head is misshapen and the short hair that's left makes a horseshoe shape around the back. I should be able to take this douchebag but for some reason it's getting harder and harder to control his wrist. This man must have no less than five niños at home because the dad strength is strong in him.

As I start to lose the grip on his wrist, the hand I'm not holding takes a big looping swing and smacks me in the temple. It's as if the connection has reminded my brain of the number of drinks I've had tonight. I am immediately woozy. The club washes in and out. A grainy picture. Gray turning black.

I try and swing back but there are three hobbit looking heads in front of me. Each punch I throw goes over their heads with a woosh until I am being rushed up the stairs, Marissa's hand in mine.

TIME UNKNOWN

Fleeting images rush toward me. I make it up the stairs. Snippets of stairs, of street, of cars, of light. I am seated on a subway, alone I think, but can't be sure. It's taking me somewhere, anywhere. All I hear is that incessant clacking of metal, a machine churning to nowhere.

Wednesday

APRIL 22ND, 2015

9:17 AM

Aisle: What happened to you last night?

VanNeece: Seriously man where did you go? I called you like 10 times.

The texts are barely readable through the phone's punishing glare. The time reads 9:17 AM, which makes me late for work, but how late I am just not sure, because there is the small problem of not being totally aware of my current location. After sitting up and rubbing a sore cheek, I proceed to do three Hail Mary's and four Our Fathers and kiss my little Elegua for somehow ending up in my own apartment. Though my belief in God has dwindled over the years, there has to be something looking out for me, because I sure am not.

Under a pile of covers and pillows lies Marissa, I hope. But I've been duped by this trickery before. I gently move a piece of comforter from her face.

Only, there is no face.

Because she isn't there.

I throw the covers at the wall, leaving an utterly depressed and naked bed.

"Marissa?" I call out to the bathroom.

There is no sound of a faucet or a flush, just the morning squeaks of trucks braking, the start of spluttering engines, sucking vacuums depolluting the Hoboken streets. The stray cats living in my building's dilapidated courtyard are crying for comfort, but no signs of Marissa.

The door to the bathroom is ajar, light still on.

"Marissa?" I knock.

There are fewer signs of life here than on the moon. The toothbrush is dry, along with the sink. I even check behind the shower curtain, as sane people do. The rest of the apartment holds no hiding places. A part of me wishes she would pop out of a cupboard, scaring me half to death. Though, if my antics last night didn't scare her away, surely a high-pitched terrified scream would.

My antics could be at fault here. Starting a brawl wasn't my intention. It was the caveman in me. Jealousy is a primeval emotion and it brings out primeval actions. Another reason why I have avoided the emotion. But what happened after?

Five minutes on the couch, head in hands, does little to recapture last night's events. Some details remain clear as day, but the plot hangs weightless in the periphery. Marissa's eyes lit by candles, the devilish shadows her cheeks made when she laughed, her dancing, her book. Such visions are engraved in my brain. But even the way droplets of tequila hung like dew from her father's mustache don't lead the way to any type of storyline. One event that couldn't be wiped away with a fifth of grain alcohol was the way she pushed me against the wall and kissed me. The rest has become fragmented.

There is no point in trying to hash it all out now, I have the entire workday to do that. A hot shower combined with an adrenaline dump kicks the hangover into high gear. My heart, soul, and health were left on that Cuban dancefloor. I'm left with one saving grace. There are no signs of Kristen here either. I'll consider that progress.

Before leaving I make a quick detour to the fridge, hoping for something to take the pain away. Behind two empty Pedialyte bottles is a small, folded piece of notebook paper.

On the front: *Lou*

In the middle: *I had a great time. Call me tomorrow.* A number scrawled.

On the back: *Marissa x*

This paper gives me a jolt that no sugary electrolyte drink could dream of doing. The fridge. Where all good things spring forth. I think I let out a "yippee" that I wish could be erased from my memory. If she were in this apartment and heard that feminine squeal she would surely take this piece of paper I'm holding and burn it.

Instead of dialing immediately, I decide it's better to play it cool. At least until tonight. Another Professor Lou lesson turned into law via experience. I've seen this go a few different ways a few separate times.

One embarrassing episode in particular plays in my head. It's stuck there for life. Lodged on repeat like a bad jingle. The same memory that recurs when I see my boss Doug. It is one of many possible catalysts for my ways and not atypical for the male species.

A sixteen-year-old boy loses his virginity to an older girl while on vacation. She sneaks him booze throughout the week, teaches him her eighteen-year-old wisdom and ways, then forgets him. She ignores his desperate texts. Blocks his incessant calls. He never so much as speaks to her again. She gains a mythic status in the boy's mind. The booze, the girl, the sounds of waves crashing on a beach…the sex, the rejection! They all culminate into poor little Lou's first lesson in the real world. Pride becomes something that slips in and out of the boy's grasp. He learns to cope with such developments. Booze, sex, rejection…

Not shocking.

I don't need a shrink to tell me what happened.

I put off the memory for the thousandth time.

10:03 AM

Just glancing at that memory secures my decision. I won't be calling Marissa today. Folding the note and placing it in my pocket takes a lot of strength, but it is the correct decision. It's not that I want to play games, over-eagerness is just unattractive.

Getting to work by 10:30 is lucky considering the night previous. I'm not totally sure when my head actually hit the pillow but there's a chance I am working on three hours of sleep. But, three hours of useless sleep and a hangover that has sunk into my bones doesn't stop me from strutting through the office with a smile on my face. The note in my pocket is involuntarily pulling at my cheeks.

My smile has become something of an endangered species around these parts. When the smile is out, it draws unwarranted attention, simply due to its rarity. The second I take a seat at my desk, a coworker approaches. The usual dread doesn't disseminate through my body. This is an odd sensation. There is even a sense of interest, of wonder, at what this nameless coworker has to say.

"Louuua Louuaaay. Oh no! Saying we gotta go! Aye, aye, yay a yay."

Just like that, the mother fucker starts singing "Louie Louie" right in my face. Normally a mortifying act. If this was numberless Lou I'd give him a stiff jab to the chin. But as I stand up to potentially square up with this sack of shit I hear myself, like an out of body experience, singing along with him.

"Louuua Louuaaay. Oh no! Saying we gotta go! Aye, aye, yay a yay."

I even get a little clap going.

The next thing I know, there are five co-workers singing along. I was not even aware there was a full song besides Loua Louay, until I hear someone belting out the lyrics.

A real laugh even escapes its cage. A true belly laugh. In *this* building of all buildings, singing *that* song of all songs. This gray box of banality coupled with my mortal enemy in song has brought my real laugh back from the brink of extinction. All due to that little piece of parchment.

After the jubilation settles, I search the lyrics to "Louie Louie". Something I've never wanted to do. They aren't so bad.

It starts off like this…

"A fine little girl, she waits for me–

Me catch a ship–

Across the sea–"

I'm not sure if it's extreme sleep deprivation or the substances still coursing through my veins, but in the small mirror on the back of my desk I can see my reflection begin to speak.

What, you think she's going to wait for you? You think this girl is actually going to wait for you? This new one. Ma.. Ma…Ma…Maranda?

Marissa. You know her name, don't act dumb. And I don't even know what you're talking about. They are just song lyrics.

Ironic song though, isn't it? A lot of ironic stuff going on in the life of Lou. I mean first, you meet this girl and she disappears on you. You go to the bathroom to do a couple nose beers and she's gone. Very odd.

Yeah, that was weird. Maybe I was in there for longer than I remember though? I wasn't exactly sober.

In all my years of nose beers they haven't taken longer than ten minutes. Ten minutes max. No reason for a girl AND this guy Christian to just up and leave. Why would they do that? Why would Christian leave with your girl?

It's all kind of a blur. But none of that night matters now. Last night happened.

Ahhh, last night. Well, that's another story entirely. It's like this girl won't make it past New York. I mean, one minute you remember the train but when it pulls out of New York it's like…poof…she vanished.

Vanished?

Vanished.

You're crazy.

It's pretty obvious I'm not the crazy one. You're talking to a reflection. What's the second part of those lyrics anyway?

"I sail that ship–
All alone–
I never think–
I'll make it home–"

Interesting.

What's interesting?

A lot of interesting stuff going on in the life of fucking Lou, I'll tell ya. So when this chick leaves you for her home, are you going to follow her? Sailing that ship all alone to Spain or what?

The note is burning a hole in my pocket. Re-reading it puts the smile my horrific reflection is so intent on destroying back on my face.

Loua Louayyy.
10:58 PM – April 22nd – 2015

Sent.

10:59 AM

It doesn't take long to harass myself into hating that tweet. No comedic value, no sense of direction, no context. The critics say, 1 star. It is quite self-indulgent to tweet a song based on one's own name, especially when no one living really knows the song except the schmos in this office.

Fucking hate that song.
10:59 PM – April 22nd – 2015

Sent.

With the note firmly in my pocket, I begin working with no complaints for the first time in longer than my brain has the capacity to remember. The first email is a reminder about a 10 AM Wednesday marketing meeting, which is something I never knew existed. My response is an attempt to play it cool.

Hi, Jim

Sorry I missed the Wednesday morning meeting. It won't happen again. Can someone send me the notes so that I can review what happened?

Thanks,

Lou

The prevailing pattern with the next few emails is frustration. Frustration at my lack of response, at my lack of attentiveness, at my…well, I get the picture. I am lacking. There is no excuse for how little I care about this job but here are a few excuses I come up with.

Excuse 1: *Courtney, I will absolutely look into this. I haven't been receiving emails this past week. I thought work was just slow as a turtle, LOL. Give me until tomorrow to get this done. I will keep you in the loop! Thanks for your patience.*

Excuse 2: *Barry, how's it going pal? Just got a chance to look at your email. It's been crazy busy! My inbox is growing like a vine in a jungle! I swear I'm covered in weeds over here, Bar! They're taking over my keyboard as we speak! I'll get this done for you later today.*

Excuse 3: *Hi, Doug. Of course I can meet any time you need to tomorrow. Just let me know, boss. I thought I had replied to this on Monday but it looks like the email never went through. My bad!*

Okay, that one was tough. Who knew the boss had emailed me on Monday wanting to discuss something?

A part of me cares but the overwhelming feeling is something akin to annoyance.

After answering all of five emails I decide to take a well-deserved break. Work is hard, it deserves rewards. I take the note out and type Marissa's number into Google. A website called Verify-Me is the first to show up. It's first search is what city the number is located in, then the carrier, then the background information on the person if available. The conclusion is well, inconclusive. The final results are that the number doesn't exist. Odd, but not game changing. It's a Barcelona number, I rationalize.

I google her name, number, and still get the same result. A whole lot of nothing.

One of those advertisements based on your own search history pops up at the bottom left corner of my screen. I know this is a scam because we employ this tactic on people. You can find any search history via an unprotected IP address and hammer unsuspecting victims with ads for your own product. And you'll know they want it because they've searched something similar to what you are offering. It's genius and dirty. For me, the ad says "Early signs of schizophrenia? Click here." I'm forced to click it out of sheer curiosity.

The top five early signs are halfway down the page.

1. Delusion/amnesia.
2. Belief that an ordinary event has
    special and personal meaning.
3. Belief that thoughts aren't one's own.
4. False belief of superiority.
5. Disorientation/hallucinations/paranoia.

Uh, oh.

Five for five.

I close out of the tabs as quick as I can and clear my search history.

2:01 PM

The rest of the day I try and distance myself from my ever-present mental disorder with mind blowing fantasies of what the call to Marissa will turn out like. Well, as mind blowing as a phone call fantasy can get.

"Hi Lou. I miss you. I'm going back to Barcelona on Sunday. I want you to come with me."

"Sure sweetheart, how long are we going for?"

"Forever."

Forever sounds like a long time, but anything is better than being stuck in this office.

My last assignment is watching a YouTube video of Guaguancó. A half-gringo must educate himself on the powers of Cuban dance if he is going to impress a girl like Marissa. While I watch the video of a skinny dark couple on a dirt road in Havana I am overcome with a feeling of embarrassment. The moves are almost identical to Marissa and the old man's. Choppy steps, hips flinging up and down, side to side, movements inconceivable to a body jammed up with white skin. After the couple circles around each other, getting closer and closer, the man reaches out to grab the woman's vagina. She laughs, blocks him, and moves sensually away. Unphased. This goes on for five minutes and each second that passes I feel dumber and dumber. The lingering slap on my cheek feels like punishment deserved.

I finally drive home, satisfied with the day's work if not totally overcome with shame at my behavior towards the poor old man who probably would have kicked my ass.

5:07 PM

But, on the way home, there is me in the rearview this time. He looks a bit haggard. He's probably still drunk even though he hasn't had a drink in twelve hours. Poor bastard.

Right now? You really haven't learned anything have you.

He's eyeing up the phone in my hand, the number dialed. To be fair, the note says call tomorrow. My assumption is today *is* that tomorrow.

First of all, Lou, assuming does two things: it makes an ass out of you and me. Second, she WANTS you to call her tomorrow. That is the exact reason why you shouldn't, Lou. C'mon man. You know the drill. How come you're able to do this with, dare I say, Kristen?

Kristen hadn't entered my mind. It never really occurred to me that I had been playing hard to get because frankly, I never wanted to be gotten. A birdie flaps its wings on the smoking peat of guilt growing in my stomach. But this isn't about Kristen, it's about Marissa, and I'm calling her.

Arianna Two.

What?

Marissa…Arianna Two…same thing. This is all heading down the same road. Haven't you learned anything since you were 16?

No, it isn't, this girl is different.

She isn't, Lou. They all want the same two things. A man they can't have and a man their friends are jealous of. It's very simple. Women are the ones that put men on a pedestal.

This is ridiculous.

Arianna Two. Arianna Two. Arianna-

Fine. Fine. I'll wait until I get home.

That's not going to happen either.

Why?

Just wait.

5:27 PM

Twenty minutes later, walking into my building, my phone vibrates.

Aisle: Lou…are you breathing?

Me: Haha yea man. Sorry I didn't answer this morning. I don't remember when I left you guys last night.

Aisle: It was pretty early in the night, man. Everything okay?
Me: Couldn't be better.
Aisle: What does that mean?
Me: I'll tell you another time.
Aisle: I'm at Wicked Wolf. Come grab a beer with me.

There is not even a slim part of me that wants to go out. Just two flights of stairs up and I'm in sweatpants, on the phone with Marissa, cross legged, giggling like a middle schooler.

Or she won't answer.

The other me, in the reflection of my phone, returns.

And then you'll be faced with a stint of no-answer anxiety. Then you'll call her again and again because God forbid someone doesn't answer their phone in a timely fashion. You'll probably text her too, you little head case. And, by that time, well, shit, she'll know you're out of your mind!

Me: I'll be there in 15.

Told you.

┌─────────────────────────┐
│   5:44 PM   │
└─────────────────────────┘

It's a balmy ten-minute walk from my apartment, just enough to pep talk myself out of mentioning Marissa to Aisle. The sky is a burnt orange smeared by ominous black clouds over the twinkling New York skyline. The clouds should be taken as a sign from Elegua. An ancient premonition of evil.

As I walk in, Aisle and an unknown male begin to kick each other's feet under the table as if I can't see. As if Professor Lou had not taught him that piece of secret non-verbal communication years ago. I watch as their legs scratch at each other like furious cats under the table. The unknown head looks familiar. The body, not so much.

A tight shirt with muscles bulging out is not the usual physique my friends are accustomed to associating with.

As I approach the table the kicks stop and Aisle, who is facing me, avoids eye contact. He's generally a squirrely character but this is strange even for him. My first thoughts are that Aisle has staged an intervention. That this muscular stranger is here to take me away kicking and screaming to a rehab facility to cure my disturbing ailment of Irish exiting. He's finally fed up. Leaving a place without telling a soul is no fun for one's friends. Though I'm prepared to fight there is not much I will be able to do with the gorilla sitting at the table.

The jacked-up ball happens to not be a zoo animal, but Brian of Brian and Jen fame. My long lost and now unrecognizable ex best friend. His cheeks are no longer soft, his chin no longer round, even his nose somehow looks as if it can bench 225. His once messy hair has been army-fied down to a tight number one all the way around. The chestnut eyes I've seen mangled beyond recognition too many times seem clear. I would never tell him this, but he looks good. Fit, healthy, happy.

He shakes my hand as if we are meeting for the first time and my knuckles climb on top of one another in the tight grip.

"Lou, long time no see pal. How have you been? You look…well, you look like you," he says.

"And you look like Lou Ferrigno. I don't see you in a few months and you grow a few sizes," I say.

"Jen got me going to the gym and now I can't stop. It's like an addiction but one that's actually good for me."

"Well, that's no fun," I say.

I call the waitress over and ask for two beers and two shots for myself and Mr. Olympia across from me.

"No, I'm good thanks," he says.

"Good?"

"Yea, I quit drinking when I started at the gym. It's impossible to work out with a hangover."

The disgust on my face must be visible. Aisle has gone uncomfortably silent. If I hadn't felt betrayed before I now feel like Julius Caesar. Et tu Brian. Et fucking tu.

"You're going to get hungover off one beer? It wasn't that long ago when you could polish off twelve and walk in a straight line," I say.

"I'm here with Jen and her family. We're celebrating."

"How are you celebrating without drinking?" I ask. "And wait, celebrating what?"

"Jen just graduated. Double major in sports psychology and fitness…"

Phew. Okay, not the worst outcome.

"…and we're getting married," he says.

My jaw is somewhere below the subway station. It may have fallen off for all I know. The waitress delivers the four drinks and I take the two shots and down one beer before speaking.

"You're getting what?"

"Married, Lou. I proposed to her after she got her diploma."

"How long have you been dating? Five months?"

"Four. But when you know you know."

I'm not sure if it's the hurried drinks or the news that makes me feel queasy. Even worse than this news is that I now have my father's voice thrashing through the wild forest of thoughts in my head.

I proposed to your mother in seven days, Lou. When you know, you know.

"You don't know shit."

┌─────────────────────────┐
│   6:07 PM   │
└─────────────────────────┘

I say this out loud. To Brian. To my father. To myself. To anyone willing to listen.

"What did you just say?"

Brian begins to puff up even larger than he already is. A bulging vein in his newly engorged neck begins to shiver.

"I said…you don't know shit."

The truth needs to be spoken, no matter the consequences. In this particular case I may be beaten to a pulp but at least I can hold my head high if it's still attached to my body. Brian gets up, walks to my side of the table. His large shadow blocks out the light. He puts his hand on my shoulder and squeezes, which will leave a mark.

"Give yourself a look in the mirror, bud. Your invitation will be in the mail."

He walks away.

┌─────────────────────┐
│   6:41 PM   │
└─────────────────────┘

"Can you believe the balls on that guy? Look in the mirror? Look in the fucking mirror? If he looked in the mirror he would realize he looks like a steroid abuser. What's he on, anyway? Turinabol? Prednisone? His sack is probably the size of two raisins which is clearly the cause of him proposing to that witch. He barely even knows the girl. He met her at a fucking strip club! And don't even get me started on that bull-shit degree. Sports psychology. What the fuck is that? That has to be fake. Is she going to work for the Yankees teaching poor major leaguers how to cope with some booing fans? Seriously, somebody pinch me."

Aisle is silent.

"Four months. Four fucking months. I was fucking Kristen for God knows how long and I never had the inkling to call her my girl-friend, let alone pop the question. Is this really happening? Brian and Jen. Jen and Brian. Engaged to be married? What are they going to do, actually get married?"

"That's usually what happens," Aisle says. He looks down into his beer.

"Aren't you a fucking brain surgeon Aisle. Look at you. Sharp as a tack. What the fuck do you know about girls anyway?"

"I know that they want to get married to guys like Brian," he says.

"Guys like Brian? Like Brian? Do you remember Brian this time last year? I'll refresh your astonishingly sub-par memory. He was us. He was us in every way. He got drunk Friday to Sunday. He chased girls. He did drugs. He was fun. Remember last summer when we went to AC?"

Aisle's eyes widen with delight at bringing up such a weekend.

"And do you remember who was crowned MVP of that weekend?" I ask.

"Brian," Aisle says.

"And do you remember why?"

"Didn't he complete the hattrick?" Aisle asks.

"The hattrick and the cycle," I correct him. "Brian was a legend. Legend's never die but this one has been castrated and all you can do is sit in silence and watch it happen. It's pathetic."

I order another two shots and two beers. I begin to play "Taps" with my mouth as the trumpet. A tear almost comes to my eye. Another soldier gone. Even Professor Lou cannot come up with a theory as to why we lose great men. It is too emotional of a topic to properly study. The only thing to do is drink and reminisce about the good old days.

"Remember when Brian left us that one night at McSwiggan's to go to New York to meet up with a girl but…" I begin but am swiftly cut off.

"But came back with a completely different girl in an hour!" Aisle finishes the story.

We laugh.

"Or that time," Aisle chimes in, "Brian did four tequila suicides in a row and the next day his eye was shut. He had to go get it cleaned out at the eye doctor and they asked him how it happened…"

"And he told them…you should see the other lime," I say.

This one has us howling. It's nonstop for the next hour. Drinks and stories. The purpose of any night out with the boys that doesn't involve chasing girls. It dawns on me that nights like this are what has kept me on this path. A time and place where nothing bad enters. The drinks fortify us from shame and guilt and the stories provide the laughs. Why would Brian give up all this? What could possibly be better?

"Where's VanNeece?" I ask. "Working late?"

"Uhhh..."

Aisle's eyes droop. Either another earring lost or something is amiss.

"Kyle..." I say.

"He's uh, out on a date," he says.

"A what? With who?"

"That girl Bridget, from your sister's party," he says.

The laughs are gone.

7:45 PM

I'm not sure if it's the drinks or the news, but I must look pretty bad for Aisle to ask...

"Are you okay?"

"No, I'm not okay," I admit.

"What's going on?"

There is sincere concern in his voice. He looks at me through watery eyes. The drinks have certainly taken their toll on him. He's currently sipping a seltzer which isn't so bad considering the high treason that has been committed by others here tonight.

"I'm fine," I say. "Just...Brian."

"That's not it. I've known you fifteen years. You've been checked out. And then last night you saddle us with a rando from your work and just leave? That's gotta be some rule in your book. Why don't you just tell me what's going on? You never tell me what's going on. You're always preaching about this and that, telling me what I should do, but you're never just honest."

"Honest? If anything, I'm too fucking honest," I say, though I did completely forget about Steven, who's services are no longer needed.

"Maybe about everyone else. Never about you," he says.

He waits for me to respond. The silence is killing me, but it looks like Aisle might be able to stew in it all night.

"Well, I've been kind of searching for that girl I met at my sister's," I finally admit.

"Really?" he says.

He sits up straight, folds his hands in front of him, and a wide smile appears on his face. I imagine this is what Delilah looks like when she is about to give someone advice over the radio. Somehow, it's endearing.

"Well, did you fuck her?" Aisle asks.

I'm taken back by the tone and the question. The smile has vanished.

"N-no. Not that I remember," I say.

"So, you left us with a fucking magician and you didn't even fuck her? Pull this girl up on Instagram? Let me see what we're working with here," he says.

"I...I can't..."

"What do you mean you can't? Do I sense some technological desperation?"

I'm not sure where Delilah went. She's been replaced by a repulsive maniac.

Aisle has turned dark. His hair casts a shadow, his cheeks look grunge, his eyebrows sit at mean angles, his knuckles are white against his glass.

"I can't find her on Instagram," I admit.

"If you can't find her on Instagram she's probably a weirdo. What's that, rule number 86? Yea, I think it is. Why even bother?"

"But I think I really like her," I say, pleading my case.

"Too bad, get over it."

I have a sinking feeling that I've corrupted the best of us. Aisle looks at me with disdain. Those words were never meant to leave Aisle's mouth but I've left him no choice. For a second there is a glimmer in his eye that says he doesn't mean any of this.

"Really like this girl…" he trails off. "Give me a break."

But the glimmer disappears.

┌─────────────────────┐
│   8:18 PM   │
└─────────────────────┘

Aisle has left me all alone for a girl he's matched with on Tinder in lieu of a second date with the crier. He said the Tinder girl was down to fuck, that he was done doing dates. Somehow Aisle finally taking my advice has left me uneasy.

The fresh Hoboken fumes wake me for my walk uptown instead of home. The streets are relatively empty. Through un-curtained windows you can make out glimpses of other lives. Dinner being prepared, dishes being cleaned, TVs flickering, kids, marriages, real life happening in every corner of every building. I'm in no mood to imagine such a life. Aisle, VanNeece, and Brian's new forms are living rent free in my head.

I must give the devil her due. Jen is a sly and cunning operator. Most gym frequenters are. They want you to believe they go to the gym for health reasons or because working out makes them feel good. What a crock of shit. In reality, they are self-conscious sociopaths. The need to look good is their number one driver. They are obsessed with how they are seen. How can Professor Lou tell? Jen's Instagram is a mixed bag of workout videos, gym selfies, and the occasional picture of her and Brian. In every gym selfie or video her boobs are pressed up to her chin in a sports bra. And then there are the skintight stretchy pants. In one specific video you can see her camel toe. She leaves nothing to the imagination and that is the point. She doesn't want the body for health's sake, she wants to be ogled at. She dangled her wears enough to steal my best friend from under my nose.

Thinking about Jen gives my walk a new vigor. I'm not giving up without a fight. In no time I am at High Noon, the strip club at which Brian met Jen.

9:03 PM

Horrific lighting, loud music, and watered-down drinks are the staple of any strip club. The bad lighting everywhere but the stage is designed to attract one into a love seat near the front row. It does its job on me.

A waitress in a shirt cut so low I can see her belly button takes my order of a beer in a bottle with the top on. She's wearing a thong disguised as shorts. Her heels are about 10 inches tall. I'm not complaining but I also don't envision bringing this one home to mom and dad. I imagine Jen was wearing this same getup when Brian met her. I'm sure this waitress is paying off her double major as well, but I must find out for certain. Professor Lou is headed to work.

"Can I ask you something?" I yell over the thumping hip-hop.

"Sure, honey."

"Are you paying your way through college?"

She lets out a deep laugh drowned out by the music as she tilts her head back.

"No, baby. I'm in stripper training. I have to start at the bar before I can be a dancer. Them's the rules."

"I knew it!" I yell.

"Why? Do you like what you see?"

"You would make an exquisite stripper m'lady. Good luck to you in all your future endeavors."

I'm not lying just to butter her up. She will make a fine stripper. She has all the necessary physical attributes. Whether she can dance or not is a moot point.

I watch a few dances, polish off a few beers, and think about how right I've been. Jen was in the stripper training program before Brian decided to become Captain Save-a-Hoe. These types of girls don't change, even if they do find a sucker that gets them out. The lingering excitement of the male gaze is something that stays with them.

I think, only for a second, that I'm being too harsh. That I don't mean any of this. That these women are just like any other. But the thought of Brian throwing his life away crushes any remaining sympathy.

As a Professor I know that one case that confirms my previous bias is nothing to hang my hat on. I must challenge these biases with study. I must think like a scientist. Further research is always warranted. I decide to buy a private dance in which I can actually hear the answers to my questions. It doesn't hurt that I will be grinded on by a half-naked lady while I ask. I tell the manager of the private rooms that he can send in any lady he chooses. I am not picky and this is strictly for study.

The first girl sent in is miniature. She is 5'5" with heels on. She's wearing a baby blue bra covering her non-existent breasts and she's covered head to foot in tattoos. Though not usually my type, she has a dangerous sex appeal. I double check that my wallet is safely in my back pocket. She gives off the vibe that anything goes, including theft.

She introduces herself as Jesse James. This is clearly her stage name and a very enticing one at that. It also confirms my opinion that she would have no problem twisting me into a position of helplessness to steal my belongings. She hits play on a hip-hop song that will last about two and a half minutes. I don't have long.

"Do you know a bartender named Jen? Jen Droule?" I ask as she places her tiny bottom directly in my crotch.

"Why? You like her or something? Just focus on me hun. I'll show you stuff none of the other girls could show you."

Like thievery, I think.

"No, I just want to know if she ever danced here before," I say.

"Jen? No. Never danced."

She's straddling me, a hand on my neck, sensually rubbing four places at once. It's very hard to concentrate.

"Never?"

"Never that I saw. But I don't pay attention to anyone except you baby."

The song fades out and another one already begins before I ask her to send in another girl. She's not pleased but takes the tip and leaves. You can't trust a klepto with tattoos to give you any accurate information, so I shun her as an outlier in my dataset.

The next girl that comes from behind the curtain is my type. A drop dead, heart-stopping woman. Her skin is the black of a freshly paved street and her fingernails and toes are painted a blinding white. Her eyes are big and sweet and if I could just look at them for one second I would see they are genuine, but she has big natural boobs and an ass that could make a man's ticker quit that gobble up my attention. The only thing fake on her are her eyelashes which extend about six inches out.

I let her dance on me for the first song uninterrogated. This is just for my own enjoyment and I wait until song number two to pop the question.

"Do you know a bartender named Jen?"

She places my hands on her ass as she straddles me. She is hoping this will shut me up. It almost distracts me from her answer.

"Yea, she quit last week honey. So just keep your hands where they are and enjoy yourself."

"Yes ma'am. Had Jen ever stripped before?"

"How would I know?"

I ask no more questions and enjoy a third song before asking her to leave and send another girl in. This is not normal strip club etiquette, but I am looking for answers.

The third girl comes in doing a cartwheel and somehow somersaults into a split on my lap. She is tall and blonde and plastic from what I can tell through the gymnast routine.

"Holy shit!" I scream.

"Never met a girl who knows how to make an entrance?"

I quickly ask if she knows Jen the bartender, terrified of anymore acrobatics.

"I don't know any Jen, but I can give you a blowjob for $100."

That's the final straw. I nudge her off me, throw the remaining cash in my wallet on the table, and leave. I'm out $200 and went 1 for 4 in my line of questioning.

11:51 PM

Back at my apartment I crack open a warm can of beer that's been sitting on my counter since God knows when. It's too late to call Marissa now. I fall asleep on the couch with only a sliver of doubt that Brian and Jen are a match made in hell. A stripper's word is nothing to take seriously, I tell myself over and over until I fall asleep.

Thursday

7:42 AM

A wake up on the couch is the equivalent of a hard workout. Muscles I was not aware existed become vocal along with a pain in my neck that feels like it may become permanent. The difference between a workout and waking up on the couch after ten too many is the temperature of pipes. Nostrils to tongue is a desert of burning sand coupled with an esophagus the degree of a furnace.

Waking up fully clothed is not ideal either but it doesn't faze me. Today is the day I will call Marissa. A girl worthy of a phone call. I take my wallet out of my pocket and it is empty. Devoid of all cash and subsequently the paper with Marissa's number. I check each pant pocket, shirt pocket, socks and shoes. Nothing.

Marissa's note is not among the garbage strewn around the apartment. I flip the couch cushions frantically and stick my hand deep into unknown crevices. Nothing. On hands and knees the search begins. Shoulder deep under the couch only yields lint and three empty beer cans. There is a half-eaten buffalo wing and a molding piece of pizza crust under the coffee table, but no note. Just how gross my apartment is does not compute. I am a one-track mind. I crawl to the bathroom and fumble through the cabinet under the sink. There is nothing but the echoes of empty spray cans clanking. The medicine cabinet is empty except for an old bag of yip. Odd, yet on brand.

My hands begin to shake, which could be due to losing Marissa's number or the extreme amount of physical activity I've endured this morning. Behind the toilet, in the shower, and back to my jean pockets again. All empty. Taking my jeans off and holding them upside down results in sixty-two cents rolling around my room but no note.

Checking the couch again is logical but this time I stick my hand so deep I jam a finger on a cold hard spring. Sucking my finger like a child, I attempt to gather my thoughts. The note started in the fridge then I took it to work. I stared at it throughout the day, which is mortifying enough, and then stared at it on my drive home.

In the car.

It has to be in the car.

8:03 AM

The car is parked at 3B. Adrenaline has enabled me to remember its exact location. In the center console is every important paper: registration, insurance, even my expired passport. These are all tossed on the floor. There is a glimmer of hope when a yellow piece of paper emerges from under the rubble, but it turns out to be a taxi driver's card. Under the driver's seat, nothing but broken cigarettes. It's confusing and repulsive all in one. Why do I smoke? Why do I drink? Why am I working this stupid fucking job? And why, of all things, have I lost this one piece of paper?

Under the passenger seat are more crushed cigs and repulsion. The glove box, when I open it, dumps an assortment of napkins onto the floor, which now have to be sifted through, one by one. Each piece with no number is discarded onto the parking lot floor. How could I care about littering at a time like this?

After the rain of napkins comes a car manual and a full pack of cigarettes. I turn each page of the manual individually, something I never thought I'd do, and still there is nothing. I light a fresh cigarette and sit amongst the napkins, lighting one by one into disappearing flames.

Maybe it's at work...

8:16 AM

Driving out of the garage at top speed has my shabby vehicle teetering left and right as if it were trying to topple over onto its shell like a turtle. The death-defying oscillation occurs until the stop sign at the exit. The sign is ignored, which almost results in a head-on collision with an elderly woman.

The first left onto Hudson Street puts me right in front of the Hoboken Police Station. They don't need to know about the close encounter with vehicular manslaughter just moments ago. They also don't need to know my plan to violate hundreds of traffic laws in the next half hour. They're probably still out there looking for me.

Personally unscathed, though I cannot speak for any pedestrians, I bring the Honda to a shrieking halt at the light on Observer Highway. This is not just an expression. The screech is piercing. A young woman lets out a surprised yell of fear as my brakes emit the sound of a prehistoric bird descending on its prey.

Parked next to me at the light is a gentleman in a high-class Mercedes. He is busy on his phone so doesn't hear me revving up my engine. Or my engine doesn't rev loud enough. My goal here is to get the man's attention because a garbage truck has just pulled into the right lane 100 feet from the light in front of me. This truck will hinder any and all speed going forward.

The light changes to green and I attempt to beat the Mercedes off the line. The man has time to hear my tires spin, look up, place his phone down, and still win, which leaves me stuck for two miles behind the stinking truck. Heart palpitations extend from my chest to my forearms and even into the pointer finger of my left hand. At around the half mile mark I break down and begin yelling at nothing in particular. If someone driving next to me is watching this scene it would not phase them, as this is a common occurrence anywhere in North Jersey.

By the time the infamous Hoboken sign passes overhead, which is just white block-lettering tattooed onto rusted metal train tracks, my freak-out has dispersed into a general sense of paranoia. My mind turns into an endless loop of places the note could be, inducing my heart rate to that of a hummingbird. It doesn't help that by the time I divert on to the Pulaski Skyway, traffic has increased three-fold.

By the end of Pulaski, five cigarettes have been smoked and half of Jeff Buckley's greatest hits album has been played. This decreases my anxiety but adds a new emotion to the mix. Angst. My eyes feel like the ticking time bomb that is Yellowstone. At any moment the water works may start flowing. As I finally pull off the highway into more traffic, it feels like my mission is losing its luster.

That is until Buckley's "Everybody Here Wants You" moans through the speakers. If this song wasn't written for a woman like Marissa, then I don't know who it could be about. The pulse returns.

8:57 AM

Head down, with no interruptions, I make it to my desk. There is enough paper scattered on top to be unsure if there is actually a desk underneath. Not only is the amount of physical trash sacrilegious at a software company, but the pages are filled with useless doodles and information which has long been forgotten. And of course, there is no note.

In one swoop, every piece of paper is slid into the garbage, leaving an almost empty desk. A crushed pack of cigarettes and a shooter of whiskey are uncovered like two dinosaur bones. Repulsion sets in once again and it is quickly growing toward self-hate.

Why? I ask. Why didn't I just call her yesterday? The palm of my hand muffles curses into unrecognizable mumbles.

There is no quit in me though. A woman like Marissa deserves nothing less. I don my Quixotic armor and tread back into the unknown of the Internet. I check my search history first and wonder why it's blank. I never clear my search history, no matter how rotten it gets.

Yes you do.

It's me in the small mirror again.

You're afraid of being schizo.

I flatten the mirror onto the desk and go through my phone, hoping, praying I can somehow find the number.

My face is buried deep into the shining light.

"What are you doing?"

"Searching," I reply to the voice overhead.

"Why aren't you working?"

"Because I'm searching, Lord. I am searching!"

Nothing can distract me – not work, not my job, not even the Almighty himself.

"Lord?"

"Yes, Lord or Elegua or whoever you are. Please help me find her. I know you guys don't actually exist. Is this girl like you? I've seen her though. I've touched her. I know she's real. But even if she is real, Lord, she is unfindable. That is not a good sign, Lord. No one is unfindable. Everyone can be found, Lord. I'm begging you. I need some advice here. Thou shall findeth Marissa on Instagrameth should be a commandment, Lord! I mean, who am I to tell you what to do? It's only a suggestion. I just need a little push, a little help. Please?"

After a minute of no answer from the almighty, I look up.

It's my boss, Doug. No lord in the vicinity.

"What the fuck are you talking about?"

"Ummm, I'm searching for this new app?" I reply. That question mark is appropriate. The inflection at the end of my response is almost a squeal.

"What new appeth? The Talketh to God app? Get in my fucking office."

11:13 AM

Doug's office is barren: a proper habitat for the Spartan-like humanoid in front of me. If there wasn't a scar under his left eye he could easily be mistaken for a robot. His spiked gray hair is in the shape of an anvil.

"How's your father?" he asks.

"Fine, sir."

"That's good. We haven't talked in a while. And your mother?"

"Fine too, sir," I say.

"Great, now that I know they're both still alive and well, what am I going to say to them about firing their son? That he's talking to himself in the office instead of working? Not just himself but to God? That he hasn't been focused since he started here? That I can look in his eyes and tell he doesn't give a shit about the company his father started, and even if he wanted to, he is too hungover? I know your Dad probably doesn't talk highly of me, we've never seen eye-to-eye, but if he still worked in this office he would have fired you months ago."

"I've been a little out of it, sir. I'm still trying to get acclimated to the business and exactly what my goals are at the company," I say.

"Acclimated? You're twenty-five. You've been working part-time since you were eighteen. Full-time for two years. And is it true you wore white sweatpants to work on Monday?"

"But...I..."

"Look, Lou. Go home. Get some real rest. Maybe stay home this entire weekend. The whole thing. Today until Sunday. Then, on Monday, either come into the office with a purpose or don't come in at all."

"Okay..."

"Get out."

As I mope to the door I decide to ask him a question that has been on my mind for a very long time.

"Sir...how is Arianna?"

"GET THE FUCK OUT!"

11:16 AM

A walk of shame requires shame. If I find Marissa, losing my job will have been worth it. Even though my brain does not compute a single care for these walls my father built, my body has received the memo. It is slumped, disheveled, and trudging towards the elevators.

"Wait! Where are you going?"

I turn around to Steven running towards me, hands behind his back, in his office clothing with his office face and his office Velcro shoes. He looks nothing like the entertainer on the rooftop bar in the city. Some of us are not always who we appear to be.

"Home, what'd you want?"

"I wanted to say thank for the other night."

"Don't mention it," I say.

From behind his back he whips out forty odd loose-leaf pages. It finally dawns on my useless brain that the real Saint Stephen has delivered on our deal. A deal I almost forgot about. A deal that wouldn't have been necessary had I just held on to that fucking piece of paper.

"Holy shit, Steven!"

"There are a lot of Marissa's and we make a lot of apps," he says.

Though he doesn't seem like a guy who appreciates being touched, I give him a big hug and a whopping kiss on the cheek.

"Where do I even start on this tomb?" I ask.

"Line by line," he says. "Just like a programmer."

The number of lines on page one are making me dizzy, but hey, at least it's a plan.

"How'd it go for you the other night by the way? You get lucky?" I ask.

"I met someone," he says, then blushes.

"And…"

I'm too tired of myself to wait for the answer. It doesn't matter.

"That's good man, congratulations," I say.

"Thanks," he says. "Let's go out again sometime."

Though Steven has held up his end of the bargain I can't help but feel angry at this request. The elevator doors shut on his innocent face and for a second he resembles Kyle Aisle.

11:22 AM

On the drive home I'm forced to acknowledge that maybe a little part of me feels bad for Arianna. Being Doug Richardson's daughter is punishment enough for all her past deeds. But maybe Doug is like this partly due to Arianna. She always found ways to make everything worse.

At the age of eight I first listened in on my mom and dad discussing the latest disturbance Arianna had caused dad's partner. At the ripe age of twelve she was caught wearing makeup in school. At fourteen she shaved her head. At sixteen she crashed the family car. This was all wild to good little Lou's ears. This was before my professorship, before my slow sink into depravity, before such a thing as a hangover ever existed. But then, at eighteen, she committed grand theft virginity and I was the unfortunate victim.

It would have been hard for a mere mortal to get away with the things she did, but she had an aura about her. She acted as if she knew what she was doing, as if the world were made just for her pleasure, as if she were divine. She got away with it because she looked the part. The truest form of privilege is the pretty kind. Her eyes, dark chocolate. Her cheeks, high and mighty. Her hair, deep brown when it wasn't shaven, looked like it had been steam pressed upon waking. And that body. Christ that body. Long toned legs, a thigh gap, tits that made the strings on her bikini hold on for dear life. Say what you want about Doug Richardson, but one thing you can't say is that he makes an ugly daughter.

It was easy to fall for such a woman. And that's what I did every summer at Doug's Florida vacation home. During these yearly treks to Mecca, Arianna became my Kaaba, albeit curvier. She was only two years older than me but it felt like I was in the presence of a starlet. She, of course, had no interest in me, which made it all the more intimidating. When she would give me attention, I'd practically pray at her feet.

By the age of fourteen I had moved on from shock at the stories that were told about her to apostolic support. Anything negative said about Arianna was blasphemy. Such a creature could never do such things and if she did, there must have been a reason. She was Arianna. She could do no wrong.

The summer I turned sixteen was when it all went haywire. When my apprenticeship to full professor began. The little seed had been planted…or spilled. The drinking and the drugging and the fear and the shame all began one hot June night, in Florida of all places. Fucking Florida…

She'd been on the phone a lot. Crossing her legs, smirking. She'd just cut her hair for the hundredth time. Her bangs hung just above her eyebrows, the back shook just above her shoulders. Oh, to be the guy on the other line. That lucky bastard. The things I would have done to be that guy would be illegal in all fifty states and in the eyes of God. The penalties would have been twenty-five to life or death by firing squad, along with a first-class trip to hell. I would have taken that chance. It wasn't necessary.

Three nights into the vacation, during another dinner that Arianna skipped, there was screaming, then snapping, then the shattering of a window. More screaming ensued. Big bad Doug did not care that his daughter had broken up with her boyfriend, did not care that she was sobbing, did not care that her life was ruined. He was more worried about the flip phone that was snapped in two and the broken bedroom window and the calculation of what this little tantrum by his one and only daughter would cost him. Mrs. Richardson might have been able to help if she wasn't passed out after five martinis and a Vicodin. If I was married to Doug I'd surely be on the same cocktail, only double the measure.

My parents and sister shuffled into their rooms, forsaking dinner to avoid the sheer embarrassment, but I sat there. I watched her grab her bag, tears falling, eyes puffed. I can still hear the angry flapping of her flip flops as she left, like a clock hooked up to an amplifier. I sat there as Doug poured himself five fingers worth of scotch and took it to bed. There was a baseball game on.

Between the waves crashing outside and the game on the TV I must have sat there for thirty minutes, maybe an hour, focused on nothing. I'd later come to know this feeling under heavy sedation. Too drunk to care. Too yipped to notice. High, drunk, and focused on nothing at all. But at this young and sober age, I was rendered motionless out of fear. I could run after her, sure, but I wasn't allowed out after dinner. Even if I was, what could I possibly help her with? Her boyfriend could drive, he smoked cigs, he probably had a twelve-inch hog that started with a pull cord.

A tapping at the window pulled me out of my reverie of having a twelve-inch hog myself. There she was. Those eyes under those bangs through glass. The original to the liquor store replica. There was no hint of the tears that had just been shed, just a little glint of chaos at the corners. Then she raised a bottle of whiskey in one hand, a pack of smokes in the other, and nodded her head to follow her.

What's a boy to do?

Not even a question.

You run out of the house while trying not to look too excited. Just like you ran after Marissa. When you get outside you can barely see her in the distance, arms stretched, long t-shirt covering her bathing suit bottoms, bottle in one hand, lit cigarette in the other, swaying freely in the night. She's almost up the dune and you can smell the ocean and the faint smell of cigarette smoke and your heart is beating so loud you can hear it and your less-than-12-inch hog is pushing against your shorts and you can't imagine how much trouble you'll be in if you get caught. You wouldn't give two shits if you were.

"Come on," she yells.

And come you do.

Not in your pants. Not yet. But you follow her route up the dune and onto the big empty black beach and you look for a little dot of orange ember and you see it high up. Higher than humanly possible and you wonder if this is all a dream. If Arianna is floating up high and away, disappearing into the ether, and this was simply a false wish, a dream played out to the laughter of a thousand stars in the sky. Maybe this is your first experience with schizophrenia? It's certainly your first experience of feeling stupid in the presence of a woman. It won't be your last.

But then you see the lifeguard stand, and the smoke of the cigarette puff from the top, and you know it's real. You know this is really happening and you can't believe it and you're shitting yourself and your legs keep walking, heavier with each step, calves tighten against the sand, until you climb up the stairs and she hands you the bottle and says, "Have some."

What's a boy to do?

Not even a question.

You take a big manly slug and feel the fire in your belly and try not to gag and you've never felt better in your life. You never will. Ever. No matter how much you drink you'll never get that first slug back with Arianna on the lifeguard stand. You take another. And another.

You finally ask, "Are you okay?"

"My boyfriend is an asshole," she says.

"What happened?"

She hands you a half-smoked cigarette. You take a puff and cough your lungs up and she laughs and your head is somewhere near the moon that is shaped like the bottom of a pregnant belly. But you hold onto the cigarette and puff again, and again.

"Is this your first cigarette?" she asks.

"No," you lie.

"Don't lie to me," she says. "Don't start this off with a lie."

You want to ask what *this* means when she grabs your face and kisses you. You can smell the alcohol on her breath and feel the smoke on her tongue and you almost drop the bottle of booze but you're holding onto it like a drowning man on a buoy. You've kissed a girl before, but not like this.

She stops, takes the bottle from your hand, puts it to her lips and takes a pull. You don't know if you've ever seen anything sexier in your life. You don't know what to do with your hands now. You fold them on your lap, then your knee, then lap again, while she stares out at the ocean. You mistake this look for wisdom. You mistake this look for an all-knowing sadness.

You don't know at the time you are being used. Even if you did you wouldn't have cared. Arianna's revenge at the expense of poor little Lou. All you can try to do is muster up the courage to kiss her again. You find that courage after she hands you the bottle and you take another rip. But the courage dies. You still don't know what to do with your hands. Do you try and go under her bra? Anywhere lower? She decides for you, puts your hands where she wants them.

It goes on like this for what seems like an eternity until she slides your pants off and straddles you and she whispers, "pull out." Those words alone can make you explode but you hold off for thirty seconds. Okay, fifteen.

This will go on nightly for the rest of the vacation. You hide the half-finished bottles in the dunes before you come back in the house and retreat to your room. Your head spins each time. You're hammered and happy.

During the day you go and take nips at the half-filled bottles to keep up an illusion of confidence until you both sneak out again. You go to the beach. You have sex. You're lasting longer now. You never thought this could happen. You are gaining confidence that will smash into pieces in a matter of weeks. But for that week at Doug's vacation home, you were the man.

She gave you her number before you left. You tried to kiss her dead sober and she turned her cheek. You rationalized that. She didn't want to get caught in front of her parents, you said. You texted her "Miss you" right before your flight took off. In VanNeece's words, "Jesus, bro." There was no response when you landed. You rationalized that too. Her phone was still broken, you said.

You called her a few days later. Followed those calls up with texts. Christ you were annoying. You wouldn't leave the poor girl alone. What was the final count? Forty-five missed calls? More missed texts? You can't remember. It's taken all the booze and all the drugs to erase it from your mind. You just know it was a lot.

When she finally responds she says, "I'm back with my boyfriend."

You try calling and it goes to voicemail.

Your poor little heart is broken. You let it eat you for a while until you realize one night at a party that you can make it all go away. You can incantate that same spell with booze and cigarettes and a woman. This habit starts in high school and becomes your personality. You wouldn't know what to do without it now. It is who you are. You've made it hard on yourself, sure. All this over a little snub? You big baby.

Doesn't matter now. You've gotten yourself into this mess and only you can get yourself out. You and Marissa, of course. Find that girl, Lou. Find that fucking girl.

11:33 AM

This time travel on my drive home is interrupted.

A text from Kristen. At a time like this...

Kristen: No call since Tuesday?

Me: Tuesday?

Kristen: Yea, Tuesday.

Me: Why would I have texted you Tuesday?

Kristen: Excuse me?

I wait as the three dots of her typing continue for eons.

Kristen: You came stumbling to my apartment like some kind of zombie. You kept saying the pizza man was chasing you. That you didn't pay. A fugitive on the run was the term. You just kept saying it. I am a fugitive on the run. You said you got in a fight. I checked for damage, and you seemed fine besides the clear mental issues. You wouldn't stop fidgeting. You fell asleep after an hour of mumbling something that sounded like Ma...Ma...Mar. I've never been so scared in my life. When I woke up you were gone.

Kristen: Oh, and I never want to see you again.

Good riddance. The liar. That is clearly not what happened Tuesday night. I found Marissa and had a night out with her and her father. I fought for her honor. We left. I got her number. That's what happened. That's my story and I'm sticking to it.

But did any of that happen?

I have no proof and Kristen is spewing a different story.

All signs are pointing to insanity.

And, if in the whole wide world of the internet Marissa doesn't exist, does she exist at all? That really is the crux of it, what this whole week of absurdity is coming down to. Is Marissa real or have I smoked, drunk, and blown my brains to smithereens?

My imaginations of being locked away in an asylum run rampant. My heart feels like fingers rummaging through a drawer.

I call Kimberly. Her phone is still off, or England's cell service is as poor as their dentistry. Either way it is a frustrating turn of events when the thread that I'm hanging on by is moments away from snapping.

In an alternate universe, Kimberly answers, and it goes something like this:

"Oh Marissa? She is lovely, darling."

Kimberly has acquired a British accent in the week that she's been there.

"Tell her Kimberly says ciao and to not break your poor little haht."

"By any chance do you have her number?" I'll ask.

"Of course, darling, of course."

And that will be the end of it. The next call will be to Marissa and an embarrassing yet endearing grovel will ensue. Unless…

Unless Kimberly has no idea who Marissa is. If that's the case I'll be locked away in a looney bin. A small acid grenade explodes in my stomach and the backs of my arms go numb at the wheel.

The only sure-fire solution here is heavy sedation. A couple of drinks is certainly better than a heart attack. The forty pages in the seat next to me do nothing to calm my addled state. Impending death, doom, and destruction can all be put off with a wee dram, or five. It's not like I have work tomorrow…

12:17 PM

There is a new kid at the cash register of my favorite liquor store. He reminds me of office Steven, a greased-up pile of bones with a zit radiating off the left cheek. "Let's go out again some time" repeats in my head. If he only knew what he was asking he wouldn't have asked. Office Steven knows nothing of the day after. The shattered shell of a human you become. There is no way to learn except through experience. After just a few years of consistency, your entire existence can change. How could he know about the real side effects? Like your brain permanently swelling or your liver turning into a hockey puck or that for some reason the longer you go, the harder it is to quit.

The kid rings up my bottle of tequila and, as I'm walking out, I hear him say...

"She isn't real."

I turn around like I'm in a Western, gun drawn.

"What did you just say?"

"Nothing, sir."

I start walking towards him.

"What the fuck did you just say to me?"

"Nothing, sir, nothing."

I grab him by the collar of his blue Sparrows shirt and shake him.

"I...need...to...know...what...you...just...said."

"It's easy for me to steal," he whispered. "If you ever need me to steal a few bottles for you I can, if you let me come to wherever you go. You're always in here buying stuff, like every day, and I'd just like to come along one time. I just turned 21 but I don't have a lot of friends, I just moved here."

"That's not what you fucking said you little shit," I say.

I let go of his shirt and speed walk towards the exit. I wonder if I have charity written on my forehead until I see my reflection in the sliding door.

She isn't real, it says.

222

1:39 PM

With every twenty lines searched on the report, I do a shot. It is the only way for me to get through this tedious work. The task goes something like this:

Find name in Column A, find social media platform in Column B, and search said name in said social media platform. It would be too tiresome if I didn't have a little carrot to help me through. For example, there are twenty-two Marissa Bongiorno's that have clicked on an Avalanche App ad, all different people and none of them are my Marissa. The only plus about the Bongiorno's is I'll have earned my fourth shot once I am done searching through them.

By the time I get to Marissa Christiano, ten pages in, I'm deserving of a break and a new angle. Christiano reminds me of the DM to Christian that has gone unanswered. In desperation I begin to comment on every picture going back months.

Me: Christian, where are you?

Me: Answer my DM.

Me: Do you know where Marissa is?

A shot of tequila, or three, smooths out the pointy edges of humiliation.

I text Kimberly and pour myself another.

Me: Hey sis.

Me: Hope you haven't died in some type of accident.

Me: I need to ask you something when you get a chance.

Me: Sorry I missed you before you left.

Patience is neither a virtue nor a sin while waiting on a text back, it is just simply nonexistent. At the fifteen-minute mark another drink is poured. At thirty minutes, and still no response, another drink is poured, and another, and another...

Carey is my last hope. Her texts are still greener than me with a hangover. I've been deserted. I'm all alone.

1:55 PM

In an attempt to go to the bathroom I am now on the floor, looking up at the ceiling. There is no indication of how or why but it's as if a one-two punch from Mike Tyson has placed me here with no recollection of the fall. Was it a fall? Am I drunk? All signs point to the affirmative. Mentally and physically, I am on a boat somewhere in the middle of the Atlantic.

Once up I take short, calculated steps to the nearest object, the refrigerator. The door swings open like a bat wing and takes me for a ride. Hanging on to the door as if it's a bull at a rodeo doesn't help the situation and again I'm on the floor. This time joined by the contents of the fridge door.

Trying to get up is a futile pursuit. Each time I place my hands to push myself up they find themselves mushed into a half stick of old butter, or slipping on an empty bottle of hot sauce. For what feels like an eternity I am like a dog wearing socks. There is no traction or brain cells, just determination. Eventually, sitting against the shelves of the open fridge, I try to sort it all out.

"Whatsth happened?"

It dawns on me, when I hear my own slobbering voice out loud, that I am properly hammered. This is the best-case scenario. Being filthy drunk can be dealt with, unlike, say, a brain aneurism. I've been here before.

An empty bottle of blue cheese dressing and the same traitorous door conspire to put me back on my ass for a third time, but I am two steps ahead of these inanimate objects. My feet are planted firmly on the ground but my upper body continues to sway like bamboo. On the table the real culprit stares at me, three quarters of the way finished, which is a surprise. Although that is quite a lot of tequila it's not nearly enough to leave me sans legs. Drunk, no doubt, but legless? This is why you should never drink alone kids. It's like weightlifting. Always have a spotter.

Experience is telling me to get into the shower as soon as possible. Walk, wobble, crawl, or hobble – but get in that damn shower.

"Age befthore beauty," I say.

Smirking, I make my way around the kitchen table like a big, dumb, easel, holding on desperately while shimmying my feet closer to the bathroom door. At the closest point to the bathroom, I stop in an attempt to restore all of my synapses' courage. Their mission, if they choose to accept it, is to carry one small message from brain to feet. Walk. Just walk, one step at a time.

When my hands let go of the table that message fails. In an attempt to stay balanced I knock over the thirty remaining pages of Marissa's and make a mad dash for the shower. My knees start forward, as knees should, but midway they begin to bend out. Along with them, my feet go ten to two and I'm waddling at top speed. I've acclimated to this new normal, when the knees shoot back inward, throwing me off once again. At every step they change direction, dancing in and out like I'm doing the fucking tootsie roll. Billy "White Shoes" Johnson would sure be proud but if this ends in the way Mr. Shoes' celebration ends, we'll have a new set of problems.

As my knees short circuit, I lean my head forward in the hope that the rest of my body will follow its lead. The rest of my body gets the hint and starts to go where my head is pointing. The only problem is my brakes are broken. I'm bumbling, stumbling, rumbling forward with no way to stop. Next thing I know I am through the bathroom door, a plus I guess, and falling through the shower curtain into the tub. An attempt to hang onto the shower curtain is made as a last resort but instead of slowing any momentum, the entire contraption ends up on top of me while my head bangs at top speed into the ceramic tub. Knockout.

3:33 PM

The shower curtain is wrapped around me the way my mother used to tuck me in before bed. It was a treacherous road with many dangers, but we made it relatively safe and intact, albeit almost two hours later. KO'd in a bathtub is depressing, but not unheard of.

Twisting the nozzle above my head releases a torrent of freezing water into my mouth. The terrifying surprise jolts my head up, banging my forehead into the metal nozzle. There is just enough wherewithal left to pull the shower diverter and check my head for blood – which there is plenty of.

Puzzled and accomplished, I sit in the cold shower wiping the blood off my face with the shower curtain. Conscious life begins to instill itself once more. The blurry edges come back into focus and the light gets brighter. In a pool of water in a small crevice of the shower curtain, my dripping blood begins to meld into a shape. First her hair, then her head, and even her smile is plainly visible in red until it finally dissolves in the water.

I am rejuvenated, if not rejoicing in the fact that I have a reason to get out of this situation.

Marissa.

Unravelling the knot of curtain around my neck and midsection is difficult but doable. Aren't all great things that way? Where there is a why, man can bear any how.

Standing up reveals that this boat has found calmer waters. It's not perfect but at least my legs are familiar with the upper body they are attached to. There are many problems visible in the mirror before me but none more glaring than the gash above my right eye. I open the mirror, oddly hoping Marissa has hidden another note, but only find gauze, a bandage, and a left-over bag of yip. Why I have these supplies but no edible food in my fridge is a question for another day.

After taking a rather large bump from the old bag of coke and bandaging my head, I am not sure what to do next. There are two problems that need solving: the need to eat and the need to talk to someone. Anyone will do. This leaves only one option, my local bar.

┌─────────────────────┐
│   3:55 PM   │
└─────────────────────┘

A pint of Guinness and a loaf of bread would be an odd order anywhere else, but not at Moran's Pub. The man behind the bar is unfazed, fulfilling one of two needs. The other need, to talk, doesn't seem likely. With half my head wrapped like a WWI vet, it's going to be difficult to find anyone willing to have a chat.

There is another person who is not keen to talk to me. She stated clearly that she never wanted to speak to me again. I don't know how permanent my ban is but I feel I need to repair some damage. Maybe my fall in the shower struck the part of my brain that has been collecting dust, my conscience.

The professor in me says there is only one way to get rid of a girl and that's to ghost her. It's best for all parties. Well, at least for one party. The ghoster. What's the point of the awkward conversation? Why break someone's heart when you can just ignore them? And considering Kristen said to never talk to her again I would be doing the right thing. But is it the right thing? Leaving a woman hanging out there unsure is a form of torture. The ghosted live in limbo. I've been ghosted before, and it fucking hurts. My faults should not be transferred to her. Somehow, I can see this all too clearly. Motive matters. Where Arianna used me for revenge, Kirsten's betrayal was different. The deception had good intent. Make Lou believe you are one thing to build something better. I just wasn't ready. It just wasn't right. It was me who put on an act. It was me who was clothed in deceit. It's been me for ten years.

Me: Umm...

After a minute long excruciating wait I dive in. There's no point in standing at the edge of a cold plunge and thinking about it. I close one eye and start typing.

Me: I know you want nothing to do with me. Neither do I, frankly. But you deserve an explanation. I thought I was honest with you from the start but none of my actions matched my words. I never wanted a relationship but acted every step of the way like I did. I said one thing but did another.

Kristen: You're fine.

Me: No. I was wrong.

Kristen: Uhhh, no shit.

Me: Sorry doesn't mean anything but I'll say it anyway. I'm sorry.

Kristen: Have a nice life, Lou.

I'm tempted to ask her if I really showed up at her house lifeless and begging for Marissa but it's now beside the point. I have to stop the hurt somewhere.

My one eye reads the last text again. A nice life. What would that even look like? There are all the transient things. Loads of money, a hot chick, champagne flowing from geysers in the wall of a mansion. But what would a really nice life look like? Probably something like my parents. Maybe a job that didn't urge me to off myself. A dog. I'd really like a dog. One of those one's that have human eyes and crazy color coats and a place where she could run and a person to share it with.

I try calling Kimberly and Carey to no avail. Instead of giving up, I begin dialing phone numbers at random. I give my subconscious full cart blanche.

The first call is met with a single dial tone and should be taken as an omen.

The second rings for two minutes straight with no answering machine.

I'm starting to think the subconscious is a crock of shit.

On the third call I decide to only use my lucky numbers: 9, 1, and 3. The phone rings and a woman answers.

"Hello?" she asks.

"Who's this?" I ask, hopeful.

I'm almost sure that it's her.

"You called me," she replies. Oh, Marissa. So witty, so funny!

I can just make out a buried Spanish accent, detectable if you know her. I know her.

"It's me, Lou. From the other night, remember? I met your father, we looked at his paintings, we danced. I don't remember the restaurant name but it was Cuban…"

"Lou?" she says.

"Yes, yes Marissa. Lou. It's me! Lou!"

"Lou," she says again, this time sure.

"YES! Yes, I was so worried. It's a long story Marissa, too long for right now. But I lost your number. I thought, for some insane reason, that it would be a good idea to play hard to get, to make you want me, you know? I was going to wait a couple days to call you. Maybe you would think I was interesting or had something better to do. I didn't. I don't do much to be honest. And lately all I've been able to do is think about you. When I finally came to my senses I lost your note. And then this girl Kristen texted me. And Christian won't answer his DMs. And Kimberly won't answer. And Carey won't answer. And I have thirty more pages to search. And…hello? Hello?"

She's hung up.

I slam my phone against the bar and by the sound of it there is no doubt the screen has shattered. Turning it face up reveals a thousand small hexagons and an unreadable screen. It doesn't help that I'm still seeing double due to the tequilas and tumble.

The bartender clears his throat. He's an Irishman with small heads for fists and 2x4's for forearms. I don't need to be told twice something that even drunk me can intuit, so I throw one of my credit cards on the bar and stumble out.

An attempt to call my friends is futile. Another look at the broken phone screen will cause dizziness and vomiting. I have a hankering to hear Aisle's voice. The real Aisle, not the douchebag from last night. But every time I try and unlock my phone my finger is cut by miniature shards of glass.

It dawns on me that there is one place I haven't searched for the missing number – the strip club, where the thief Jesse James is likely the culprit. Though 4 PM at a strip club is an ugly place, I turn my compass to true north and begin stumbling.

4:01 PM

A cab pulls up next to me assuming my outstretched hand for balance was an attempt to hail him down. I would have walked the mile and maybe gotten there by sundown had the cabby not assured my timely arrival.

"High Noon. Thtat."

He drives the two minutes down Washington St. and in the rearview my reflection tells me to go home and go to sleep. My reflected self has been nothing but a nuisance and I am glad to see him leave with my exit from the cab.

I try to open the door to the club but it won't budge. I bang on the door but there is no reply. I, for one, am stunned. A strip club closed. How could they? What if someone were in desperate need of a life-or-death lap dance? Or, what if some drunk asshole lost a number in the private room? It is simply irresponsible.

I continue to bang on the door for ten minutes to no avail and then take a seat on the curb.

I weigh all my options when I hear a voice behind me.

"Were you just banging on this door?"

"Marissa?" I ask turning.

"Who? Were you just banging? We're closed."

It is the gorgeous stripper from last night sans the six-inch eyelashes. My saving grace. I explain my predicament, and she lets me in to search the premises.

"What are you doing here anyway?" I ask while rummaging through couch cushions in the main room. A strip club is a depressing enough place when it's packed. It resembles a mausoleum when it is empty.

"Practicing my routines. You think spinning up and down on a pole comes naturally? This shit is harder than you think," she says.

"Can I watch?" I ask.

"If you got money," she says, laughing.

I explain that all my cash is gone, along with the number of a girl who may not be real.

"I know what you mean," she says.

With an understanding pat on the shoulder and the relaxation of her suspecting eyes she looks nothing like the stripper I remember.

"That stuff happens all the time here," she continues. "You meet a nice guy with lots of cash and he pays you all his attention. He says he wants to meet the real you, not the stripper you. He wants to take you on a date. Wants to get you out of this place. He puts his number in your phone and you call, and the number doesn't exist. And then you wonder if he ever existed. And if that night ever existed. And then you're back on-stage dancing for a bunch of faceless men."

Her speech brings water to my eyes. We are two people in an ocean hanging on to wreckage. Her flotation device is a pole, mine a bottle. I nod in acknowledgement. She nods back.

"You mind if I check the private room?"

"Go ahead."

The private room is grimier and less private than I remember. It's really just a curtain and thin sheet rock walls. There are four identical barn-like stalls and I pick the one I think I was placed in last night. Turning the place over in minutes provides nothing. Instead of Marissa's number I find a used condom and almost vomit. My hope is dwindling.

When I walk out, Wonder Woman is practicing her flawless routine. She moves as if there were no gravity. Her body resembles a black jaguar's, aware of just how extraordinary it is.

"You were the one grilling the girls about Jen last night, right?" she asks.

"Uh, yea," I say.

"Well then you should probably know she's just about the nicest girl I've ever met in this place. Every time a girl got off the main stage she'd have an ice water waiting for us and she'd always buy us drinks off her own paycheck. There were plenty of guys that came in here to watch her bring the drinks out instead of the girls dancing. She's a hot one that Jen, but she never paid them any mind. If you're contemplating whether you should be with her or not, I'd say go for it, but that's just me."

"I'm not with her. It's my best friend I'm looking out for," I say.

"Looking out for? How old are you?"

"Twenty-five."

"Aren't you a little old to be questioning how your friend lives his life?" she asks.

"I'm a little old for a lot of things."

"Just so you know she never stripped once. But why would that matter?"

It wouldn't. She could have been the Michael Jordan of strippers or a nun and it wouldn't have mattered. I have just been pulling at strings ever since Brian decided to run away from the life we built together. The house of fun we ran like thieves has crumbled. I knew this already. Somewhere deep inside. The whole charade about disliking Jen because she could have been a stripper was just that, an act. I was searching for the flaw in Jen to get my friend back. But what would I be bringing my friend back to? Drinking until our livers explode, hangovers that last days, brain fog that covers you like a gray blanket. If I was a true friend I would understand that this life is not worth it. The fun times don't equalize the pain. But misery loves company.

As I begin to leave she yells out, "You find that number you were looking for?"

"Nothing," I reply.

"Next time you come, you owe me $20 for that show I just gave you."

I shut the door on her cackling laugh and take a seat on the sidewalk. Across the street is a shrink's office.

4:58 PM

Clinical Psychology: Doctors Herzon and Henry.

Hours:

Sunday–Monday: Closed

Tuesday–Thursday: 10–2 PM

Friday–Saturday: 12–5 PM

What a schedule.

The shrink won't do me any good closed. And besides, the shrink is for insane people and I'm fine. I'm fine. I cling to the only rational thought I have left. The babalawo. Five days to see Marissa again. And I did. I think? The Babalawo will know how to handle my current predicament. She has to. I can take the PATH Train to 33rd, then another train to the Bronx, or....

Oh, no. A cardinal sin. It's a rookie mistake. Maybe I am insane because this thought has never crossed my mind. Don't drink and drive, Lou. Don't ever drink and drive. Unless...

Unless it's to find your one true love. Yes, that's it. A made-up lesson from a doddering drunken professor. My mind is made up. My chariot in the make and model of a Honda Accord awaits. Don me my lance, grab me my cape. This won't end well. The walk itself will be long and arduous, but worth it.

[6:15 PM]

Behind the wheel I feel as if I'm in a video game. Fake hands, fake wheel, fake seatbelt. The speedometer, I am aware enough to realize, is not fake. A clutch observation. Follow the speed limit, use your turn signals, fake hands at 10 and 2. This is no time to get sloppy. But sloppy is as sloppy does, and as I back out I smash the back left bumper into a concrete piling. This is no time to get out and assess damages.

It's sad my career as a professor has come to this. A teacher of life and love, history and woes, rules of responsible social action both in real life and on the internet, is now tarnishing his good name with an atrocious act. Breaking a code of conduct. There's a saying about reputations that I'm too drunk to remember.

Somehow I make it out of the parking garage. It takes about ten minutes but I am maneuvering this vehicle with tender love and care. All of my focus is on the tight circular turns that when I finally get to the end I look down at my phone for directions and it hits me. I couldn't possibly get to the Bronx without my phone. And I'm drunk. Two very major problems. I make a hasty decision. Marissa must be where I am headed. Why? No clue. See schizo sign number two.

[6:27 PM]

The Holland Tunnel throws me for a loop. It's the damn lights. Every ten feet they go ticking above my head like God were flicking them on and off. It's going to make me sick. And don't remind me I'm under water. A thought like that could make me park the car and run in the opposite direction.

There are visions of a wall bursting, waters flooding the tunnel, and poor little me drowning in the green muck of the Hudson River. Though the tunnel with light traffic takes three whole minutes, it feels like I've been holding my breath for world record time.

A deep gulping breath when I enter New York briefly revives me until I realize I am in New York and there is construction work on my predetermined route. A devastating blow. I keep my hands firmly at ten and two. Any lapse in concentration could put my life – and pedestrians – in danger. I may be a menace to myself but try my best not to be a menace to society. I am just a man on a personal mission. No one need get involved.

Final destination is sister Kimberly's. Why? Not sure. That's where this whole thing started and where it must end. There is a significance to this Mecca of my defunct life.

I turn down a one way that I can't catch the name of. Not like it would matter. My dashboard tells me I'm heading east, which is not the way I want to be going. I head east for far too long. Finally I build up the courage to follow a few more one-ways until the dash reads W. I stay on a one way, heading west with windows down, until I smell the river.

The important decision comes when a sign appears in front of me reading North or South with urging arrows pointing left and right and nowhere else to go. No other information is available. The street signs seem to have been stolen and New Jersey across the river is covered by the sheer size of this North/South monstrosity. Maybe I could have triangulated my location based on what Jersey building was directly across from me, but who am I fooling? I'm still trying to figure out if my hands are real. Elegua, grab the wheel.

The car begins to move to the south exit until a last-minute jerk to the north almost takes out a bum walking with a shopping cart. In the rearview mirror I see his pants down at his ankles and a middle finger high in the air. For the first time all day I let out a laugh that comes out like an old lady's.

7:39 PM

I park outside Kimberly's. Making it in one piece was my intention, but even I am surprised at my success. Though I imagined being here since the inception of this awful plan I have no idea what to do now. Was Marissa to magically appear? Was the party supposed to still be "raging" on from last Friday? What could I possibly think this horrific plan would net me?

My legs wobble as I exit the vehicle. I'm still drunk, of this there is no doubt. I walk up to her door and ring the bell. No one answers. This isn't shocking because no one's home. It occurs to me that I must head to the back, the porch in particular, where it truly all began.

I climb the fence, slip, and crash into garbage cans. The same garbage cans I envisioned dirty things with Marissa just six nights ago. The place I was supposed to leave my phone.

Climbing the wooden stairs is an easier task and I plop into one of the Adirondack chairs. The sun has set. I've brought my handy dandy pack of cigarettes to conjure up the same spell. What was it last time? Two cigarettes and a prayer?

I smoke two cigarettes fairly quickly and recite the incantation.

"Who has a deck in Manhattan?" I ask the cosmos, again.

Silence.

"That's exactly what I was thinking."

To my right there is a faint trace of yellow. A brown wisp of...

Oh, what am I saying? Shut the fuck up, Lou. Just shut up. She's not here. That's a lamp post glowing and a brown pigeon circling overhead wondering if you're going to feed it. I throw my cracked phone as hard as I can at the garbage cans.

She doesn't exist. Give it up. There's no way she ever existed. Your faulty head has made it all up. A sick and twisted game that came from somewhere inside and then played out to a single audience member... me. I should go get checked. Schizophrenia is no joke, especially in a man's twenties. Maybe stop drinking too. Yea, stop drinking. Drugs, also. Yes, stop doing drugs. Yea, yea...

10:03 PM

I wake up a few hours later in the same chair. Something I hadn't realized when I first arrived was the line of beer bottles on the side of the wooden railing. I'm reminded that I told Kimberly I'd clean the place for her after she left in exchange for bringing my friends to the party. Otherwise, they weren't invited and I would have had to roll solo to that pathetic event. I hadn't told them that. I didn't want them thinking I was that desperate to have them around.

As I stare up at the one star the smog will allow, I realize that's all Marissa is. A hope. A wish. A figment out in the distance that calls to me but resembles a flipped magnet. Constant repulsion wherever I go.

The shameful reality is that now I have to get back home. I'll come back tomorrow to clean. The key is somewhere in my disaster of an apartment and I'm not in the mood to get arrested for breaking and entering. If I'm ever going to get arrested, it better be for something worth it. I wobble back to my car.

10:37 PM

"Do you know why I stopped you, sir?"

"I do not. I had my hands at ten and two. Going the speed limit. Using turn signals. The dashboard is rea..."

"Your taillight is out. Looks like you might have hit something," the cop says.

"Oh, yes officer. Backing out of a parking garage. I hit one of those concrete pilings..."

"Have you been drinking sir?"

"Have...I...been...drinking..."

Friday

[10:37 AM]

Concrete is cold. Metal is cold too, but at least metal can get hot. There's life inside metal. It has the ability to change. Anything that can change has some life left in it. But concrete is lifeless. And being lifeless on top of concrete myself is the last straw.

There was no point in resisting. Yes, officer, I have been drinking for the last…checks watch…decade. It was quite the wakeup call when I was told to step out of the vehicle and walk in a straight line. Utterly impossible. The line was moving and he shined his light in my eyes so forcefully that it knocked me over. The ABCs were easy but backwards? I couldn't do that dead sober. When I was placing my fingers to my nose I heard a car beep in my direction and waved without looking or thinking. Zero for four. They placed a pair of cuffs on me and threw me in the back of the car. I had just made it back through the Holland Tunnel into New Jersey before getting pulled over.

It was a mellow night in the Hoboken lock up, all things considered. I was so damn close to being in my bed I could almost feel the covers. If I hocked a vicious loogie from where I was arrested I could probably hit my apartment. Instead, I am waking up on this cold dead concrete.

Getting booked was fun. I always dreamt of taking a funny mug shot. When I lined up for the photo I let out a short and sad yelp. As the camera flashed it could have only captured a look of distraught sadness. I couldn't help it. It shocked me that I was even taking a mug shot. I asked if I could re-do it. The woman who I had reported Marissa as missing to just laughed and refused my request.

Between the bars in my cell I can see the clock. I've slept soundly for twelve hours straight. In spite of the concrete, I haven't had that good of a night's sleep in quite some time. The concrete was dead and cold but at least it was a floor. There was a roof over my head. I'm actually sober.

Habit in me, that evil circadian rhythm, realizes it's Friday and wonders what the plans are for tonight, but something tells me that Professor Lou is going to need a few nights off. Maybe weeks, maybe months, possible early retirement. It's not so much that a DUI has scared me straight, but that I had a particular vision of myself which is now gone. Some say you are not a true professional unless you've gotten a DUI. I see it quite the opposite. A true professional never gets a DUI. A DUI is a sign of weakness, of stupidity, and above all a lack of being able to hold your alcohol. It's a sign that maybe, just maybe, you are a washed-up old fool who's looking for an out.

11:01 AM

I am filled with despair at the location of the impound lot and that I am legally not allowed to touch the car for another twelve hours. That's probably for the best. I should not be driving or drinking in any order for the foreseeable future. On top of that is the $2,000 impound fee and impending legal penalties my drunken nightmare has bestowed upon me. I know I deserve it. The drunken driver is one of the worst criminals there is. The utter selfishness. The sheer lack of care for others. An infant blinded by drink avarice or liquid confidence. Looking at a drunk driver is like looking at a five-year-old who takes pleasure in torturing animals. All the potential for harm is staring you right in the face. At least I didn't kill anyone. I was just…

Even the thought of Marissa couldn't wipe away my guilt. The walk of shame back to my apartment is one of epic proportions. I can hear people talking about me. I see them stare. They know what I've done. The community is ashamed of their Professor emeritus. The closer I get to my apartment the more abhorrent I feel. Everything is a reminder of all that I've done.

My apartment is its own abhorrent mess that must be dealt with. A fumigation team may be in order. But for now, I readjust the fallen shower curtain, wash the grime off myself, and pray, really pray, there's still time to make it. I grab the key to Kimberly's apartment on the nightstand before hailing a cab. As I wait outside they're still talking about last night on the street. They speak in hushed tones in order for me not to hear but I hear, loud and clear. There goes Lou, the fool. There goes Lou, the clown. There goes Lou, the jester. He's not a professional anymore. He's been dropped down to the amateurs. This is no place for amateurs. Even mothers place their hands over their mouths and wonder how they ever let the Lou's of the world educate their kids.

2:05 PM

My parents have a standing two o'clock lunch every Friday for eternity. It is one of those gushy romantic gestures that I hate and wish I had. They have a table reserved for four at the Bryant Park Grill in case either of their children would like to join. One occasionally does, the other has never attended. Friday at two could bleed into Friday at five and I have been preoccupied on this day at that time for longer than I can remember. I'm sure my friends are furiously texting me as we speak. The broken phone is in Kimberly's garbage pile. It feels like a blessing. This Friday my streak must end.

I've decided to dress appropriately. Wing-tipped shoes, blue slacks, brown belt, white button down, even a blazer. I feel uncomfortable in this get up but that seems appropriate. Growing up is uncomfortable. It should be uncomfortable. Otherwise, what's the point? I must fake it until I make it.

When I arrive at the restaurant I am glad I eschewed the pair of stained joggers and white t-shirt I had originally planned on wearing. I would have stuck out here more than I did in jail. The Bryant Park Grill is a building that eases and awes. There are tall windows bordered by thick iron scaffolds covered in ivy. There is a rooftop surrounded by fresh flower beds. Lamp posts are dropped at random intervals from Victorian-era England. And it all sits in the shadow of the New York Public Library. This is where I should have taken Marissa. This is where you take someone you think is worth it.

The maître d' points out the two love birds in a booth near a window looking out at the park. I make my way through lines of white linen tables, guests eating with pinkies extended. The clinking of champagne glasses makes my teeth feel like they are being scraped by a sickle probe. The look on my mom's face when she sees me is one of utter shock. My father has a look of confusion, like when you run into someone from home on vacation. The prodigal son doesn't look the same out of context.

"Oh, mi hijo! What are you doing here? What happened to your head? Is everything okay? Aye probecito," my mother yelps.

She squeezes my cheeks as if I were still her little boy. In a way I still am. A chick stuck under her sheltering wing. I didn't come to feel her warmth, though it is tempting. I could nestle under her protective bosom, order a glass of wine or three, make a couple jokes at my father's expense and continue on with my life. But I came here to talk to him.

It occurs to me that fathers are exactly like jail cell floors. They are cold and ruthless because they have to be. They are there to teach lessons, not to coddle. At least the good ones are.

"Why aren't you at work?" he asks.

"I knew you'd say something like that," I say.

"It's Friday at 2:30. Don't you have a team meeting to discuss next week's plans at 3? That meeting was my idea."

"So you could get away from the office for lunch with mom?" I ask.

"Absolutely," he says, touching my mother's hand, smiling. I realize my father can be just as mischievous as me, though he has harnessed the power for good.

"Touching," I say, ready to gag at the public display of affection.

But what is there to gag about? A couple in love. A human necessity older than time. The love that keeps the whole thing going. The love that made me. The love that keeps on making. That terrifying prospect of giving your life to someone else. There is nothing on planet earth less gag worthy.

"Seriously, what are you doing here?"

"I want to talk."

"Sit then. What do you want to drink?"

"Just a water."

His eyebrows rise to the gleaming golden rafters. He knows something is amiss. The get up, the abstinence – the whole thing reeks of desperation.

"I think I want to quit my job," I say.

My mom smacks her forehead. A nice meal ruined once again. She crosses herself once, twice, and a third for good luck. She looks up at her deity, the ones that have brought me to this, until my father brings her back to earth.

"Honey, why don't you go for a walk around the park. By the time you get back everything will be fine. No one can ruin our Friday lunch. Not even our own idiot son," my father says.

She looks at me as if she needs permission to leave or permission to stay. A mother until the bitter end ready to protect her one and only son from infanticide. I just nod my head knowing it's the only way.

When my mother is out of eyesight I feel the back of my head skimmed with the palm of my dad's hand. It's not a smack but more of a graze. It sounds and feels like a bee sting. I actually laugh.

"What was that for?" I ask.

"I eat. I sleep. I work. And I am happy. I get this one lunch with my wife a week and here you come waltzing in, trying to ruin it."

"I'm not trying to ruin it. I just needed to talk."

"You know how a phone works, no?"

"Lost it," I say.

"What happened?" he asks.

I recount the bare minimum. There is no reason to mention my faulty reality. My rationalization that a girl doesn't exist because she can't be found won't resonate. It also makes no sense under the sober lights of Bryant Park Grill.

"So you got suspended and then celebrated by getting a DUI? You are such an asshole. You could have killed someone. If you weren't my son I would ask who the hell raised you. Sometimes I wonder what I could have done better with you and then I realize there is nothing. I raised you as best I could. I was there for every game, every practice, every question. I tried to show you how to live by example. What else is a father supposed to do?"

"Nothing, dad. You didn't do anything wrong. You've done everything right. Too right. Too perfect. Everything I do is going to fall short."

"That's foolish," he says.

"Maybe."

He looks out the window, thinking. My mother is walking near a carousel, watching the kids glide up and down on antique unicorns and horses. She counts her rosary beads with a little mermaid dangling at the end of it. Yemaya and Jesús Cristo. She is probably praying that her family will still be intact after this walk.

"You never had older brothers," he says. "And maybe you're better off for it, maybe you're not. But I see all three of us in you and it scares the hell out of me."

"What do you mean?"

"I wish you got to meet them because they would have loved you. You're so much more like them than me. You're wild, you're fun. You're like a big wobbling middle finger to the world of worries and cares. It's terrifying, Lou. Because that's exactly how they were and then they died, and I was just this young kid watching it all."

"You don't ever talk about them," I say.

"What's there to say? They were my brothers and they died when I was sixteen. The papers said the roads were slippery that night and that's what I've told you and your sister but I'm not stupid. The papers were just being nice. They knew my mother and father and saved them from any reputational harm, but I knew the truth. My brothers were always drinking and driving. It didn't have the same stigma back then but it had the same consequences. And after they died I started going down the same path. I wanted to be like them. And then your mother saved me…"

"Why didn't you tell me any of this?"

"I didn't think I would need to. I thought that maybe if you watched me like I watched them, you would follow what I did. But brothers and fathers aren't the same."

His hands start to shake as he takes a glass of water to his lips. I've never seen him like this. He puts the glass down and collects himself with a couple deep breaths. The corners of his eyes look like a bird's footprint in sand. His eyes are gray as rain-filled clouds.

"I don't know if I ever told you this," he says. "But I have a reoccurring nightmare. I'm at my own wake and there's your mother, you, and Kimberly sitting in the front row. You're crying, as you should be. You are all devastated, which makes me happy. I'm sorry, but it does. If your family isn't sad to see you go then who is? As I look up from the casket there is no one else there. Just you three in the front row crying your eyes out. I get out of the casket and I walk through the aisles of empty chairs. The chairs go on forever. Empty of all the friends that should be mourning my death had I done life differently. It makes me sad. But as I walk back towards the casket the chairs begin to fill up. I can't see their faces until I climb back in the casket for my final rest. I take one more look back and the seats are filled with your friends. All the people you've touched in this world. That's when I realize I'm jealous of my own son. That you have this way of connecting to people. That they love you. I'm no longer jealous, just proud of you. I am proud to be your father. Proud I made a son that connects with people. I look at them and they are all crying just as much as you and your sister and your mother, and they are all crying for you, Lou."

Tears have built up in the slits of my eyes and two big droplets fall onto the clean linen covering the table. I could use a drink but instead I wipe the fallen tears with my napkin until they are just smeared wet streaks.

"I'm sorry," I say.

"Me too."

"I'm going to quit my job," I say again.

This makes my dad snort with laughter.

"After all that you still want to quit the one thing holding you together? Oh man. Just wait until you're a parent. Imagine your son who has just been arrested saying he's now going to quit his job? It's like talking to a fucking wall."

For the first time ever the thought of being a parent doesn't make my stomach convulse.

"Don't curse at the table," I warn him.

He puts his head in his hands, half laughing, half yelling his frustration into his palms.

"So what are you going to do?"

"I don't know. Just somewhere you're not involved," I say.

"Is that what this is about? Because that's all bullshit, son. When I was a kid working for your dad was a cool thing. If you were the son who got to keep the business in the family you were the lucky one. You shouldn't feel bad about that. What's the point of all the work I do if I can't give it to someone?"

"I just want to start something untainted. Something for me and me alone."

He nods his head in approval.

"You're still an idiot," he says out of the side of his mouth, waving my mom back in.

My mom creeps towards us. Weary. I give her a hug.

"I saw your babalawo," I whisper in her ear.

She holds me back at a distance.

"Iyalawo Isla?" she asks.

"The women in the Bronx," I say.

She touches the cut above my eye, pats my cheek.

"Iyalawo, mi hijo. She's an Iyalawo."

My dad's right. I am still an idiot. As I walk out my mother crosses herself three times and smiles.

3:15 PM

Before making the trek to clean my sister's apartment I stop at the Stephen A. Schwarzman Building of the New York Public Library. They don't make buildings like this anymore and I don't know why. It's better than any church my mom has dragged me to. The walls are so tall it's like they are reaching towards God with their fingertips outstretched. And the books. Hundreds and thousands of books. If I do ever get my shit together long enough to buy a house the only accoutrements I'll need are books. They are more beautiful than any decoration Kimberly has designed. It's not her fault. They are mesmerizing.

There are twelve long wooden tables laid out like work benches. People are reading and writing, coffees and waters strewn around, ear buds lodged in. There is more concentration packed into this room than I've ever seen in an office. These people are filled with purpose. They don't look happy necessarily, just content. I am envious of these anonymous faces.

I ask the librarian where the children's section is and she looks at me like I'm on some sort of list. I tell her I am looking for a book for my nephew and her stern eyebrows relax.

The walls of books are shorter in the kid's section. So are the chairs and the tables. It's like everything has been shrunk down to miniature size. I feel like I'm in a doll house. The colors on the walls are prime and bright and make you want to break out into song and dance. There are hideous yet endearing pictures children have painted with toothbrushes on the walls and in-between bookstacks. I glide my fingers along the books and make my way toward the S section. I'm looking for Maurice Sendak, author of *Where the Wild Things Are*. The popular book has not been taken out or they have more than one copy in rotation. It's a book that I don't remember except for the sad looking bull on the front cover. The bull reminds me of me.

I slip the book off the shelf and take a seat at one of the empty tables that hover at shin level. My knees press up against my chin as I crack open the book. One ass cheek slips off the side of the tod-dler-sized chair. I feel like an ogre. I feel like a wild thing.

The book starts with the protagonist Max getting sent to his room with no supper for acting like the little nut job he is. In his imagina-tion his room turns into a forest, a boat appears out of nowhere, and he's whisked away to the island of the Wild Things. I connect with this Max. I myself am having trouble differentiating what is real and what is not.

The Wild Things are an amalgam of different animals cut and spliced onto one another. There's a skinny dragon with a slicked back main that looks like Aisle. The short rotund one with hair growing from every orifice is a dead ringer for VanNeece.

Max is faced with a dilemma. Return home or stay on the island of the Wild Things. I have to admit, the island seems like an awesome time. If this was an adult picture book I imagine it would look like the Playboy Mansion. The 'wild rumpus' would resemble a Greek orgy of beautiful women and booze flowing like the Mississippi. Before I can continue my imaginings of debaucherous bliss I feel a mini hand on my knee and look up from behind the book at a little tyke. He seems lost. His eyes are big and round and questioning. His blonde hair is cut as if a bowl were placed on his head.

"Those awe monstews," he says, his r's turning to w's.

"That's right kid. Big, scary monsters. But Max tricks them," I say.

"How does he twick them?"

"Well, here, look," I turn the book toward him and keep reading. "He stares at them without blinking once."

"What happens next?"

I read the ending to the kid. Max gets a whiff of his mother's cooking, realizing he doesn't want to be stuck with the Wild Things on the wild island. That the smell of a home-cooked meal could bring someone back to their roots is something I inherently understand. When you need life lessons from a children's book you've really lost the plot.

"How do you like the ending?" I ask.

"My mom's cooking smells like fawts," the kid says, and runs away.

For the life of me, I can't stop laughing.

4:15 PM

When I get to Kimberly's apartment I rummage through the garbage cans and find my phone. Through the mini hexagons I can see it has 1% battery left. Then it starts to ring. Though barely readable I can see the incoming call: Carey. It takes seven swipes of the shattered screen to finally pick up.

"Lou!" she yells.

She sounds like she is far away from the phone. I'm worried she's been kidnapped. The sounds in the background are joyous as if her captors were holding her at a bar on a beach.

"Where are you?" I ask.

"I'm sorry I just left you. Matt called me and said it was an emergency. I guess it was. He surprised me with a trip to the Bahamas and we had to leave for the airport in twenty minutes. He told me to turn off my phone."

"That's nice, Carey. Have fun," I say, ready to hang up.

"Wait. Before we got on the plane he proposed to me. When we landed both of our families were here. It's like a dream."

"That's…that's amazing Carey. I'm so happy for you."

"You get it Lou," she says.

Then my phone dies. I drop it back in the garbage heap.

I don't know why but my eyes are filled with tears that won't fall.

4:22 PM

The glorified professor has turned cleaning lady. Rubber gloves are not a good look but neither is a DUI. I've lost more than a professorship overnight, I've lost self-respect. But maybe, just maybe, I've gained perspective.

The bulk of the mess was cleaned by my sister's co-workers. Why they couldn't finish the job I'll never know. If it were up to me they would all be fired. A line of garbage bags, filled to max capacity, leans against the sturdy end of the sliding glass door to the porch. Not on the outside. On the inside. Animals. For some reason the brilliant minds over at Kim Kennedy's could not take the bags the extra foot outside.

Small puddles under the garbage bags have formed over my week-long absence. It smells like my apartment. I take two of the bags to the trash, dripping sediment up and down the outside staircase. The third and last bag, as my luck would have it, splits and regurgitates its contents over the floor. The sound of smashing cans and bottles seem like it might ring out forever. When gravity finally settles things there is only the sound of a rolling can or two and a pathetic grown man crying. I can't help it. It started in the picture booth at the jail and the emptied garbage bag finished the job. My tears add to the depressing wetness of the room.

One by one I empty whatever liquid didn't make it on the floor from each can and bottle into the sink, crying as I go. The emptied cans find a new home in a fresh bag. I find a mop in a closet, fill a bucket with water and dish soap and take to the floor. What a nuisance I've become. I'm not crying for the wasted alcohol. It's not a cry of self-pity either. It's a cry of exhaustion. A life of effort put into a whole lot of nothing. Cleaning my sister's apartment might be the first productive thing I've done in months.

In Kimberly's bedroom there are a few empty beer bottles on her dresser next to bottles of perfumes and lotions, and Creag's quarter-filled bottle of Johnnie Walker. The bed is unmade. There are clothes scattered on dresser drawers. Kim seemed to have left in a hurry. I'm tempted to take a drag from the bottle...

5:01 PM

But I don't. I look the monster directly in its eyes, just like Max, and say no. I am the king of all Wild Things.

I finish the job, spraying down the place with two bottles of perfume in hope that by the time Kimberly comes home the smell of a weeks' worth of rotting will be masked. Then I hear a phone ring.

It's not mine, dead and at the bottom a pile of garbage, but Kimberly's house phone. I'm not sure whether it's Jesus or Elegua or just my own conscience telling me to answer it. I pick up the phone.

"Hello?" I whisper.

"Lou?"

"Who's this?"

"It's Kimberly you moron. Why are you at my house?"

"Uh, just checking in," I say.

"Don't tell me you're cleaning my apartment. It's been a week."

"Of course not. Why are you calling your own apartment?"

"Checking my messages?"

"You really are a hipster."

"Fuck off," she says.

"How's England?" I ask.

"The food's not as bad as they say. And the tube is great. Less confusing than New York. And the pubs are…"

"I mean how's Craeg?"

"Craeg…has to stay for another year," she says, letting out a sad yelp.

I'm filled with intense anger and wonder if I'll have to beat the shit out of another ex-boyfriend or die trying. Craeg is a behemoth but I don't care.

"I'm sorry," I say.

"It's okay," she says. "But thanks Lou. We'll see what happens. I'll call you tomorrow."

"Wait, I have to ask you something."

My hands are shaking.

"Ask it already," she says.

"Do you know a Marissa from Spain?"

Her pause is all of two seconds. I almost puke.

"Yea she's staying with Lauren from sales like three blocks away from me. 329 West 30th I think."

I hang up and run.

5:33 PM

I'm in front of the apartment door. I've thought of a thousand things to say on the run over but as I knock and she answers I'm dumbfounded.

"Marissa?"

The real thing, in a purple sundress this time. She looks more human in the daylight. The idol I've built up as flesh. A real girl who, it occurs to me, I know next to nothing about.

She still looks elegant but less queenlike, more rustic. The dress waves at her knees. Her bare arms have a light layer of hair. There's a freckle I hadn't noticed in the shape of Michigan below her right eye. She's more beautiful now than she's ever been.

She looks at me as if I'm the mirage. As if I'm the one who is not real.

"Lou?" she asks. "Why are you here?"

"It's a long story. I...I'm sorry I didn't call you," I say.

"It's okay. It's only been what, three days?" she laughs.

She doesn't seem as stressed as I've been. Only three days? It felt like an eternity.

"You know my dad proposed to my mom in seven days," I say.

"You aren't going to propose to me, are you?"

I get down on one knee.

"Oh no," she says.

I pretend to tie my shoe and stand up laughing.

"Thank God. I don't even know your last name," she says.

"I don't know yours either."

We both laugh.

"Pero, I know you like boxing," she says.

She puts her guard up like a fighter and starts throwing ones and twos, laughing.

I pretend to grab her between her legs and she quickly blocks it with a forearm.

"I need to really teach you Guaguancó Mr. Lou," she says.

"Please."

"Do you want to come get a drink with me and my friends? I was just about to leave."

"That's the last thing I need. Can I walk you there?" I ask.

Every night does not start the same.

"Si," she says.

As we walk, she holds my arm as if to hold me up. These are my first steps into this new enlightened life.

"Why *didn't* you call?" she asks.

There's more than a hint of jealousy. It's kind of frightening. There's a weight of responsibility behind it. A new knowledge. It's not as horrific as I once thought it would be. Considering someone else before me is not a burden, it's a relief. But that doesn't mean I can come clean with you yet, Marissa. I'm not sure how to word this…I lost the number and then I thought you weren't real. I thought that you didn't exist. I thought that my life of drinking and drugging had finally caught up with me. I thought I needed a shrink. I thought I needed a straitjacket. I thought I'd wake up one morning and find myself in a padded room. No Twitter? No Instagram? Not even Facebook? You couldn't be more real if you tried, Marissa.

"I lost the piece of paper," I say.

"Ay dios mio," she laughs.

"I've been running around like a crazy person trying to find you. I didn't know where you were staying or how to get in touch with you," I say, creeping closer to the truth.

"I thought I told you I've been staying a few blocks away from your sisters?"

I finally let my guard down. The cool, impregnable Professor is officially retired. I rub my temples and ball my fists into my eyes, trying to come up with something to say.

"You probably did. I've been somewhat of a mess," is all I can manage.

"It's okay," she says.

She squeezes my arm.

"How long are you staying here for?" I ask, terrified of the answer.

"My father wanted to go back to Spain next week and start on a new collection. I usually go wherever he goes but right now he doesn't have anything to sell. And I'm in my twenties. Do you remember my father's lesson about your twenties?"

"I do."

"Egoista," she says.

"Selfish?" I ask.

"Si, selfish. So, what should I do?"

"What's something really good and selfish?" I ask.

"Maybe I stay right here in Nueva York," she says.

"Yes, what else?"

"Maybe I finish my book?"

"Yes, I'd like to read it. Anything else?" I ask.

"Maybe you meet me at my father's gallery tomorrow night and then after we go out to dinner?"

"Or maybe I cook you dinner?" I say.

"Si," she says. "I'd love that."

"Can you write down the address to the gallery? I lost my phone."

"Is it still in the garbage pile?" she asks with a smirk.

"Something like that."

She takes out an identical piece of paper to the one I found in the fridge and writes the address down.

"Write your number down too…just in case I get lost."

Marissa Elena Cifuentes. Full name and number.

It occurs to me I'll have to get a new phone. Then I'll have to delete every app I have. Arianna's number along with them. I'll have to tell my friends about Marissa. I'll have to save her number. I'll have to attend Brian's wedding. I'll have to tell Aisle he was right all along. I'll have to do brunch. I'll have to do a whole lot that Professor Lou would not approve of but…

Professor Lou's final lesson – if she's real, always get her number.

And then call her the next day.

She kisses me on both cheeks, laughs, then kisses me on the lips as I leave her at the bar.

There's one last errand I must run.

I have to see a murderer about a job.

Acknowledgments

When you've worked on your first book for ten plus years, you are bound to have had some help. First and foremost, I'd like to thank all the authors who made me fall in love with reading and subsequently writing. Though I must have been pretty naïve to think I could do what these giants of literature have done, without them this book wouldn't be possible. To list them would make this book run another hundred pages, but I am forever indebted.

I've written and rewritten the book in your hands a hundred times. Every time I wrote or rewrote a part is because something or someone pushed me in that direction. The novel really took its final form after attending the Curtis Brown Creative Edit & Pitch Your Novel course. I'd like to first thank all the other students who attended that class. When you've written a book like mine and you're the only male in a class of nine women, you might think you're going to be laughed or shamed out of the class. These women did neither. I still talk to them and they have been nothing but encouraging in my quest to get this book published.

Laura Pearson, the teacher of the class, changed the way I thought about my novel and ultimately helped me set a clear vision of what this book was trying to be. On top of that, she tried her best to help me get an agent. I am grateful for all her work and care.

As for actual editors, the two that helped me get this book over the finish line are Vanessa Ogle and Adam Pearson. I am eternally grateful that they saw my vision and helped me get there. Vanessa deftly cut the book from its once bloated state to what it is now. Without Adam Pearson, and his aggravating questions, I might not have understood the layers (both physical and philosophical) that my book was working towards. Again, I am grateful. Without Substack I wouldn't have met either of them. Long live Substack.

The behind the scenes to get a book to its final stage is crazy, and I could go on and on with people to thank, but the ones I really want to acknowledge are my friends and family. If you think I could've written this book without the best group of friends then you are sadly mistaken. You don't get characters like Lou or Aisle or VanNeece if you haven't been surrounded by characters your entire life. Smitty, Pecs, Dinks, Kev, Eddie, Dan, Ryan, Rob, Tom, Brandli, Spill, Brandon, Jetter – without our banter I could never have become a writer. You've sharpened my pen by giving me shit and taking it in return. If this novel made you laugh, you can thank these guys. That's why I started writing. That's why I continue to write. To get a laugh from the boys. Love you guys.

To Nana – You'll probably never read this book but thank you for leaving the Dominican Republic, not knowing a stitch of English, and creating a life for your family. And, of course, thank you for teaching me how to cook.

To Grandmom – I learned more about life and love and forgiveness from listening to you than reading any books. But then again, you self-published one yourself and there is more wisdom in that small, wonderful book than in anything I've read before or after. You really were *An Uncommon Everyday Woman*.

To Popop – Thanks for handing down your gene of stubbornness. Without it, this book would have died on the vine.

Mom. Dad. If you've gotten this far, I apologize. I couldn't have asked for better parents. Not only have you employed me, but you've also been nothing but supportive of me following my own dream. Luckily this book is self-published, so if it affects business, we can always cease and desist. I could never thank you enough, but hopefully one day this book will generate a couple hundred bucks and I can take you both out to dinner.

Tara. My Tara. I know I scared you half to death when I asked you to read this book. You figured the drunk moron you were falling for was about to ruin it by asking you to read something truly awful and you'd get *The Ick*. Luckily, you believed in it from the first sentence. You've sacrificed more than any other person to help me follow my dreams. From watching the kids for a weekend while I went to pitch this book (only to be rejected), to putting the kids down many nights alone while you let me edit, to keeping them occupied if they happen to wake up before 7 AM (my writing time is 4–7 AM). Without you this book has (and had) a completely different ending. Without you no happiness in my life is possible. Without a woman that a man looks up to, and wants to be better for, he is nothing. I could write another novel right here but all I am going to say is thank you for our two beautiful daughters. I still can't believe we get to be mom and dad together. I hope I've written a book they can read some day (when they are MUCH older) and be equally embarrassed and proud that their dad wrote it. I love you three girls more than you'll ever know. Everything would be pointless without you.

P.S. To the hundred plus literary agents that rejected me, from the bottom of my heart, thank you. This self-published book you hold in your hands is going to do better than any debut writer you currently have on your roster. Your rejections only made me more confident.